EVIE'S VICTORY

As a new year begins and the world is at war, Evie Yeo is turning over a new leaf. Her nearest and dearest in the little Devon village of Lymbridge, the war effort for the boys on the front, and her class of infant pupils will be getting all of her attention this year. Though rations are slim, and work is hard with the men away, Evie knows she's lucky to have her friends and family around her. But as the snow falls, Evie realises it might be harder than she thought to put the past behind her and find her happy ending.

EVIE'S VICTORY

EVIE'S VICTORY

by

Kitty Danton

Magna Large Print Books
Long Preston, North Yorkshire,
BD23 4ND, England.

British Library Cataloguing in Publication Data.

A catalogue record of this book is
available from the British Library

ISBN   978-0-7505-4390-3

First published in Great Britain in 2017 by Orion Books
an imprint of The Orion Publishing Group Ltd.

Published in Large Print 2017 by arrangement with
The Orion Publishing Group Ltd.

Magna Large Print is an imprint of Library Magna Books Ltd.

Printed and bound in Great Britain by
T.J. (International) Ltd., Cornwall, PL28 8RW

For Josie and Louis, with all my love

Chapter One

The year 1942 was going to be very different to its predecessor, Evie Yeo decided resolutely as she was getting ready for bed.

Gone would be the slightly feckless Evie who had spent too much time mooning over one faithless man after another. This thankless behaviour had wasted *far* too much of the previous year, and had caused her an unhappiness that very much outweighed the fleeting moments of pleasure.

And in would come a bolder and more positive Evie, she decided, giving her dressing table just the smallest of thumps with her right fist as a sign of her resolution. She felt very determined that before the first week of January was out she would be a new, stronger and generally much improved Evie.

A man would not be the way to happiness, quite obviously, and so she was going to stop looking.

She was planning to pin-curl her hair every evening as (she hoped) this would be an obvious sign to friends and family of a fresh and rigorous self-discipline. Evie thought that to pay more attention to her hair would have the benefit of killing two birds with one stone, as in addition to signifying the new Evie, the government was encouraging women left on the home front to look as well as they could in an effort to boost the morale of all of those who felt jaded – and let's be honest, who didn't? – at facing the third year of keeping the home fires burning whilst their beloved country was still at war against the Jerrys. Evie wanted very much to show her support for the war effort, and although keeping her unruly hair in order might seem a small contribution, at least it was a step in the right direction.

In addition, Evie pledged to herself that she'd read at least one mind-improving book each week, and make sure she always got eight hours of restorative sleep, even if that meant being the first of the paying guests to go to bed every evening.

Evie leant closer to the angled mirror attached to her dressing table and peered at her image intently before carefully selecting a section of hair, although she then jabbed a hairgrip sharply into a finger as she tried to tame the unruly tress. There had been a time she would have clenched her jaw with impatience and then, most likely, given up on the pin-curling almost before she had started, with a petulant slinging of the offending hairgrip into some dark corner of her low-ceilinged bedroom.

Not so tonight.

With an enviable serenity Evie swapped the hairgrip and the swirl of hair to the opposite hand, and once she had wound the curl back up, she was able to secure the grip without bother. One down, she thought. And then, only another thirty or so of these dratted things to go. She smiled. At least she had allowed a small but nonetheless significant pause before becoming just a trifle impatient.

Self-discipline is a wonderful thing, Evie told herself ten minutes later without a trace of irony. Only a stray strand or two had avoided her assiduous pinning, except for the final section still to be done.

Routine and planning ahead would be the key to a calmer, less up-and-down way of going about things, Evie was sure. And it was going to make her feel much better, and perhaps after a bit of practice, possibly even a little contented. She wasn't certain she could aim for anything as lofty as 'happy' yet.

In fact, she wasn't going to dwell on her feelings, good, bad or indifferent.

Instead she was planning to jam-pack her days with a whole host of things. January, with the short days of a West Country winter, could be dreary, with time seeming to stand still. The clouds would feel heavy and low above her home village of Lymbridge, she knew, with the imposing granite tors sometimes hard to see despite standing craggily tall on top of the surrounding moorland peaks. The moor's heather and gorse would have shrugged off their violet and golden hues of summer and autumn to merge into something that looked uniformly dark and spiky, and potentially more violent, while the weather would feel unrelentingly grim and always chilly. But none of this would matter this year, not if Evie Yeo had any say in it.

Evie tamed the final – and, as it turned out, particularly troublesome – whorl of hair, and exhaled audibly as she pondered the things she thought she should do if this different and more controlled Evie was to announce herself to the world as someone who had turned over a new leaf.

So, in order, she should:

1. Be better at going to bed early, and looking after herself generally. Evie knew too that she had allowed herself to become very run-down over the autumn, with the result that she had ended up spending close on a fortnight laid up in bed feeling too feeble to care much about anything. Although it had seemed just prior to becoming poorly that she was putting others' welfare before her own – which was a good thing, surely, as it was selfless, a trait she had always been told was good to strive for – would in fact another view be that for Evie to have persisted in this behaviour at the expense of her own well-being was in reality little more than outright selfish behaviour? In these trying times other people had more important things to do than concern themselves with looking after her once things had descended to a level where they had to step in. Whatever the truth concerning her own motivations, Evie rather thought she had pushed things too far in this respect recently.

2. Be a better teacher. Her class of infants at Lymbridge Primary School were demanding and had a range of abilities. They were very sweet too, of course. But Evie was still relatively green when it came to teaching, having only the two terms' experience under her belt, and the children had seen nothing yet as regards how she was going to knock them into shape, that was for certain. She was going to plan ahead more effectively, and work harder every day. (Evie gave her dressing table another little thump with her closed fist, just to drive this point home.)

3. Be a better sister. She had rather neglected her

youngest sister, Pattie, in recent months, which
was unfair, especially as Pattie had been most
diligent in caring for Evie just a week or two earlier
when she had been struck down with the nasty
bout of influenza over Christmas. And, of course,
before that there had been that dreadful argument
in Lymbridge's only public house, The Haywain,
between Evie and her middle sister, Julia. And
although she and Julia had tentatively started to
build bridges between each other after the hideous
Fiona – and Evie wasn't going to waste time thinking about her right now – had given the still-wan
Evie a most awkward moment on New Year's Eve,
there was a long way to go yet before the two eldest Yeo sisters had anything approaching the easy
way with one another that, once, Evie had believed
could never be lost. (How sadly mistaken that
assumption had turned out to be.) And as for her
little brother, James, well, Evie had taken him so
for granted for such a long time that she really
didn't know very much about what he was up to
these days. What a shame it was that she hadn't
paid more attention to her siblings over the previous autumn; they deserved more from her as
their eldest and hopefully wisest sister.

4. Be a better daughter. Evie didn't care to think
too deeply about how shocked Robert and Susan
had been when their daughters made a complete
show of themselves in The Haywain fracas. Even
to acknowledge now the unexpected fisticuffs after
Julia had refused to be at all contrite at her wanton
behaviour, which Evie had felt at the time (and
still did, if she were honest) was the least that
should happen on Julia's part, flashed a rise of

15

nausea to Evie's throat and a hot slash of shame across her cheeks. She didn't think she'd ever forget the horrified looks her parents had given her when she shot into the kitchen after the brawl, her skirt grubby and patched with damp from rolling around on the floor of the ladies' bar as she and Julia tussled. Evie was convinced that the once-close relationship she had enjoyed with her sensible and always loving parents had been altered irrevocably for the worse through this moment of completely uncharacteristic loss of control on her part. Not that Julia had helped things – although that was another matter, of course.

5. Be a better friend to Tricia. Okay, there was a history here, as Tricia had been made pregnant by Timmy whilst he was engaged to Evie. But still... Evie knew that, deep down, she hefted around her neck rather a large albatross of emotional turmoil as a result of this particular pickle that she was somehow reluctant to package off into her past. She wasn't at all comfortable about this, no matter how pleased she was that Timmy had done the right thing and made an honest woman of Tricia. Evie knew she must make sure not to patronise Tricia, and that she must always treat her as an equal. It wasn't Tricia's fault she was less educated than Evie, and came from a more modest background, and Evie wondered if in the past she had allowed herself to feel slightly superior, which wasn't at all a nice thing to have to acknowledge. Tricia, after all, had the wedding ring on her finger, and Evie most certainly did not. The truth of it was that Evie had never cared to think too closely as to precisely what Tricia had known of

Timmy and Evie's engaged status when Timmy had tempted Tricia to accompany him late one evening behind the village hall for a little slap and tickle. However, since then Tricia had rather won Evie around with her forthright and down-to-earth view of the world. Tricia was kind and she always made Evie smile, and now that Timmy was never going to walk again, Evie thought those qualities Tricia personified counted for a lot more than coming from a respectable family and speaking with a posher voice.

6. Be a better friend to her faithful old school pals Sukie and Linda. Evie wasn't quite sure why she had added them to her list as, actually, she thought she *had* been quite a good chum as far as they were concerned. Perhaps 'Be Better' point number six was more for safety's sake, as it never hurt to remind oneself of the value of true friendship.

7. Be better at dealing with the older people in the village who were important to her. As far as Evie was concerned, Mrs Smith – her headmistress and, trickily for Evie at times, Timmy's mother also – and her new husband, the kindly and sanguine Mr Smith, fell into this category. And then, of course, there were also Mr and Mrs Worth, the owners of the rather grand Pemberley guest house where Evie lodged, who had decided to stand by their unexpectedly wayward young paying guest after she so disgraced herself at The Haywain. Julia had not been so fortunate, and had been asked to leave the comfortable lodgings Pemberley had once offered to her too. Evie's middle sister had had, therefore, no alternative but to move back home to Bluebells, the Yeo

family home, in order that Robert and Susan might prove a stabilising force. At the time Evie and Julia couldn't have countenanced spending a single night under the same roof; but that was then, and now Evie felt differently, although she wasn't completely convinced that Julia quite shared her softening feelings.

8. Be better at organising her time. This needed to happen, definitely. For, under this 'Be Better' point, there was a ream of tasks that were waiting for Evie to turn her attention their way, including, but not confined to:

• pushing hard at upping the fundraising for buying a Spitfire to be donated to the RAF. (This Spitfire plan had been her idea, but Evie knew that she hadn't given it too much thought since even before her influenza, let alone lending any practical muscle on her part.) The sum needed was £6,000, and right now this felt like an unclimbable mountain;

• helping Mrs Worth find some more paying guests to fill the empty bedrooms at Pemberley where Evie so enjoyed living. It would be too bad if the authorities requisitioned the large house for the war effort because of a lack of PGs, not least as Evie would have to find somewhere else to lodge. Nowhere could be so convenient as Pemberley, as its grounds abutted Lymbridge Primary School, meaning each morning Evie only had to walk down the graceful drive and then less than a hundred yards along the road before she was at the school gate. Requisition was a real danger if those rooms remained empty, Mrs Worth never seemed to tire of saying;

• cracking on with putting together the series of fundraising talks Evie had discussed with the *Western Morning News* well before Christmas, gaily promising at the time that she would arrange a programme of interesting debates that would be sure to draw a crowd over the spring in nearby Plymouth (ideally the audience would have deep pockets out of which they would make significant contributions to the Spitfire fund). But so far Evie had done nothing to sort out the programme of speakers;

• making sure the Lymbridge sewing circle kept up its enthusiasm for Make Do and Mend as part of the war effort. After all, it had been Evie's idea originally that they should meet at Pemberley, as the wooden dining table Mrs Worth would lovingly buff until anyone could see their face in its shiny surface was so massive that it meant all manner of patterns could be carefully laid out as the village's needlewomen discussed how to get the most out of even the smallest bits of material in these times of utility outfits and clothing coupons, and endless scavenging, scrimping and saving;

• thinking about what to do about Keith's three adorably playful kittens, who would be big enough to leave their mother in all too short a time. As always, the mere thought of the little tabby school cat made Evie smile; she could never help but be tickled that the mannish-sounding Keith was, in fact, a female;

And so on.

Taken as a whole, number eight on her 'Be Better' list was rather daunting, Evie sighed to herself, as she could think of several other things she really should put in this section too.

9. Be better as a member of Lymbridge village. The war was dragging on and on, eliciting a high cost from everybody in oh so many ways, and clearly now was the time for everyone to look out for each other as perhaps they never had before, and to work together in the war effort. There was always the underlying worry of loved ones, friends and acquaintances being away fighting, and although people were used to this unsettled feeling, it remained thoroughly unpleasant. Evie feared that she had been very distracted recently and so probably hadn't really been pulling her weight in being an active and good member of the community left at home in Lymbridge. Even though she had organised a fundraising school carol concert that ended up being quite a big do over at The Grange, which was the newly opened recuperation hospital where Timmy was now a patient, really it had been Sukie who had lifted the evening into something special. And then dear Sukie had had to come to the rescue once again to save the New Year's Eve dance too, this time by finding a band at very short notice, as Evie's raging influenza had meant she was good for nothing in the Christmas run-up. So, although Lymbridge villagers had congratulated Evie for her hard work, really all the credit for either event actually happening should have gone to the long-suffering Sukie.

Just as she came to the end of re-pinning several of the more defiant chestnut waves, as they had already started to spring loose – were they playing with her? – Evie was busy lining up in her mind 'Be Better' points ten, eleven and twelve when she noticed that Keith's three inquisitive kittens had made a pincer attack on her sleeping scarf, and were now dragging it away between them across the floor in an admirable display of teamwork for such little balls of fluff.

Oh well, thought Evie as she leant down to retrieve the scarf, much to the obvious disappointment of the kittens, maybe that's enough organisational thinking for me right at the moment.

And then as an afterthought she added, I probably shouldn't get my mind too overactive just before I settle down for the night.

The clarion call of 'Cocoa!' drifted up the stairs from the kitchen just as Evie was about to wind the now slightly dusty sleeping scarf around her head as a means of keeping the pin-curls snug, and (hopefully) avoiding uncomfortable hairgrips digging into her scalp when she was trying to sleep. This was normally a fiddly process as Evie knew she should take care also to make sure that all the pinned curls were lying in a manner that would create an impressive hairstyle the next day. Julia had a real knack with hair, and had used to come to the rescue for this bit on the rare occasions Evie made an effort with her hair before bedtime, and once again Evie felt a pang of sadness that Julia and she were no longer sharing the bedroom tucked under the eaves at Pemberley.

However, Evie was very fond of cocoa, even though the weak and grimy-looking night-time beverage they were all used to drinking now under the guise of 'cocoa' was nowhere near the rich, dark treat of pre-war days that the local Devon milk seemed absolutely perfect for. Clotted cream, tasty butter, and thick and velvety milk were, pre-war, one of the benefits of living in the West Country, where the soft-eyed cattle produced a rich and tempting array of dairy products.

Evie's mouth watered as she thought briefly of the delicious cream teas, with scones and heaped spoonfuls of her mother's homemade jam that the Yeo family had used to enjoy. She swallowed as she wrenched her scarf tight, with the pins any old way, and knotted its ends haphazardly into a perky bow above her forehead, and then trotted swiftly down to the warm kitchen to make sure she wasn't going to miss out.

Finding a comfy spot close to the warm kitchen range, she stayed chatting with the other residents at Pemberley as Keith and her kittens darted around their feet, having raced Evie to the kitchen; Keith was teaching them that the nightly call for cocoa might mean a dash of milk in their saucer too.

In fact, Evie was enjoying herself so much that she didn't look towards the kitchen clock on the mantelpiece above the range until well past eleven thirty.

It was only as Evie wended her way back up the final flight of stairs to her room right beneath the eaves, where its comfy bed nestled in a nook under the window, that she remembered her 'Be Better' list.

Hadn't early nights been at the top of her agenda?

Chapter Two

The spring term had started a couple of days earlier, although not quite as Evie had anticipated, which was more than a trifle irksome for her as this was her third term as a teacher and so this time around she had pinned her hopes on her new term feeling a little less like the fraught and uncharted territory the previous two terms had done.

Even though the start of the year had been both up and down for Evie in a personal sense – up, as the man she loved admitted finally that he cared for her too; and then down, as immediately Peter had confessed his feelings, he announced he had requested from the Ministry that he be transferred to another part of the country, and so he and Evie hadn't been able to pursue their feelings further – Evie refused to allow herself to feel totally demolished, as had happened previously when relationships had faltered with Timmy and then, later in the summer of 1941, hiccupped with Peter.

Evie supposed it was different for her now as, even though she had fallen heavily for Peter over the summer, during the autumn she had had time to get used to the idea of them *not* being together, largely because of the looming and distasteful presence of the devilish Fiona, Peter's horsy-faced former fiancée, who always seemed to be hovering somewhere in the wings.

Peter and Fiona (the tiresome woman having unceremoniously dumped Peter a year or two earlier when she had thought she could do better) had started seeing each other once again when Peter had transferred temporarily to London the previous summer. Hastily moving out of his lodgings at Pemberley without so much as a by-your-leave to Evie, Peter had believed mistakenly at that time that she was poised to marry Timmy; and Fiona meanwhile had come to the conclusion that maybe Peter was the better option for herself after all.

Predictably Fiona had hated Evie on sight – and the feeling was pretty much mutual, it had to be said – when Peter returned to Dartmoor early in the autumn, with Fiona tagging along, with everything about her grating on Evie's nerves. Naturally Fiona had wasted no time in showing Evie just how deeply she had got her clutches into the admittedly rather too biddable Peter.

Then there'd been a few weeks when Evie found Peter hard to read as he seemed to be backtracking with Fiona just a little, and yet not making a play for her.

And even when – finally! – he had told Fiona it was over between them both as the clocks were striking for the New Year, he still hadn't made his move properly with Evie, other than to say to her the following morning that he'd asked for a transfer elsewhere. Well, he'd mentioned, far too casually in Evie's opinion, that he loved her (almost as if Evie should have known this), but it was a declaration accompanied by the rider that Fiona was the type of determined woman who would make it impossible for he and Evie to be happy together, and so for them to remain apart was unfortunately the best solution on the basis that it would lead to the least unhappiness all round.

At this Evie didn't know who she wanted to slap more: Peter for being so spineless, or Fiona for being such a witch. Of course, the slapping was purely fantasy; that night in The Haywain with Julia was the one time in her life that Evie had given in to violence, and Evie was determined it was going to be a once-only occurrence.

So somehow Evie had dredged up a new resolve over the past few days. She simply wasn't going to allow herself to be knocked sideways by Peter moving away. Everything she had experienced with Peter in the eight months since they had met had been too much of a rollercoaster, with precious little reward in the emotional sense. Now Evie had had enough.

Although Peter said he loved her, apparently for him it wasn't the sort of love that just wouldn't be denied, Fiona or no Fiona. Whatever he really did feel, he'd chosen retreat as the better option.

So although upset, Evie was going to show some backbone in the face of Peter's feebleness, and the result was that she was determined on no more snivelling and sighing over a man she couldn't have.

It had been, therefore, a more upbeat-seeming Evie who had welcomed her infants several days earlier on the first morning of the spring term with what she hoped sounded like a heartfelt 'happy new year' to each of them and whichever parent was delivering them to school, as she stood in the playground with her winter coat neatly buttoned and her scarf wrapped cosily around her neck.

In the face of the pupils' excited exclamations of what they had got up to over the Christmas holidays, and the presents they had received, the melancholy experience of recent months of thinking about Peter and her unrequited feelings had, Evie discovered, not been too difficult to push to one side of her mind.

Thoughts of what was about to occur at Lymbridge Primary School were harder to cast aside, though, and however cheerful she might have looked on the outside, deep down Evie felt as if she were in a not particularly nice dream.

This was because of an announcement she had been met with on arrival for the first day of term.

'Evie, it's good you've come in early,' Mrs Smith had boomed briskly in her direction an hour before the first pupils were to arrive, when she first caught sight of Evie, 'as I have important news to share.'

And with that inauspicious greeting, Evie's day took a distinct turn for the worse.

Mrs Smith continued, 'I heard late last night that Lymbridge Primary School is, as I warned you might happen just before Christmas, indeed being merged. The good thing is that the two village primary schools we are amalgamating with shall be coming to us, with the new pupils being integrated into our classrooms. But make no mistake about it, my dear, it will mean a huge upheaval for everybody.'

Evie felt her cheery new year's salutation to Mrs Smith evaporate on her lips, despite it being the first time Mrs Smith had used the affectionate 'my dear' when speaking to her.

Evie was such a homebody that she always felt apprehensive when faced with news of any change, and so she was perturbed to see that there was something odd still about her headmistress's expression.

Evie knew already some local schools might merge, and so why was Mrs Smith looking as if there was something else that Evie needed to be told about?

It was a something that might not be very pleasant for Evie to hear, to judge by her headmistress's increasingly grave expression and wrinkled brow.

At the moment there were thirty pupils in the school: fourteen in Evie's class of five- and six-year-olds (there had been sixteen up until they had broken for the festive holiday, but two of the children had been moved with their parents to another part of the county and as their new home was quite a long way away they would be joining a school that was close to Exeter on the other side of the moor); and sixteen in Mrs Smith's class, which covered from age seven until eleven.

Now, Mrs Smith went on, the number of pupils at Lymbridge Primary School would be swelled by eighteen children from one school, and eight from another. This would make a total of fifty-six pupils in the school.

Evie frowned, not least because the two-classroom school building felt small enough as it was, and she couldn't imagine how these extra pupils would be squeezed in, unless some were taught in the Nissen hut at the bottom of the school field, just on the other side of the school's 'Dig for Victory' communal vegetable patch (and incidentally the place of Evie and Peter's first kiss). But the Nissen hut was a dank and dingy space, and would be murder to heat over the coming term.

Then Mrs Smith dropped a much more explosive bombshell. These new pupils weren't going to be accompanied by their previous teachers, as often happened when schools merged.

'You will be surprised and probably a little shocked, Evie, but Mr Leonard Bassett is going to return to Lymbridge Primary School as a teacher...' explained Mrs Smith, although Evie couldn't hear what the headmistress then went on to say, as she was so taken aback. This was perplexing and devastating news, and for just a moment Evie felt as if she was going to faint.

Leonard Bassett?

Words completely deserted Evie, and she could only look at Mrs Smith with her eyes wide and mouth unattractively gaping.

Evie was plunged back into gloom-inducing recollections.

For it was Leonard Bassett who had come so decisively between Evie and her middle sister, Julia.

The long and short of it had been that when Evie's former fiancé, Timmy, who'd been badly injured on manoeuvres abroad, was lying close to death in Stoke Mandeville Hospital in Berkshire late the previous summer, Mrs Smith had taken a sabbatical from the school in order to be near him. Timmy was Mrs Smith's only child, and they were exceptionally close (at least on Mrs Smith's side), in part because Timmy's father, Mr Bowes, had deserted the family home when Timmy was only six, a young and rather buxom employee at Spooner's store in Plymouth having proved irresistible, and so mother and son had been left to face the inhospitable world together.

With Mrs Smith otherwise occupied cheering up Timmy, Leonard Bassett had been the replacement head teacher drafted in to cover for the long-time headmistress.

Mr Bassett had lodged at Pemberley, and Evie had never taken to him. It hadn't helped that the day Leonard Bassett had moved in had been the day following Evie's discovery that Peter had rekindled his romance with Fiona, and she was feeling at a particularly low ebb.

Anyway, try as Evie might to think positively of him over the coming weeks as the autumn term rolled forward, Mr Bassett had remained firmly taciturn, with no sign at all that he found Evie to be interesting in the slightest, or even just the once, even the tiniest bit funny.

In addition to these failings, Leonard Bassett had shown a dull obsession with cricket and, much more disturbingly, he'd had strange moments when he was teaching at the primary school when he seemed lost and totally wrapped up in sad thoughts, sometimes meaning that he would just walk out of his classroom to leave his charges unattended and able to get up to who knows what. Twice Evie had found him crouching behind the Nissen hut, his head in his hands, looking as if he were drowning in turbulent emotional currents.

Evie had been unsettled at first, and then very concerned by Mr Bassett's unpredictable behaviour while teaching, fearing that any blame parents might have for slipping standards might, in Mrs Smith's absence, instead be laid firmly at Evie's door as she was so new to being a teacher and was at Lymbridge Primary School only on a temporary basis. She was also anxious about the safety of his pupils when he wasn't at the head of his class, of course, but frankly – and Evie wasn't proud of this – it had been a lesser worry in the face of her fear that she might be in some way held responsible if anything went wrong. After much agonising, Evie had confessed to Mrs Smith that she thought there was something very wrong with Mr Bassett.

And there was, as it turned out.

Aside from poor eyesight that meant he couldn't sign up to fight, Mr Bassett had revealed – when confronted by Evie's father, Robert, following the shocking revelation that he and Julia had taken their relationship to the level of being married but, scandalously, without the benefit of a marriage certificate – that he was suffering with a long-held nervous complaint, the symptoms of which included struggling with responsibility and being prone to reckless behaviour.

Unfortunately this impulsive conduct turned out to include him making overtures to Julia, and the pair had taken to sneaking around together in secret.

It was when their friend Linda made a casual comment that the clandestine relationship was brought out into the open and it all became shocking to a quite appalling level, as far as Evie was concerned. Evie was told that Mr Bassett and Julia had had two nights at The Griffin in Oldwell Abbott, sharing the same room exactly as if they were Mr and Mrs Bassett, and Julia were wearing his wedding ring on her finger. Which she most certainly was not.

The two blissful nights had been her own idea, Julia was happy to boast, and she had thoroughly enjoyed every moment of what she and Leonard had got up to.

Evie had discovered this news at a time when she was feeling particularly vulnerable, as besides the fact that Timmy had made Tricia pregnant while he and Evie were engaged, Evie knew that she herself had given Peter mixed signals and had allowed him to think her single when she had foolishly promised herself to Timmy. Predictably, the consequence of this was that her fledgling relationship with Peter had gone wrong too. Evie had just been facing up to the uncomfortable truth that she was guilty and confused about the mere idea of sexual intercourse (she wasn't quite sure why, but that was how she felt). And she was realising that her determinedly prim and perhaps rather priggish behaviour – she insisted to herself that she wanted to be a virgin when she married: how quaint! – might well have led ultimately to her romantic unhappiness. Actually, Evie knew it wasn't quite that simple, but then neither were these assertions to be totally disregarded.

Anyway, to learn that Julia, always the more staid and sensible sister of the trio of Yeo girls, had dared to behave so outrageously and without an iota of shame, felt like a knife twisting in Evie's gut. It had all proved too much for her at that particular moment, and she had let rip at her sister in no uncertain terms. And Julia had stood her ground without any obvious signs of embarrassment, before launching into some home truths that Evie hadn't enjoyed hearing a bit. To make it worse, the argument had degenerated into a fight, and it had been so public, in the ladies' bar at The Haywain. And all over Leonard Bassett – Evie cringed still at the very thought.

The result was that the sisters had been the unwelcome focus of rather a lot of scurrilous village gossip for a short while. Evie had been formally reprimanded at the school as her position was one of responsibility, and Mr Bassett had resigned from his post as temporary head teacher even though technically he hadn't broken any of the rules of his employment.

The tangle thickened as Leonard Bassett asked Julia to marry him, belatedly, and she accepted but then, the very next day, she refused his proposal, suggesting instead they just lived as man and wife, and she call herself Mrs Bassett. Evie could still hardly believe that her ordinarily sensible sister had behaved so rashly by turning down the chance to become the real Mrs Bassett after having given herself so freely to him. But a heartbeat later Evie had to admit to herself that, in reality, she didn't know Julia as well as she thought, for she had happily been making assumptions for years about her younger sister, probably with the tacit complicity of Julia herself, who'd clearly not cared to set Evie right about any of her misperceptions.

As it turned out Julia and Leonard Bassett setting up home together hadn't actually happened yet, but Pattie, who still lived at the family home where Julia had moved back to, had recently confided to Evie that Julia no longer spent every night at Bluebells...

Evie and Julia hadn't spoken for weeks after their scuffle, and it was still only a week ago that Julia had leapt to Evie's defence when the odious Fiona had warned Evie off Peter a bit too loudly in front of everybody at the New Year's Eve dance in the village hall. It was fine for Julia to tell the world what she thought of Evie's supercilious and unbearably smug attitude, as had happened that fateful evening at The Haywain, apparently. But woe betide anyone outside the Yeo family who attempted to criticise Evie in public, such as Fiona sniping at Evie on the dance floor at New Year, seemed to be the message Julia was keen to reinforce.

As the clock ticked towards the first pupils arriving for the spring term, Evie shook herself inwardly and tried to concentrate instead on what Mrs Smith was saying. The headmistress was still talking about the practicalities of the merger.

Deeply shocked by the news that she was going to have to face Leonard Bassett on a daily basis, Evie forced herself back into the here and now, and told herself that she really must get a grip on herself.

She sighed with a jagged depth of emotion. For a moment it all felt too much, and she couldn't bring herself to look at Mrs Smith.

Mrs Smith, who knew about the tension between Evie and Mr Bassett, paused her monologue to look at Evie. And then the older woman patted her arm in comfort. 'Evie, I know. I know,' commiserated the tweed-clad older woman in a much gentler tone than was normal.

Evie had never previously thought Mrs Smith to be a particularly sympathetic woman, and so it looked as if she were probably going to be wrong about that too. Oh dear.

'It's absolutely not ideal, and nor is it nice for you,' said Mrs Smith. 'You and I both have had a dicey history with Mr Bassett, as aside from your, er, your spat with your sister about him, I myself deeply resented the time I had to spend away from Timmy when Mr Bassett then left the school so abruptly, meaning that I had to step in without so much as a by-your-leave in order to hold the fort once more when my dear boy was lying gravely ill and needed me by his bedside. But this is a time for everyone to make sacrifices and I did my duty as I saw it, as you must now do yours. We are in a time of war and must all pull together. And the shortages of qualified teachers locally are such that I've simply had no other option than to bring Mr Bassett back. I do apologise, Evie, but there it is.

'If I try and find the silver lining in this particular cloud, even you acknowledged that when his mind is on the matter, Mr Bassett is an able teacher and that the pupils respond well to him.

And my job is to make sure he keeps his mind where it should be, while your job is nothing more nor less than for you to go on as you have been doing as I believe wholeheartedly that you have it in you to be a wonderful infant teacher.' Mrs Smith paused for breath. It was a short pause.

She went on, 'I'm sure Mr Bassett is not delighted at the prospect either, Evie. But when I explained the situation to him in person at an embarrassingly late hour last night the poor man was in his pyjamas, and no, there wasn't any sign of Julia, before you wonder – even though he has a private income that means it's not imperative that he has to work, he knew he had to help us out as we are in a hole, and so he said he was happy to come back once more to Lymbridge Primary School. He will be joining us next week when the new pupils will also arrive. We must all make the best of a bad job, and we should remember that Mr Churchill would expect no less from all three of us.'

Evie still couldn't trust herself to speak.

It wasn't until the next day, when Evie had had twenty-four hours to get her thoughts in order and to become more used to the idea, that she felt calmer about the prospect of having to see Mr Bassett on a daily basis.

Then Mrs Smith gave Evie another surprise.

Evie would remain as teacher to the infants class, which would swell only to seventeen pupils with the addition of just three youngsters.

Mr Bassett would be allocated the seven- and eight-year-olds; there were fourteen of those, and they would now be called 'juniors middle'.

And Mrs Smith would teach the nine-, ten- and eleven-year-olds, in a class of twenty-four, the class now called the 'juniors top'.

The juniors middle would take up residence in Evie's former infants classroom.

And Evie's infants class would move to the church hall that was situated along the single road through the village, further down and towards the shop. Morning and afternoon playtime, and lunchtime for the infants, would all still take place at the school. And in order to account for the few minutes' walk between the church hall and the school several times a day, Evie's class would start fifteen minutes earlier in the morning, and end fifteen minutes after the main school finished for the day.

'I appreciate that this is adding another half an hour onto your working day,' said Mrs Smith, 'and unfortunately you won't receive any additional payment for this. And I daresay parents with children in both the infants and the juniors will be irritated. But I think you will agree with my opinion that it's important that your class still feels part of the whole school, and that we should organise a more structured period of activity after they've eaten their packed lunches to ensure this.

'For reasons you know all too well and that I don't need to go into again, I must be able to keep an eye on what is going on with the juniors middle, and I trust you meanwhile not to get up to too much mischief when left to your own devices.'

Mrs Smith dropped her grandiose voice to a level that sounded grave but much less portentous, and she peered deeply into Evie's eyes as she added, 'I'm very much hoping you prove worthy of my trust, Evie, and this increased responsibility, which you should take as a sign of my belief in you. Please do not let me down.'

Evie assured Mrs Smith that she would do her level best to be a credit to her headmistress and to Lymbridge Primary School. She meant every word.

Evie told herself stoically that she must try to think positively about these changes and to embrace the extra workload rather than rail against it. Mrs Smith had, after all, all but told her she was doing quite a good job with her infants, and the older woman had made it clear too that she felt Evie could be trusted. All of this was positive, Evie knew.

Still, the reality was a further squeeze on Evie's spare time, while she would have busier lunchtimes too. And it was going to be unavoidable that she would run up regularly against Leonard Bassett. All of this might require a great deal of self-control in order for Evie to work efficiently and smoothly, something that Evie had struggled with in the past as she wasn't naturally a particularly organised sort of person, but something nonetheless that Mrs Smith, and Evie's pupils and their parents, would both require and expect.

Oh, what an exasperating start to a new year this all promised to be!

They still had almost a week's grace before the

new regime would begin, and naturally there was a lot to do in the meantime.

Mrs Smith announced she would teach the whole school as one large class in the interim. This would leave Evie and the elderly school caretaker, Mr Cawes, to organise the church hall (which also served as the village hall), and then for them to go to the two outlying schools to bring as much equipment over to Lymbridge as they could.

At the weekend, there would be a vehicle available that Evie and Mr Cawes could use to ferry the bigger items such as desks and chairs around.

The more Evie thought about it the more she realised that this was going to be a more complicated job than she had at first assumed, as it wasn't simply a matter of bringing the desks and chairs from the two schools straight to the village hall. Irritatingly, all the equipment would have to be taken to Lymbridge Primary School and then divided into small, medium and large, with then only the smallest desks and chairs being transported to the hall, along with various wall charts and alphabet and sum posters that Evie had made.

How exceptionally vexing it all was, especially as Evie knew that in all probability she and the occasionally grumpy Mr Cawes would barely be speaking to each other by the time they had got everything sorted, and that then she probably wasn't going to be in the best frame of mind for getting off to an equable start with Mr Bassett either.

Chapter Three

As usual when she felt discombobulated, Evie headed to Bluebells for tea, looking forward to the warmth and familiarity of her family home's slightly shabby kitchen, and her mother Susan's steadying presence.

Evie felt shaken still over the news that Leonard Bassett would soon be a part of her daily life, and she hoped very much that Julia was at Bluebells when she arrived as perhaps enough water had passed under the bridge that they would be able to find a quiet spot for a chat. Although Julia had sprung to Evie's defence at the New Year's Eve dance, and they had hugged each other the next day when Evie had bumped into Julia as they went about their business in Lymbridge, they hadn't yet had the opportunity really to clear the air with one another.

This was a situation that absolutely must be resolved, and as soon as possible, Evie thought, as she walked briskly towards Bluebells. Although nowhere near four o'clock yet it was pitch dark already.

The milder weather of the last two days that had led to the remaining snow from December disappearing almost overnight felt now as if it was being pushed aside by a fast-approaching cold front. Evie fancied she could sense the barometer drop minute by minute, and that the familiar moorland sounds around her were taking on the distinctive quality that heralded a forthcoming brutal winter snap. In fact, she decided she could hear drumming hoof beats in the distance, with the occasional neigh, and so she thought that maybe somewhere out in the darkness two rival herds of Dartmoor ponies were squaring up over the same patch of winter grazing, keen to eat as much as possible while the ground was free of a fresh fall of snow.

But Bluebells turned out not to be the sanctuary Evie envisioned. The bumpy white cob walls shaded by the almost black overhanging thatch, its small windows and battered front door had been so much a part of Evie's growing up that long ago she had virtually ceased to notice any of it or indeed listen to her father Robert with his oft-repeated refrain of the need to re-thatch or to repaint the front door. Despite it being dark and poky inside (although not more so than other traditional cottages in Lymbridge), Evie loved everything about Bluebells with its lived-in look abutted by a rather untidy front garden and weather-blasted orchard behind, and a ramshackle wooden garage away to one side.

For Evie knew that the way the thick-walled cottage looked gave little hint as to the happiness and the warmth of family life inside.

But now Evie arrived to nothing short of a sense of pandemonium.

Susan's eyes were unnaturally glittery, and she was squeezing and fiddling with a tea towel, and pacing awkwardly about the small kitchen without seeming certain where she wanted to go.

Normally her mother was unflappable and calm, and seeing her behave this way gave Evie a sinking feeling in her tummy.

What was even odder was that Robert, who was usually at this time of day to be found reading the newspaper as he sat in his favourite chair to one side of the kitchen range while Susan prepared the family's supper, looked to be making a cup of tea for his wife.

Evie couldn't remember having witnessed the like before as, excepting on Christmas Day after the festive lunch had been served (as then Robert and her brother James would take over the kitchen for the rest of the day), Susan or the girls were the only family members who would prepare food and drink. This was a fact that had led to many moans over the years from Evie and her sisters, especially when they were busy and James had been ostentatiously lounging about in a way he knew would infuriate them. Little brothers could be very annoying at times.

Pattie wasn't at home, and Julia couldn't be seen either. But James was cleaning shoes as he sat on the window seat near the kitchen table, and he rolled his eyes when he caught Evie's glance, and then nodded skywards. Evie realised he was indicating that whatever was wrong was something to do with what was occurring upstairs.

Frank and Joseph, the evacuee lads from Peckham in London who now shared the Yeo family home at Bluebells, were playing cards at the table and although Evie noticed that their game was accompanied by none of their normal boyish banter, it didn't look as if the problem lay in their direction. Instead, they glanced quickly at Evie with pained expressions and immediately turned back to concentrating on their game with downcast gazes.

Evie wasn't used to walking into Bluebells and nobody greeting her or seeming pleased to see her, and so she didn't know what to think.

'Mother dear, whatever is wrong?' Evie asked in what she hoped was a caring way. 'Is there anything I can do to help?'

Susan stopped her pacing when she saw Evie and immediately her eyes started to glint with tears, and then she said, 'Evie lovey, you'll never guess. We've just had a visit from the authorities – we're going to lose Catherine, and Marie too.'

'Oh no!' said Evie, her heart sinking uncomfortably, deep in her chest. In an instant she felt a real sense of loss.

Catherine and Marie were the two small evacuee girls from Plymouth that the Yeos had taken in not long after Easter in 1941. They were both infants in Evie's class, and after a period of being very withdrawn and quiet, they had become noisy and full of fun and naughtiness as six-year-olds should be. They'd been cheerful and lively earlier that day, and clearly had had no idea of what would be happening to them in only a matter of a few short hours.

They weren't sisters, but they were absolutely devoted to one another. Both their fathers were away fighting, and Marie's mother had been seriously injured in the severe bombing campaign that Plymouth had endured the previous year, which had killed Marie's dear brother, who had only been a mere eight years old, and destroyed their house. And dear little Catherine's mother had been run over by an ambulance driving in the dark (no street lights and only the faintest beam allowed on headlights made being out and about in night-time quite precarious) and pronounced dead at the scene of the accident; the ambulance had been on its way to attend those injured by the bombing that dreadful night. Catherine was an only child, and aside from her absent soldier father, nobody had been able to trace any other relatives. Obviously traumatised, the two little mites had been taken to the police station together, and had been inseparable ever since, each taking comfort in having the other around.

Plymouth had proved to be a terrible target for repeated bombing attacks, no matter how many barrage balloons had been placed as a deterrent. It hadn't taken the Jerrys long to work out that strategically Plymouth was immensely important to Britain. Its large port and location to the western side of Britain made it ideal as a Merchant Navy centre as ships from abroad importing goods into the country didn't have to risk sailing further up the English Channel; and Plymouth had all the facilities required for being an important Royal Navy base too.

And so for their safety, Marie and Catherine had had to be evacuated. They had been sent with a group of children to Dartmoor, an area that although relatively close to Plymouth was much more sparsely populated, being made up mostly of small villages, farms or great swathes of open moorland, with therefore few reasons to

43

attract the attention of the bombers.

The two little girls had ended up at Bluebells when no other local berths could be found for them, and within just a couple of weeks they had sneaked into everyone's hearts and were soon thought of by the Yeos as fully paid-up members of the family clan.

'Marie's mother has been in hospital and then nursed back to health in Goodleigh, I think they said, with her own kin,' Robert explained as he looked over to Evie across the top of his wife's head, as he gently manoeuvred Susan onto his favourite chair at the kitchen range and then passed her the cup of tea he'd made. Evie was touched to see that he'd used a cup and saucer reserved for visitors, rather than their common or garden everyday crockery. In a quiet voice Robert added, 'But she feels well enough to have Marie back now, and she's happy to take Catherine too until her father comes home, as the powers that be think the wee maids should be kept together.'

'Goodness,' said Evie. 'What a wrench for us all, and you especially, Mother, as they've really come to be part of the family. You've been so wonderful with them and have very much helped draw them out of their shells. And they've been stalwart members of my class too, so we're going to miss them terribly. When are they going? It would be nice if we can give them a little party to send them off.'

'That's the thing, lovey,' said Susan, her voice growing increasingly shaky. Her hand was trembling as she placed her half-drunk cup back on its saucer with a short clattering sound. 'A car's coming within the hour, and so the poor little mites are going tonight. They're not going to be able to say goodbye to Pattie, or to their friends at school – and it's fair breaking my heart, although at least they will be able to say farewell to you. Julia is helping them pack right now, not that they've got much to take with them.

'Evie, I'm ashamed to say that I felt proper peculiar about losing them when I heard, and I just couldn't face doing the sorting for them myself. Julia saw this and stepped in to do what needs doing. It just won't be the same here without them. Anyway, you stay and talk to your father, Evie – I really must go and see how they are getting along.'

Evie was surprised at the size of the lump in her own throat. Marie and Catherine were adorable little girls, and Evie realised that in all likelihood no one at Bluebells would see them again after tonight. It was easy to think they would, but with everybody's busy lives and petrol rationing, the girls being not seven years old and probably not yet up to writing even short letters, and with Plymouth having to undergo a massive civic re-structure and rebuild because of the bombing, which meant that many families had become peripatetic, with the best will in the world it would be hard to keep in touch.

Glumly Robert gave Evie her own cup of tea (she got an 'everyday' cup and saucer, she noticed), and then her father nodded towards a loaf of bread sitting crust end up on the breadboard, with the cut side downwards to keep it as fresh as possible, to see if she was hungry.

Evie shook her head as food felt like the last

thing she could stomach just at that moment.

Meanwhile Frank and Joseph were still unnaturally quiet. Ordinarily they were boisterous and lively lads; they were brothers, and had originally been called Franz and Josef. They had been ferried out of Europe by train when it became clear that to be Jewish was to be very vulnerable, and tragically they'd had to leave the rest of their family behind. On their arrival in London they had lived in a traditional working-class area in the south-east of the city, although they had then been evacuated to the West Country with the rest of their school not long after war had broken out. But when their London home was bombed out and their foster parents found themselves homeless, even though all the other boys who had been evacuated along with them to Devon had long since returned to London to be with their own families, Frank and Joseph had made it clear they wanted to stay in Lymbridge for the duration. Frank was now at the 'big school' in Oldwell Abbott that James attended, and Joseph would be joining him there in September.

Privately Evie thought the lads would never leave Bluebells – it was over two years since they had arrived and they were so embedded now in local life that if they were to go too, an even bigger hole than the one the loss of Marie and Catherine was making would be left. It would be quite unfillable, and in any case it wasn't as if they had their own family waiting for them in London. They didn't talk any longer of their life before they came to Dartmoor, which Evie liked to think, although she wasn't sure, was a good thing. She knew that when

46

the war ended Robert would move heaven and earth to find the boys' relatives in Europe, but sadly Evie didn't bear much hope that they would have made it, as the news filtering through suggested that huge parts of Europe had been decimated and many lives lost, although of course Evie hoped very much that there would be a happy outcome for the lads.

Evie went and sat with them, and asked if she could join their game of cards. Once the game had got going again, Evie said to them that it was understandable they would feel strange at Catherine and Marie leaving Bluebells. She admitted that she felt very peculiar too.

'You do both know, though, that your home is here with us, don't you?' she said gently, as Shady, the family dog, came up to stand close beside the boys, his damp nose nudging at each of their elbows, as if Shady were agreeing that Frank and Joseph were part of his family too. Evie added as she dealt a new hand, 'Me and Julia, and Pattie and James, think of you as our two youngest brothers, proper job Yeos through and through. And along with Mother and Father, we hope that you each understand that you can always make your home at Bluebells.'

Boys being boys, they didn't really say anything much to this. But Evie fancied their shoulders relaxed and that after a long while they started to take a bit more interest in their card game, although it was only when their normal accusations of cheating began that Evie felt she was able to make her excuses and leave the table.

Less than an hour later Evie stood with the rest of the Yeos in the road outside Bluebells to wave Catherine and Marie off. Marie's mother was a passenger in the car that arrived to collect them and Evie was shaken to see how thin and careworn she looked. She had been so emotional when she spied her daughter that she'd barely been able to speak.

At the first glimpse of her mother Marie had stood stock-still and stared at her, as if she couldn't believe her eyes. Then she burst into tears and flung herself into her mother's arms to be enveloped in the warmest of hugs. It was the first time the pair had seen each other for well over six months, which must have seemed like a lifetime to the little girl. Catherine had watched the reunion with rather a pensive expression, holding on to Susan's hand very tightly. But then Marie's mother, while keeping an arm tightly around Marie, opened her other arm so that Catherine could have a hug too.

Evie's heart went out to Susan who reluctantly let go of Catherine and gave her the gentlest of nudges in the other woman's direction. Susan was trying to smile through it all, but Evie could see how sad her mother was. The little girls had clearly wormed their way very deep into the heart of the Yeo family.

As the girls' small amount of luggage was stowed in the car – just the one very small cardboard suitcase between them – Evie crouched down to say how much she'd enjoyed teaching them, and that the next evening perhaps they could recite the alphabet and say some tables, so that they could show off to Marie's mother what they had been learning. Nodding very seriously, they promised they would do as Evie suggested. They looked utterly bewildered at what was happening to them, it was all so very sudden.

It was too nippy standing outside Bluebells to eke out the parting longer than need be, and it was with heavy hearts that the Yeo family stood in the road waving until well after the car had disappeared, even though with no street lights and no illumination coming from the house as the blackout curtains were so effective, they knew they could no longer be seen by Catherine and Marie.

'Julia, might you and I have a cup of tea together, and a word?' said Evie, as they all trooped back inside. 'I know you'll want to sort your bedroom out, but I really would appreciate it.'

Catherine and Marie had been topping and tailing in Julia's bed since their arrival, which was why Julia had moved over to join Evie at Pemberley in the first place. Since her return to Bluebells in disgrace, Julia had been camping out on the uncomfortable sofa in the parlour. Evie had slept on it the night of her and Julia's fight, and she knew how hard and lumpy the sofa was, and so she thought that Julia must be looking forward to getting back to sleeping in her own bed once again (when she wasn't staying at Leonard's rented room, that is, Evie thought with a small moue of distaste). Julia worked for the Post Office, delivering mail around the village and to the outlying farms. She would cycle energetically for miles, up and down some very steep hills, and so she needed

49

a good night's sleep, especially as in her free time she was kept busy too doing the hair of some of the village women.

'Why don't you come up upstairs and help me?' suggested Julia.

Evie thought her sister sounded reasonably cheerful, and so she hoped this equable mood would last. She smiled in reply, and followed her sister up the narrow stairs, stopping off at the cupboard where Susan kept the clean bedlinen to get two clean and pressed sheets and some pillowcases.

Neither of them said anything for a while, and Evie busied herself stripping off the used linen, and then making up the bed, while Julia moved things around in the chest of drawers, and dusted off various surfaces with a feather duster.

'Julia, I don't know that I thanked you enough for standing up to Fiona on my behalf at the dance on New Year's Eve. You didn't have to step in as you did, and I want you to know I very much appreciate it,' Evie said, breaking the companionable silence at last, as she started to sweep the linoleum-covered floor.

Her sister laughed, and said wasn't that Fiona a piece of work? 'She might be wearing the latest fashions, but she's all teeth and too many angles, if you want my opinion. I've no idea what's been going on, but it's as clear as the nose on your face that she's got it in for you. I guess there's some sort of history between you and Peter.'

And with that Julia stopped what she was doing so that she could look at Evie with a searching expression.

'Not any more, there isn't,' said Evie.

To judge by Julia's ordinary-sounding tone, it didn't look as if she had grasped too much about what had been going on in Evie's life. Actually, Sukie was the only person Evie had confided in fully about Peter, and now she sensed the confidence had held.

It struck Evie suddenly that she had been over-critical on the night of the tiff regarding the 'crime' of Julia and Leonard Bassett creeping around together behind everybody's backs, as, if Evie were honest with herself at this point, she could see that she also had been guilty of playing her Peter cards very close to her own chest. And so had her own behaviour been any more exemplary in this respect than Julia's secrecy? Probably not by very much.

Evie added gloomily, 'Actually, there's not really much "history" between Peter and me – and certainly nothing near your Griffin escapade...'

Julia stopped what she was doing as she tilted her head to one side and looked at Evie with an arch expression, chin dropped deliberately to-wards the collar of her pretty cotton blouse and with comically raised eyebrows. She clearly hadn't expected Evie to allude to her and Leo-nard Bassett's first sexual encounter quite so soon in their conversation, or so bluntly.

Evie tried to hold Julia's gaze, but in what she hoped was a non-challenging sort of way as she didn't want to provoke any tetchiness.

There was a tense pause for a pulse or two, and then Julia started to smile before miming licking the tip of her forefinger and drawing it down-

51

wards in a vertical direction, indicating that Evie had scored the first point but that Julia was amused rather than angry. Consequently Evie's responding laugh of relief reverberated with only the slightest edge of hysteria.

With a small jolt Evie sensed suddenly that this release of tension between the sisters made her feel unexpectedly quite brave.

'Darn it,' she said then, 'I'm going to come clean to you about Peter and me, Julia, and you can tell Pattie if you want. I've only told Sukie, but now I find that I don't really care who knows.'

Julia sat on the bed and patted a spot on the bedspread beside her. There was no heating in the room, and their breath was showing in little puffs of steam, and so Evie grabbed the spare eiderdown lying folded over the wooden frame at the end of the bed. She sat close to Julia and draped the vaguely damp-feeling eiderdown across both of their shoulders, and began to confide in her sister all that had gone on with Timmy and Tricia and Peter and herself. As she talked Evie realised how very entwined the lives of the four of them had become over the last six months.

Evie spoke for quite some time, and Julia didn't say anything, although she did at one point inch closer to Evie and put her arm around her shoulders under the quilt.

'And then you and I had that horrid argument in The Haywain. I think my complete loss of temper – and I do feel very ashamed of my screaming like a fishwife at you in such a public place – was as much my own frustration at myself as it was jealousy that you had dared to do what I hadn't been brave enough to, not that I had quite had the chance, although I had certainly thought about it,' confessed Evie. 'I'm not going to say I approve of what you and Leonard did, but I'm not sure I quite disapprove of it any longer, if you know what I mean. There's even been the odd moment when I wish I'd done it too, and so now looking back, I think I was mostly jealous.'

Julia didn't reply immediately, although she clasped Evie tighter to her for a moment. 'Oh Evie, I wish I'd behaved differently that night too, as I've hated the fact that we fought. I don't know what it is about Leonard. But when I think of him, or he is near me, I suppose the best way that I can describe it is that I feel as if I'm a stronger and braver person. I feel diminished without him, and I want to be with him every minute. I feel as if I could lay down my life for his.'

Evie knew of the power of what Julia was describing. The thought that it was Leonard Bassett who ignited this depth of feeling in her sister was hard for Evie to square, but she supposed that love drove reason galloping away.

'So what is going to happen? Are you going to live with him? And why did you say yes when he wanted to get married, and then no?' asked Evie. 'Pattie's been useless for gossip, and I've been longing to talk to Mother and Father about you two, but they made it clear that the pair of you are a no-go area for discussion with them as far as I'm concerned.'

Julia gave a rueful snort of humour, and said, 'Well, they certainly haven't taken the no-go route with me, as they've talked at me about it for hours.

They think I'm a fool and that I'll probably regret it, but they are also taking the view that it's my life and I must do as I think best and be at liberty to make my own mistakes. They've been at pains to point out that of course their door will always remain open to me, not like some families, I know, as many a daughter has been thrown out and told never to darken the family home again for much lesser indiscretions. All that Mother and Father have asked of me is that I don't flaunt what is going on in front of James or the evacuees when I go to spend the night with Leonard.'

Evie squeezed her sister's chilly fingers, as Julia went on, 'And to answer your question about whether Leonard and I will move in together ... we'd love to, but it turns out that our fame precedes us now, unfortunately. Property for rent around here is in very short supply at the moment because of the number of people who have been brought into the area to work at Plymouth docks, either for the Navy or on the merchant shipping side, and we're yet to find a landlord who will rent to us as an unmarried couple. Leonard says we should marry, but I want to wait until the scuffle in The Haywain is just a footnote round here in most people's memories; and then I can have my dream wedding day with everything just as I want it.

'I don't regret going to The Griffin with Leonard – I can't tell you how amazing those two nights were – but I was too hasty in saying yes when father more or less bullied us into the proposal after you and I scrapped in the pub. What a mistake that was, as I just didn't realise how very much I wanted a day as perfect as when Linda married Sam, which wasn't going to happen at that time.'

Evie wasn't quite certain whether the mistake that Julia was referring to might be the sisters' tussling, or the hasty acceptance of Leonard's proposal, and so she decided just to nod wisely as if she was completely following what Julia was saying. They'd not talked for such a long time, and now Evie didn't dare interrupt the flow.

'I do want to marry Leonard in the future, Evie, really I do. But a good marriage has to get off on the right foot, and while I'm happy that everyone knows that he and I are committed to each other in *all* senses already, I felt that to marry in haste seemed as if it would be merely because I'd made a disgrace of myself by screaming like a harridan in The Haywain. And what I want so badly is that when Leonard and I tie the knot everyone knows that we are a true love match,' Julia said.

Privately Evie thought her sister was being rather optimistic as Julia was very likely severely underestimating how deeply shocking people had found Julia daring to have sexual intercourse without any sense of apology or the sanctity of a wedding ring. Lymbridge folk had long memories and Julia's casual flouting of social conventions would be gossip fodder for quite some time, Evie feared. Still, she was determined not to be the one to rain on Julia's parade with any gloomy comments.

Evie realised Julia was still speaking.

'Meanwhile Leonard rejoins Lymbridge Primary School on Monday, as I'm sure you know by now, and so I definitely don't want to ruffle any feathers until he's settled in. All in all, we're intent on keeping a very low profile just at the moment.'

Evie relaxed a bit more; Julia had given her the perfect way in to mention her own feelings of trepidation about working with Leonard Bassett again.

When Julia heard how nervous Evie felt at the prospect, she admitted that Leonard was feeling worried about it too, although he was determined that it would all go much more smoothly this time around. His doctor had given him a series of physical exercises to do each day, and Julia had been instructed in how to massage his back – the aim of this was to give an outlet for his stress, in the hope that his unpredictable behaviour would be easier to manage. When the weather improved Leonard had told Julia he was going to have a bash at long-distance running around the moors as he was sure this would be good for him too.

The sisters were cold right through now despite the eiderdown draped across them, and they fancied a hot drink. But before they went downstairs to the warm kitchen, Evie had one more question.

'Julia, I hope you don't mind me asking, and of course I'll understand if you don't want to say anything. But what was it like when, you know ... er, you know ... you and Leonard did, er, did *it* for the first time?'

The cup of tea and the warm-up in the kitchen had to be delayed for a good twenty-five minutes further, and more than once downstairs Susan and Robert looked at each other askance when hoots of laughter drifted down to them from Julia's bedroom.

It was a much happier Evie who hugged her sister goodbye that evening before heading back to Pemberley. While there was undoubtedly still work to be done in restoring their old relationship, both she and Julia seemed to have deliberately shrugged off many of their gripes of the previous year, and that could only be a good thing.

Chapter Four

Once they got down to work preparing the new classroom – although getting down to it required two cups of tea first, as well as some plain biscuits that Evie had been able to scrounge from Pemberley – Evie was surprised at how smoothly, and how companionably, she and school caretaker Mr Cawes got along. They'd had their run-ins in the past, but not now. Mr Cawes was a very elderly man who had fought in the Great War, and as they worked he started to speak about this time. Evie found it really interesting the more he told her, and she began thinking about the parallels with what Britain was currently facing.

Just as fascinating was when Evie discovered as they chatted about Lymbridge during the 1920s that Mr Cawes had an enviably encyclopaedic knowledge of who'd got up to what and with whom in Lymbridge over the last fifty years or so. It was mainly trivial gossip but it was enjoyably scurrilous, and the pair of them laughed out loud more than once. She was surprised at how quickly the hours passed, and she thought Mr Cawes probably felt the same way too.

They decided to sort the village hall first, and so they spent a good hour tidying it. Then they brushed and scrubbed just about everything they could see, making sure everything was as spick and span as they could get it, and the floor was as clean as possible.

James gave them a hand with moving bits and pieces that had been left languishing around the hall to a small room tucked away at the back, where Evie decided the children could also put their coats and scarves during the lessons, while the larger items stored at the hall that wouldn't be needed too soon and that wouldn't perish in the damp conditions were lugged over to the Nissen hut at the bottom of the school field.

Evie thought she'd get used to moving things around over the next few months as the school wasn't to have exclusive use of the village hall. School would end for the day at three fifteen, with everyone out by three forty-five and the whole place tidied, and at four o'clock groups such as the Women's Institute or the physical fitness classes would take over. So, on a running-late day (of which Evie hoped there wouldn't be too many), she would only have fifteen minutes to get the hall ready for whatever would be happening later in the afternoon. It wasn't ideal, but it was a condition of the school being able to use the hall.

Meanwhile sorties were made by Evie and Mr Cawes back to the school for a blackboard and chalk, and then a very old and no-longer-used map of the world, a spare first-aid kit plus, of course, the awards chart of stars Evie had laboriously designed for the start of the Michaelmas term as an incentive for good behaviour and solid learning.

Evie remembered that she'd need soap for the lavatories (the primary school was allowed its own supply, despite the nationwide shortages), and some towels. And a stash of spare pants and knickers, just in case, as some of her little ones couldn't be totally relied on in this respect. There weren't any spare boxes of Izal toilet paper Evie could take for the lavatory, but Frank and Joseph earned a half crown each by cutting up a very large pile of old newspapers and threading the cut squares onto lengths of twine that they then knotted into a loop so that Evie could hang the prepared paper in each toilet cubicle. And James earned himself a florin too for cutting down several beer crates so that the smallest infants could have a sturdy helping step up to the full-sized porcelain toilets with their thick wooden seats. Evie could see, though, that the round wooden handles on the chains hanging down from beside the almost ceiling-height cisterns were too high for her charges, and so she told herself she must go into each of the cubicles at least every hour in order to flush the lavatories as she wanted to make sure that the more squeamish of her infants wouldn't be put off if they needed to spend a penny.

Robert arranged for a farmer to visit both of the other schools with his van during the week, which although smelly looked to have been specially cleaned inside for the transportation, and any desks and chairs that weren't being used at the other schools for their final week were stowed inside, as were various books and stationery. One of the schools had smallish football goals, with rope netting attached to the heavy wooden framework, and a chalk marker for a pitch and some footballs, and so Evie decided that the sports equipment should come with her back to Lymbridge too. Maybe she could persuade the Worths that when the worst of the winter weather was over the bottom of the lawn at Pemberley could be loaned to the school as a small soccer pitch. (There was a little bit that abutted where the stable block was, which Evie thought would be perfect as it wouldn't really be noticeable from the main house.)

At each of the schools she and Mr Cawes visited, Evie made sure she said hello to the children who would be joining them the following Monday, and she told them how very much everybody at Lymbridge Primary School was looking forward to their arrival. Most of the children stared back at her with a look of disbelief that was bordering on apprehension.

On the Friday afternoon Evie mustered her sweetest voice to ask if it was at all possible for Mr Cawes to get up early on the Saturday so that the kindly farmer could collect them once again to do the run to pick up the remaining tables and chairs. Rather to Evie's surprise Mr Cawes didn't put up a fight, which was handy as the farmer had other things to do later, and so it was still dark when they drove through Lymbridge on their way to the two schools. Mr Cawes was quite cheerful about losing his Saturday lie-in, all things considered.

At one school Evie had a slight altercation with her opposite number from a school near South Molton that was also being allocated some of the pupils and equipment. This other teacher said grumpily that *they* were to have the bulk of the chairs, and for a minute or two the situation looked a little fraught and as if it could develop into a stand-off between the women. It was when Mr Cawes and the farmer came into the classroom to see what was keeping Evie that the other teacher backed down, and Evie got her way.

The trio from Lymbridge chuckled as they drove back to the village with their booty, making the odd comment that the rather snooty maid wanting Evie's chairs must have thought they looked 'proper fearsome' to judge by the speed she gave up on the tussle and scampered away on her bicycle. Evie thought it was probably more down to the fact that the unintentionally but nonetheless rather comical outfits the farmer and Mr Cawes had been wearing as their weekend mufti, combined with them coming into the classroom and stopping in their tracks to stare gormlessly in silence at Evie's adversary, were what had done the trick – the other teacher probably thought they were all too odd a bunch to waste any more of her own weekend free time on.

Mrs Smith was waiting back at the primary school. She was leaning over the playground wall to watch for their arrival, her imposing physique able to be seen from a long way away. She relieved a thankful Evie with a promise that as long as Evie sorted her classroom the following day and set the tables and chairs out for her class in a welcoming manner all ready for the pupils, then Mrs Smith would take over from here this morning and would make sure the appropriate number of chairs and tables would be waiting for her.

Mrs Smith promised to ensure too that an oil heater would be taken over to the hall, which felt draughty and cavernous in comparison to the much smaller classroom the infants were used to; there was only one heater spare and it wasn't very big, unfortunately. Mrs Smith said she wondered therefore if Evie could persuade James to cycle later that afternoon around the farms and homes of all of Evie's pupils, with a note that Mrs Smith had already written for the parents of each infant pupil to say that double vests or liberty bodices were to be the order of the day, and if their parents wanted and there was an older brother for a hand-me-down, then the girls could wear boys' trousers for the next month or two, to keep warm until the milder spring weather came.

How daring, thought Evie. She had never put on a pair of slacks herself, but she rather thought she might run herself up a pair the following week, if she could find a pattern and forage some material. The land girls who were round and about wore trousers made from strong, heavy-duty cotton, and Pattie, who helped out on various farms, loved her working trousers, as did Linda, who was a farrier.

But Evie or her friends had never worn trousers as an ordinary item of clothing. Would she be allowed into The Haywain if she were wearing a pair? Evie pondered. And what would Mrs Smith or the parents say if they saw Evie wearing trousers when she was about to teach the infants?

Evie had to confess to Mrs Smith that she thought James would be difficult about her idea for his long cycle ride. It would probably amount to about twenty miles, and the route was very hilly, and some of the parents wouldn't be at home, with the result that it would almost definitely be a most trying day for him. James was well known at Bluebells for being incredibly lazy on his Saturdays and Sundays, but Evie didn't think Mrs Smith needed to be told that as well.

Mrs Smith pursed her lips, but opened the clasp on her large brown leather handbag.

She drew out a one-pound note and looked at Evie.

Evie gave a small grimace to show she thought James would feel the job should earn more than that. 'It will be a lot of hilly cycling,' Evie then tentatively reminded her employer as Mrs Smith held her stare.

With a frown of exasperation, Mrs Smith pulled another note, this time for ten shillings, from her handbag. Evie nodded, and quickly pocketed the money before her headmistress could change her mind.

'Evie-Rose!' called Sukie quite loudly as Evie walked into the ladies' bar at The Haywain later on, just as the church clock struck six. Evie immediately noticed the wattage of Sukie's broad smile beaming in her direction.

63

As was his wont during the cold months, land-lord Barkeep Joss had made sure there was a cheery fire burning in the black cast-iron grate, which was open on front and back below the chimney stack to ensure that both the main bar and the ladies' bar could benefit from the warmth of the same blaze. The kindling was crackling invitingly, and there was a faint smell of pine cones, as Joss liked to bung a couple in for fragrance. The fire was throwing out a good heat, which was just as well as a quickly developing frost that evening was already turning the heather and the gorse white-tipped, and Evie had taken care to wrap herself up very warmly before she dared venture outside to walk from Pemberley across the village to The Haywain.

Linda was standing at the bar waiting to be served, the heel of her right foot lightly tapping on the stone flags of the floor as she was obviously keen to rejoin her friends, and as Evie disrobed herself of coat, woolly neck scarf, hat and gloves, Linda nodded over to enquire what she was drinking, to which Evie mimed a weak lemonade shandy. They were such long-standing friends that this silent exchange only took a second or two.

Evie sat down next to Sukie. The last time they had met had been on the afternoon of New Year's Day, when Evie had visited Sukie at her home on the way back from counting the takings from the New Year's Eve dance at the recuperation hospital. The totting up had been done at The Grange so that for safety's sake Peter could then stow away the cash from the night before in the safe that had been installed in the secret part of the building he worked in, deep in the basement beneath the hospital. Evie, who still wasn't certain as to the precise nature of Peter's job, had wanted to tell Sukie that afternoon that he'd informed her he was going to leave the area, and she was feeling dejected and in need of her friend's reliably comforting words.

Sadly, it hadn't been a particularly satisfying conversation for either of the pals. Sukie had been uncharacteristically pale and silent. She normally never had more than one or two drinks of an evening, but as it had been New Year's Eve she had imbibed more than that and had been left feeling very fragile the following day as a result of the festivities, as she had been dancing until well into the small hours after welcoming in the New Year.

Evie meanwhile had felt completely thwarted over the failure – yet again – of her and Peter to work things out between them, and she knew that Sukie thought Evie hadn't been cross enough with Peter during their discussion, or quite sympathetic enough over Sukie's pounding head.

But this Saturday evening Sukie looked full of beans and back to her normal cheerful self, with clear bright eyes and her lustrous blonde hair looking particularly bouncy and shining with health, despite the style it was in being a trifle windswept.

At the sight of Sukie's gleaming mane, Evie couldn't help but put her hand up towards her own hair. She had worn a scarf to keep the worst of the dust off her hair when moving the desks and tables, and when she and Mr Cawes had cleaned the hall. That afternoon she had had a bath in the usual tepid two inches of water that everyone was used to these days, and she had used an old and chipped glass to sluice water over her head, but she wasn't sure it had done the trick. The problem was that shampoo was nothing but a distant memory, and soap was scarce too, with shortages in all the shops.

A few months ago James had come up with an ingenious idea. He'd gone around the village begging for the tail ends of soap bars, and as he had a knack of being very charming he had managed to talk his way into quite a haul. He had subsequently pressed the heels of soap together into one large piece, which he then divided into small bars, placing each one in a metal contraption he'd made – a small globe constructed from chicken wire, attached to a long wooden handle. He'd then been able to sell these soap-in-a-baskets off to people in Lymbridge for a shilling apiece.

The idea was that one should swish the contraption in a little water, making a weak soapy solution that could be used for washing hair or clothes; James had carefully worked out a way the wire bit could be opened to take a new piece of soap when the first one was finished. As a design, it worked surprisingly well, and a small amount of soap could thus be eked out to last a very long time, although of course the watery concoction it made had nowhere near the cleansing properties of a bar of soap used directly on dirty clothes or one's skin, or – fond sigh at the thought! – the pre-war glug of shampoo in one's hand that would be rubbed into dirty hair, with the process

66

being repeated and then the residue carefully rinsed in endless pints of clean warm water until the hair-washer was sure every bit of dirt and soap scum was gone.

Luckily everyone was in the same boat, and these days it was deemed tactful by all not to mention if anyone's hair was looking a little dull or greasy. Scarves and crocheted snoods were the popular choice when a hairstyle really needed a bit of help.

But unfortunately that afternoon Evie has discovered that her own clever contraption – which had been James's first prototype – was bereft of even the tiniest sliver of soap. It had been a very frustrating moment.

'Sukie, what have you done to your hair?' Evie was unable to resist saying now, as she continued to inspect her friend's gleaming head from several angles.

'You'll never guess!' Sukie replied as she shook her head, deliberately making her golden hair shimmy attractively. 'And then I've got news to tell you after that. It's news that you are going to want to hear.'

Before Evie could try to guess, Sukie's teasing tone gave way instantly to one that was distinctly more gushing. She said that on Wednesday a mysterious brown-paper parcel had arrived for her at the office where she worked in the administration department at the recuperation hospital. She'd been about to file some patient records but had naturally been diverted by the parcel, as she'd never had any personal post sent directly to The Grange, or indeed any parcel ever sent to her by post before.

At first Sukie hadn't been able to work out who the package was from, but she was delighted to find that inside was a bottle of luxury shampoo, and then she unearthed, nestled under the tissue paper that had been scrumpled around the precious cargo to keep the bottle safe, a card with 'Sukie' written on its envelope in flamboyant script.

It turned out to be from Wesley, the leader of the band that Sukie had managed to book for the New Year's entertainment. The card thanked Sukie for their booking – it was The Swingtimes' best-ever engagement, Wesley claimed – and at the bottom he had left a telephone number he could be reached on.

Without more ado, that lunchtime, when her supervisor, Miss Davis, had popped to the lavatory, Sukie had rung Wesley from the office telephone to say a heartfelt thank you for the shampoo, and now they were going to go on a date.

'Goodness!' exclaimed Evie, as she remembered how very good-looking Wesley had been. Although she had still felt feeble after her influenza for the New Year's dance, this was one thing she had noticed about him. 'What a charmer!'

Then a look of surprise flitted quickly across Evie's face, followed by a slightly bleaker expression as a troublesome thought struck her.

Sukie didn't notice as she was craning over to see if Linda was on her way back yet from the bar.

Evie wasn't surprised in the slightest that Sukie

had been asked out, as she was tall and slim and impossibly beautiful, and so it was to be expected that she had many admirers. In fact, Sukie had had the opposite sex eating from her hand for many years, but Evie knew that although Sukie frequently went on dates she was very well behaved and never overstepped the bounds of what was deemed proper as she was acutely aware of the need to keep her reputation intact.

Evie's surprise was more because Wesley was black, his family originally coming from the West Indies. He was, in actual fact, the first coloured person Evie had ever seen up close or spoken to. And while she had admired him, Evie realised that she had never countenanced that a black person might want to go on a date with a white person, or vice versa. Evie realised suddenly that she was very parochial when it came to things like this, and that maybe she needed a little time to get used to what felt, at this moment, to be a radical proposition. It wasn't that Evie thought it was wrong, and she could completely see why both Sukie and Wesley might be attracted to each other. It was more that Wesley's sculpted darkness and Sukie's creamy pale skin and blonde hair were the biggest contrast there could be, and Evie worried that it would seem locally to be an emphatic statement of something. And although Evie wasn't quite sure what this something might be exactly, she felt almost certain that to many people on Dartmoor this 'something' would have a distinct sense of challenge about it. In such a conservative area as the moorland reaches of the West Country in 1942, to see these two spending time together would be bound to cause gossip and consternation, although of course Wesley lived in the city of Bristol and there Evie supposed people might arguably be much more used to this sort of thing.

'I know! He could charm the birds from the trees, Evie-Rose. But he's lovely, and so handsome, and a perfect gentleman, I'm sure. We talked for ages on the telephone, although I had to hang up quickly when I heard Miss Davis coming back to her desk. And then the next morning he telephoned me again and I had to speak in a whisper so that nobody caught on that I was being so bold as to take a personal call. I pretended it was from the bandages supplier,' said Sukie breathily, although still without paying any real attention to Evie.

Normally Sukie was a devoted and responsive comrade at arms, and so this sight of her friend almost lost in her own world struck Evie as most definitely unsettling.

And the more Evie looked closely at her best friend now, the more Evie noticed that Sukie seemed to have an unusual sparkle about her, despite the fact she was wearing a skirt that had seen better days as well as a rather humdrum old cardie, and she was still sporting a pink nose from being out in the gusty moorland wind.

Sukie was normally a cool customer when it came to men, and Evie couldn't remember her having quite this excited, vibrating tone about her voice when speaking of a man before. Whatever was up with her?

Linda was now sitting with them, and Evie

could tell that she didn't know what to think either, to judge by the way Linda's eyes kept flicking between the drinks and Sukie.

Sukie was a playful and daring person, and she liked to push a boundary or two, they all knew that. But this Wesley business seemed something potentially more risky than single-handedly taking on the local lads in a game of skittles, or leaning across the horseshoe-shaped bar that connected the main and the ladies' bars to make a slightly risqué quip at the expense of one of the local farming chaps standing across in the other bar.

'Sukie lovey, I don't want to be a dampener, you know that, my sweet, don't you, but have you thought this through?' began Evie in a gently cautious tone. Upsetting Sukie was the very last thing she wanted to do, but she didn't think she'd be a good friend if she didn't at least highlight how such a relationship, if it progressed as far as the status of 'a relationship', would be taken by some of the people living in Lymbridge.

Evie's reward was a withering gaze, and a pursing of Sukie's generous lips. 'Of course, Evie, I'm not a fool, and I don't doubt that the colour of his skin will cause a ripple of gossip. But it is just a single date, that's all. I've not promised to marry him. And frankly, if we decide we like each other, I doubt I'll worry what anybody thinks, or that anybody will give us much thought as I'm sure that these days they've all got much more important things to concentrate on, such as the war and the dangers we and our loved ones are all facing.' Sukie's words were delivered calmly enough, although her posture had stiffened, and so there was a distinct hint of rebellion, Evie noted.

'Of course, Sukie. But you know how stuck in their ways people are around here, and it won't be a surprise to somebody as clever as you are that people would think it odd if you cast aside the local men who are still around here for someone like Wesley, as attractive as we could all see at New Year that he is,' Evie pressed on, making sure she kept her voice soft and without any hint of confrontation.

Sukie snorted. It was quietly done, but it was a snort of defiance, most definitely.

This didn't bode well and so Evie remained concerned, particularly as when she probed further it was revealed that 'just a date' had been Sukie slightly underselling what she and Wesley had actually agreed.

He was going to come down to Lymbridge for two or maybe even three days, and Sukie had arranged for him to have a berth in the attic at the hospital where the crew for the airfield were staying until the hospital needed the use of the rest of the vacant rooms upstairs at The Grange.

As Sukie worked in the lower rooms of The Grange at the hospital office, it was a convenient arrangement as far as she and Wesley were concerned.

But, thought Evie, it wasn't necessarily an arrangement that would be particularly well chaperoned, and while there was nothing about Wesley to suggest anything ungentlemanly (not at least that Evie had noticed in the short amount of time she had spent with him, when in fact she'd been struck by what an extremely nice chap he seemed), Evie could only hope vehemently that Sukie wasn't going to do anything rash or that might compromise her reputation. People could have long memories for this sort of thing and be very petty-minded, even in wartime.

Evie's thoughts jumped to her own sister. Julia and Leonard looked to be weathering the storm, just about, that their own impetuous romantic behaviour had provoked. But if Sukie were to push to, or even beyond, the edge of good behaviour, and with a man from so obviously a different background, then Evie was concerned that even Sukie, who was so used to being lauded, might discover her place in local society to be severely diminished, and from there to experience a loss of reputation that she would find very hard to recover from in both the practical and the emotional senses.

Linda looked to be equally as cautious about the idea as Evie, to judge by her refusal to offer an opinion either way. She tried to change the subject with some anodyne chat about the weather, but the conversation didn't really take hold and soon Linda gave up.

Clearly this wasn't the reaction that Sukie desired from her friends, and she was distinctly frosty with them for ten minutes or so, before suddenly announcing it was time for her to call it a day and go home.

Linda pointed out it wasn't yet half past six, and Sukie looked back at her huffily.

At one point Evie dared to ask what the other thing was, the 'news' that presumably related to

Evie too, that Sukie had mentioned, only to be told in no uncertain terms, 'Oh no, you don't deserve to know, Evie. You've made me feel irritable and tired, and I don't feel like talking any more, and so I'm going to drink up and head to my digs for an early night.'

And with that Evie and Linda could only look at each other helplessly as Sukie stood up and rapidly shrugged herself into her coat, which she didn't bother to button, before striding purposefully from the bar and away from the pair of them, without so much as a backward glance, moving so quickly that her coat spread out behind her like a sail caught in a breeze.

Sukie was usually the most reliably cheery of all of them. Evie knew that Sukie's feathers must have been well and truly ruffled by what her friends had said for her to have been so sharp with them.

Chapter Five

The following morning Evie went to the early service at church and then, after breakfasting at Pemberley (and what a slimmed-down number they were sitting at the dining table these days, she couldn't help but think, as former Pemberley PGs Peter and Mr Smith were long gone – Peter to who knows where, and Mr Smith to move in with the new Mrs Smith – as were Mr and Mrs Wallis, who had returned home to Kent, while WVS girls

74

Sarah and Tina had now left for London), Evie headed over to Mrs Smith's cottage.

Evie wanted to see if Tricia fancied walking with her across to the recuperation hospital to see Timmy. Actually, Evie would prefer to see Timmy on her own as they didn't chat as freely or make each other laugh in quite the same way if Tricia were there. And after the disquieting evening the day before, Evie knew that if anyone could lift her bruised spirits it was probably Timmy.

However, bearing in mind her 'Be Better' list of a few days earlier, she wanted both to extend the hand of friendship to Tricia, and especially to make sure that Tricia was in no doubt that although Evie was friends with Timmy, who was of course her ex-fiancé, there was nothing more to their relationship now than simple friendship, and absolutely nothing of the romantic persuasion, and so Tricia didn't have a thing to worry about with Evie in that respect.

It was ironic, Evie sometimes considered, how much better she and Timmy got on with him being married to another woman. If she and Timmy themselves had gone on to marry, it would have been disastrous, Evie was convinced, and she believed Timmy was now of this opinion too. She could imagine that they would have bickered about something or other, probably always trivial, almost every day, and that ultimately they would have had to settle for an increasingly tedious existence together with only the odd flash of un-complicated fun they could share.

And the wonderful thing now was that even though Timmy had made Tricia pregnant by accident (and while still engaged to Evie), and although at first sight he and Tricia seemed not particularly well suited to each other, now that Timmy and Tricia were married and devoted parents to their dear baby daughter Hettie, Evie suspected that he and Tricia were rather growing to like each other, and maybe even love one another a little.

Tricia, although not educated, certainly wasn't stupid, and she had an appealing down-to-earth attitude towards life that probably came from her having worked previously as a dairy parlour maid. Evie was finding Tricia an increasingly interesting person to spend time with, and she thought Timmy would come to appreciate and find Tricia's openness invigorating too. As it had sadly become clear in recent months that Timmy's injuries meant that he would never leave the confines of a wheelchair, Evie felt that Tricia's sense of humour and her certain grittiness in the face of adversity would come into their own, and mean ultimately that Timmy would just get on with living his life to the full and not in as compromised a way as they had all assumed he would not long after he was injured. Well, he would be compromised to the extent he'd no longer be able to walk or drive a car, but Evie could see that with a bit of practice he shouldn't be prevented from continuing with all the other things he liked to do.

What was obvious was that both Timmy and Tricia delighted in baby Hettie, as Evie did too. The doctors thought Timmy almost definitely unable to father any subsequent children, and so this made Hettie especially precious.

Evie had had the extraordinary experience of almost seeing the dear thing being born, when Tricia had gone into labour on the back seat of Peter's car, much to Peter's horror. Evie couldn't help but smile at the memory of Peter's tense shoulders and his desperate attempts to keep looking forward and concentrate on the road ahead as he raced his car to the hospital, even though there were all manner of uncomfortable sounds going on right behind him as Tricia lay on the back seat with Evie holding her hand as Evie crouched in the footwell beside the terrified mother-to-be.

Now, although Evie had once heartily disliked Tricia – or, more accurately, she had disliked the *idea* of her, as she hadn't actually known her personally – that had been an attitude that had changed significantly over recent months, to the point that Evie was very proud to be Hettie's godmother and she felt growing warmth towards Tricia who, like Timmy, just had the knack of making her smile.

Meeting Fiona had helped Evie put her feelings into perspective. An able-bodied Timmy was always going to have got up to the occasional naughty peccadillo with the opposite sex, Evie suspected, with it being almost certain that at the time of their tryst Tricia had been little more than simply a means to an end for him. By chance one evening Tricia had been at The Haywain, and Timmy had been there without Evie – and the result was history. Evie had thought about it a lot and had come to the conclusion that being married to Evie was unlikely to have curtailed many of Timmy's amorous rompings, and at least now she wasn't locked into an unhappy marriage, which meant that she could at some point try to find a man who would value and love her whole-heartedly. Tricia was made of sterner stuff than she, Evie suspected, and was much better equip-ped to deal with any shenanigans that Timmy might care to put her way.

Anyway, in comparison with the somehow guile-less Tricia, Evie felt that Peter's former paramour, Fiona, had something that was much more calcu-lating and unpleasant about her.

Yes, Fiona was the cold and scheming type of person who certainly deserved Evie's ire, Peter or no Peter, Evie felt.

Most definitely.

And the fact that Peter had picked up again with Fiona indecently soon after his and Evie's secret kisses at the summer Revels at the primary school the previous July still rankled heartily. Fiona seemed most assuredly an unpleasant sort of young woman, if Evie were any judge of char-acter; and the fact she wasn't even pretty was just another point stacked against her, as while Evie knew she was no raving beauty herself she liked to think of herself as sweet-looking. But if Peter thought she and Fiona had looks on a par with one another, then Evie supposed she would have to disabuse herself of that thought, which was a further burr under her saddle.

'Evie, hurry yornself inside!' cried Tricia in cheerful greeting, as she opened the front door of Mrs Smith's cottage to her and unceremoniously plonked Hettie in Evie's arms before Evie could so much as say hello or why she had called around.

Tricia went on as she led the way to the kitchen, 'We're jus' fixin' t' date for 'Ettie's christenin', and it looks like a fortnight t'day, or maybe a month, or six weeks, an' so yorn be pride o' place as 'Ettie's godmama. We might 'ave a knees-up at T'Aywain dreckly after, if Timmy can sort it, an' 'Ettie's goin' t'wear Timmy's christenin' robe. I 'ad a word wi' yorn photographer chappie up at Pemberley an' 'e's down for markin' t' day for us. Indeed he said we might get a photo in t' *Western Morning News* of me and Timmy an' 'Ettie.'

As Evie gingerly manoeuvred herself and the baby onto a sturdy chair – Hettie giving a vigorous wiggle in protest at Evie's inexperienced handling of her – Evie thought that Mr and Mrs Smith might have hoped for something more traditional to commemorate such a special occasion, such as a genteel tea party at their pretty cottage. In Evie's experience Mrs Smith did like to make others aware of her position in local society, and a shindig at The Haywain didn't quite fit the bill.

But when Evie looked towards her headmistress, Mrs Smith was smiling benignly at little Hettie, appearing for all the world as if a knees-up at the local hostelry was precisely what she and Mr Smith would have chosen to mark this celebration.

And so Evie made herself grin broadly, and she told Tricia as enthusiastically as she could that it was wonderful news, and that Timmy must be looking forward to it immensely, and she herself could hardly wait as it was bound to be a lovely day, and that she felt very honoured to have been asked to be one of Hettie's godparents.

Timmy's friend Dave Symons was going to be a

godparent too apparently, although Evie doubted he'd really embrace the role as he liked to think of himself as something of a lad about town with a love 'em and leave reputation. (He should be so lucky!) He was singularly unsuccessful with the opposite sex, and Evie thought his cavalier attitude didn't bode well in a godparent. She decided to keep this thought to herself, however, and managed to keep smiling as Tricia chatted away about him. It had been Dave Symons who had told Evie in what could only be described as a gleeful fashion about the five minutes that Timmy and Tricia had shared behind the village hall that had led to the birth of Hettie, and so at the thought of this there were moments when Evie felt her smile in severe danger of slipping.

To change the subject Evie jokily asked if Hettie was going to have her dancing shoes on too for the christening party?

It was exactly the right thing to say, and Tricia and Mrs Smith vied with each other to tell Evie about the things they'd been thinking of they could do to celebrate the christening, and then all about the new things that Hettie could do, which seemed to be to guzzle a lot of milk while nursing, sleep the sleep of the dead and smile on command, as far as Evie could work out.

As they chatted Evie was able to find out what was expected by Tricia and Mrs Smith from her as a godparent – aside from making a promise in church to be a good moral example to the little girl and to look after her spiritual well-being, she would be expected to give Hettie a small gift to commemorate the day.

Everybody in Lymbridge attended church regularly, of course, as it was frowned upon if one didn't. However, as she sipped from a cup of tea at Mrs Smith's kitchen table, Evie realised that she had never thought too deeply about this weekly routine. It was just what everybody did on a Sunday. If Evie were honest, she had never considered herself particularly religious, and she would often find that the Rev. Painter's lengthy and invariably dull sermons had been subsumed by thoughts of her own forthcoming lunch or something else equally trivial.

But Hettie's christening meant that she would be making a solemn public promise to be what could well be the spiritual backbone in Hettie's life, and Evie felt this was a serious commitment. She didn't think she'd ever be properly qualified to talk about questions of faith with Hettie (this war having thrown up a whole raft of questions and uncertainties as to God's intentions, at least as far as Evie was concerned), and so Evie didn't feel she'd want to stray into this territory when Hettie was older. Faith was such a personal thing, and Evie believed that everybody should make up their own mind as to their beliefs. But she did feel that over the coming years she could try to encourage Hettie towards always thoughtful and kindly behaviour as regards her treatment of those around her, and Evie could ensure that Hettie would be in no doubt too that whatever difficulties life might have in store for her, Evie would always be standing in her corner, come what may.

It was only when Hettie began to grizzle for a feed that Evie reluctantly handed her back to

Tricia, who to Evie's surprise immediately unbuttoned her blouse right before Evie; and before Evie could look politely in another direction Tricia popped Hettie's rooting little mouth efficiently onto a brown and bulging nipple she had proficiently hoicked out of her underwear.

Evie felt herself blushing although she couldn't quite pull her eyes away, and then she admonished herself for being far too old-fashioned and reserved. She had watched Tricia breastfeed when she was still in hospital just after the birth, but Evie thought it had seemed more appropriate in that setting. In Evie's opinion Mrs Smith's cottage seemed more a place for tea served in dainty bone china, accompanied by polite conversation, but then Evie told herself that *she* was the snob and that of course Hettie wouldn't be interested in a cup of tea or whether Evie was feeling a bit hot and bothered about something that was very natural but that was usually carried out in private. There were only the three women there, Timmy being at the hospital and Mr Smith currently away working in London, and so what on earth was there for Evie to be embarrassed about if Tricia and Mrs Smith weren't feeling awkward? And Hettie wouldn't care either way, that was for certain, just as long as she got her tucker, to judge by the contented nuzzling sounds she was making.

Tricia winded Hettie, and decided that she'd go to see Timmy in the afternoon as she wanted to put Hettie down for a nap first, and so she said that Evie should go on without her.

And as Evie headed down the road to the recuperation hospital at a prompt enough pace that she hoped would make sure she kept warm, she mused that there was a sweeping sense of change about the way people were living.

There was Sukie excited about seeing Wesley, while on a bigger canvas, Evie intuitively felt that women were feeling differently about themselves with every passing month that most of their menfolk were away fighting for King and country. Feelings of independence and self-reliance were becoming contagious amongst the women remaining on the home front.

When Evie looked about her, she felt the womenfolk she knew were no longer always quite the biddable sorts she could remember from her formative years, who back then, before the war, had mostly seemed content to be subservient members of the family. Their new responsibilities and their changing roles were responsible for this shift in attitudes, Evie could see, and she felt that although everyone was anxious as to what the war might deliver to them personally, nevertheless there was a new tide of feminine fulfilment just starting to make tiny waves across society.

Then Evie considered that when the war was over – and it would be one day, wouldn't it? – it was very possible that quite a large proportion of women wouldn't be content just to resume their old, more compliant place in society as if nothing had happened to them while their men were battling forward. And what would happen then? Evie wondered.

I doubt I'd ever feel happy about feeding a baby in front of other people, though, Evie admitted to herself. Assuming I ever manage to find a husband, and that I have lassoed him and firmly tied him to the bannisters so that he can't escape, I'm certainly going to make sure that he makes a cup of tea quite regularly for me, and even occasionally does the washing-up. So there!

Frustratingly Timmy was nowhere to be found when a rosy-cheeked Evie arrived at the recuperation hospital, and so she wasn't sure what to do.

There was a time when she would have nipped around to the back of the building, to the virtually hidden entrance to the basement, and knocked on the unobtrusive wooden door to be found there. This was the way into the supposedly top-secret subterranean warren of rooms that had become Peter's domain, and where everyone who worked in the basement took care not to catch Evie's eye, or would gently push a door closed, she'd noticed, if they thought she was looking at what they were doing as she passed in the corridor.

At the memory Evie felt her heart sinking, and she couldn't prevent a sigh escaping her lips – she hadn't expected that simply being near where she had recently spent time with Peter could cause such a rapid plummeting of her spirits.

Timmy's small ward, which usually held about five or six injured servicemen besides him, who were all adjusting to life in a wheelchair, was on the raised ground floor of the hospital, and not only was Timmy conspicuous by his absence, but none of the other patients usually to be found on the ward were present either. It was the once-grand room from which Timmy had watched the point-to-point racing in the early autumn, when

Sukie had beaten all comers in one of the races.

Evie wandered over to the window and stood staring out at the airfield. From here, she noticed if she looked one way she could see the next village, nestled between the moorland hills, the church with its famously crooked spire in dark relief against the sky. This was the church that had refused to remove its spire when requested by the authorities to do so, claiming that the aeroplanes on the airstrip headed off in another direction, and so it was an unnecessary waste of money and effort.

If Evie looked in the other direction, she could see the country road wending its way up to Lymbridge. The view from The Grange really was spectacular, even at this dourest time of the year when the majestic moors of the summertime had given way to something much darker and ominously brooding. Evie found herself calmed by the spectacular view, though, and she hoped Timmy and his fellow patients felt likewise too. The nurses were used to seeing her around and so nobody seemed to mind her presence.

After a while Evie noticed as she gazed around that the front door to the hospital, which she could see from her spot in the window bay, now had a wooden ramp leading from it and traversing the steps down to the circular gravel drive that circumvented a formal rose garden at the top of the drive to the house. Perhaps this was a clue, Evie thought, as she went to investigate.

And so it turned out to be. Evie inspected the ramp, and then noticed what she presumed were wheelchair tracks in the drive's gravel that then changed course so that they were heading off in the direction of the recently constructed airstrip that had been levelled close to the hospital.

Following these tracks took Evie to the largest of the huts on the edge of the strip, and there she found the other patients from Timmy's ward, and various members of the ground crew and what looked like a few pilots all to be engaged in a raucous tournament of table tennis. The games were taking place on three different tables, with all the other furniture in the hut having been bundled to the edges of the room to clear enough floor space for the wheelchair users, and the results had been chalked up on a blackboard attached to one of the hut's walls. Able-bodied people were playing against wheelchair players, although it looked to Evie as if those who could stand up had been handicapped by having to hop on one leg and keep their other foot off the ground at all times, and there was quite a lot of shouting and ribald commentary. To judge by the warm fug in the room and the noise, it looked as if everyone was having a jolly time and that the matches were being hotly contested.

Timmy was on the far side of the hut, his sweaty brow and damp hair intimating that he'd already played, and he waved happily across at Evie. Then he indicated she should wait where she was, and he'd come to her. He picked up a couple of blankets that had been discarded on an old couch, and wheeled himself over to her.

Evie noticed with pleasure the strength he had regained in his arms, and how much he had improved his manipulation of his wheelchair. Every

86

time she saw him she could see a marked in-
crease in what he could do, although she did
notice that quite often his face would wrinkle in
what she thought looked like pain, even though
Timmy would always deny this if Evie asked if he
was hurting somewhere.

She stood smiling down at Timmy as, in silence,
he neatly folded one of the blankets, pretending
for Evie's benefit that he was doing a silent demonstration of laundry folding, complete with comical faces, wagging of fingers and much smoothing
of imaginary creases, and then he placed the
folded blanket over his legs and tucked it in. He
was, as always, quite the comedian, and Evie
thought that Stan Laurel and Oliver Hardy
themselves couldn't have put on a better comic
performance than Timmy had.

Evie had to resist the urge to help him, though,
and this was difficult as she longed to do something that could show him that she wanted to
share a sense of solidarity with him. But she knew
it was more important that Timmy, and all the
other wounded people like him, learnt to look
after themselves in order that they could become
as independent as possible for when they left
hospital to return to life back at their homes.
Timmy made less of a fuss about folding the other
blanket, which was for his shoulders, although
naturally he couldn't resist throwing the end of it
across his chest and over his shoulder in a theatri-
cal manner and pulling a funny face as he did so.
Evie thought that, almost definitely intentionally,
this funny face bore more than a passing resem-
blance to one of Mrs Smith's more extravagant

expressions, and she laughed at Timmy's cheekiness as he grinned back at her.

Timmy allowed Evie to hold the door of the hut open for him, and one of the pilots heaved the chair over the wooden lip at the bottom of the door frame, but after that Timmy insisted on wheeling himself even though the way wasn't very smooth and he had to use a lot of upper-body strength when his chair's wheels found the rutted ground hard-going. It looked to be with reluctance that he admitted he would need Evie to push him up the ramp to the front door of The Grange.

As they headed back to the hospital together, Evie listened to Timmy saying that the pilots got bored easily. They had to wait around for days at a time in uniform, ready to take to their planes at a moment's notice; and it had apparently been Peter's idea that table tennis might be a good thing and would maybe help dispel the anxiety they would naturally feel while they were sitting around with nothing much to do.

Evie caught her breath at the unexpected mention of Peter's name, but Timmy didn't notice. She swallowed and collected her thoughts, and then asked Timmy how he was.

'I'm looking forward now to being at home,' he admitted. 'It's been fun here but increasingly I want to strike out on my own. Hettie's growing by the day, and I want me and Tricia and her to be in our own home by the time we're ringing in 1943.'

He added that his mother had decreed that Timmy would have a specially adapted home built for him. It would be a dwelling with no steps and doors wide enough for a wheelchair, and with special appliances in the bathroom so that Timmy could do all that he needed to do there unaided. The kitchen table and the cupboards would be lower than usual, as would the butler sink, and Mr Smith had found an American firm who made cookers for people in wheelchairs, and was investigating having one imported. Evie said that having friends in high places, like Mr Smith was, was very useful at times – she had had recourse herself to ask Mr Smith several favours over the past months, and she knew very well how resourceful and how helpful he was.

Timmy told Evie then that Mr Smith had gone so far as having architectural drawings completed for a single-storey building. It had been Mr Smith's suggestion that rather than building the home in the orchard to Mrs Smith's cottage, as had been the original idea, it might be a better scheme if a plot of ground should be purchased elsewhere in the village so that the newly-weds could begin their married life not *too* close to Mrs Smith. According to Timmy, Mr Smith had worded this very tactfully so that Mrs Smith didn't take offence. Evie thought that must have been a diplomatic feat of the highest order.

'Mr Smith is a wily old bird,' laughed Timmy. 'He said to me on the Q.T. that Ma wouldn't stop coming around if we were too close, and the trick would be to find somewhere close enough so that I can wheel myself to theirs, but just that bit too far to discourage her from too much dropping in unannounced as she might if we are all cooped up at the bottom of the garden. And so you'll never guess – but we've made an offer for that patch of scrubland that's set back a bit to The Haywain, which owns it, and they've accepted so the paperwork is just going through. We've got plans for the new house as well, and so it should be all systems go before too long.'

'Timmy, you are the only person alive I know who could manage to actually build their home right next door to the pub. Poor Tricia!' chuckled Evie. 'She doesn't know what she is in for.'

Evie then had a good idea. She told Timmy about the shortage of PGs at Pemberley.

He laughed and said, 'Too easy, Evie Yeo, too easy! There's several round here who'll leap at the idea of such a posh bunker, I'm sure. You know, doctors or those running the airfield or so forth. There's going to be lots of people brought down here very soon for training, so I hear, and my guess is that those with scrambled egg on their caps will be looking for somewhere refined to live. I'll put up a notice in the hospital staffroom, and at the airstrip mess. And then it will be mission accomplished, Miss Evie Pee Gee Yeo, you'll see!'

They'd reached the ramp, and Evie tried and failed to push him up it as it was steeper than it looked. To get the chair up it she would have to push harder than she had done the first time. Timmy suggested she take a run at it with the chair. This worked, although there was a sticky moment just as she managed to get the chair almost to the top, as Timmy was shouting encouragement as if she were a horse winning a race he was betting on. Evie couldn't help but belly-laugh, with the predictable result that she came over all weak and nearly let Timmy and the chair slide gently back all the way down to the gravel drive again.

'Phew, that was hard,' Evie admitted as Timmy and she headed at last down The Grange's generously proportioned hall and turned into his ward.

They spent a little time talking about the forthcoming christening, and the probability that Dave Symons would be pretty useless to Hettie as a spiritual guide.

'Yes, he'll be tragically bad,' agreed Timmy with a chuckle. 'But the great thing is that Hettie will have you. And you'll be marvellous, won't you?'

Evie gave Timmy a gentle push on the arm as she agreed that she would do her best. She thought then that he looked tired, and so she said that she should go.

'By the way, Evie, you do know that Peter is still working downstairs, don't you? He's not here today as he's gone over to Plymouth, but I thought you'd like to know. He told me yesterday that the Ministry had refused his request for a transfer,' said Timmy, with a mischievous glint in his eye. 'I asked him about you and he wouldn't be drawn, but he had that look – and you have it too when you think about him, and you believe I'm not looking. Just like now! Anyway, I thought you might have been told he was going, and that you might like to know that he's not after all.'

All the oxygen in the room seemed to have been sucked away. Evie's ears filled with the sound of her racing pulse.

'Evie! Evie, you've gone very white. You'd better

91

sit down as I don't want you fainting on me,' came Timmy's voice from what felt like a long way away.

Chapter Six

Later that afternoon Evie settled down in the empty dining room of Pemberley and began to write a list.

To Do
1. Welcome new children tomorrow.
2. ~~Organise a spitfire fundraising meeting~~
3. ~~Put together a list of speakers to run past the Western Morning News.~~
4. See Peter and ~~tell him what I think~~ clear the air.

Five minutes later she realised she'd ground to a halt on writing her to-do list, as thoughts of what she might say to Peter now that he hadn't gone, but hadn't deigned to be in touch with her either, had proved just that bit too distracting.

Carefully Evie ripped off the strip at the top of her piece of paper where she had written this so-far-unsatisfactory list, screwed it up and threw it on the embers of the dying fire, although she took care to keep the lower portion of the page as she had learnt to try to avoid any sort of unnecessary waste. She began her list anew on this lower piece of paper, hoping that an underlined heading would nudge things along more effectively.

TO DO

1. Bake biscuits for my infants.
2. Welcome new children tomorrow.
3. Be pleasant to Leonard Bassett.
4. Go to see Sukie.
5. Go to see Peter!
6. Get somebody else to organise the Spitfire fundraising meeting. Mr Worth? Mr Smith?
7. Ask Julia to sort the next meeting of the sewing circle?
8. List of speakers for the *WMN*.
9. Christening gift.
10. PGs.
11. Spitfire cake competition – anything to do?
12. Put on another dance?
13. Put on series of films in the village hall?
14. Rummage sale?
15. Sunday teas for the hospital patients?
16. Maypole?
17. Scavenge hunt?

And as an afterthought:

18. Learn to drive.

Evie wasn't quite sure how she was going to fit all of this in, especially as she would have longer days over at the village hall with her infants from the morrow.

She also wanted to spend a bit more time with her family at Bluebells as she was missing them, but that had felt like an odd thing to write on a to-do list and so she hadn't included it.

Evie exhaled and her chest felt a little tight with sudden longing at the thought of what they were probably all up to at Bluebells. She went to the kitchen to see what the position there might be in terms of biscuit ingredients, with her fingers crossed that there would be something nice she could use for her baking as, being Sunday, she wasn't going to be able to go and buy anything if the cupboard proved to be bare. And that was even if there were any spare food coupons left – these were all pooled so that Mrs Worth could cater for the whole household – which there almost definitely wouldn't be. Still, making the biscuits might well prove to be the least arduous of the tasks on her list, Evie thought.

Irritatingly the kitchen at Pemberley offered scant pickings. This was an all-too-familiar experience for everyone these days, even though country areas tended to have more advantages in the food stakes than the towns and cities, often reflected by the talk around the Pemberley dining table turning to how on earth did people manage if they couldn't keep chickens or have a vegetable patch or could come by a rabbit for the pot? Everyone could see the point of rationing, but nobody liked the smaller portions or the limitations on ingredients. Evie had tried to get used to the fact of never feeling she'd had quite enough after eating, and when Julia was at Pemberley quite often they'd talk about dreams they'd had of eating abundant feasts or, once in Evie's case, a whole meal made of raw onions.

Although it was not that long after lunch, and Evie would much rather be curled up in a chair by the fire with the wireless on and a book in her hand as she was feeling weary and it looked very cold outside, she slipped into her coat and scarf and headed to Bluebells.

She arrived as James abruptly pulled the front door shut in temper and stomped down the drive, giving only the slightest of nods in Evie's direction as he passed.

'Father, what's wrong with James?' said Evie a moment later, when she went into the kitchen and saw Robert on one side of the table, and Susan on the other, both leaning on it as they faced each other with rather cross looks on their faces. 'I thought right now he'd be pleased with the cash he's earned for cycling about at Mrs Smith's whim.'

It was Robert who replied to Evie. 'James is like a bear with a sore head these days. I mentioned that he probably had homework to catch up on, and it was as if I'd suggested he take all his clothes off and run completely stark—'

'Robert!' cut in Susan sharply, to stop the rude word poised on her husband's lips.

'Er, stark ... naked up the road through Lymbridge.'

Evie and Robert smiled at each other, both knowing what he had really been poised to say. Evie could hear the muffled sounds of Pattie and Julia upstairs and thought she'd go to say hello.

But then Susan lifted a teacup and saucer to see if Evie fancied a cup of tea. And of course she did, and so she sat down at the kitchen table.

'I was telling your mother, it's his age,' continued Robert. 'We had the odd tantrum and slamming of doors with you three maids, but you girls weren't too bad, all things considered. I think there's a lot of change going on that's unsettled him, while James is feeling his age too. I remember being fifteen, and it can't help either that I told him earlier he's got to be an example for Frank and Joseph as otherwise he'll set them off too, being all shouty and mardy.'

'I'm sure James is feeling his hormones, but it can't be easy being close on sixteen, with a war on,' said Evie. 'It's not much fun for him, or anyone else that age.'

'That's as maybe,' said Susan firmly, 'but it's no excuse for him to behave badly. Anyway, you come and sit by the stove as there's something your father and I want to tell you.'

Evie felt a tremor of apprehension close to her heart as she went to sit down.

Fortunately there wasn't bad news to hear.

Instead Susan said that Mrs Coyne, the elderly owner of the village shop where Susan worked behind the counter, was finding it too much to keep on, and so she had asked whether Robert and Susan were interested in buying her out and taking over the business.

'Goodness me,' said Evie. She knew the family didn't have any savings or spare cash, and also that since her father's garage he had so enjoyed owning had folded during the depression of the 1930s, they would be all too aware that running a small business in the countryside, let alone when the country was at war already, was by no means a safe

96

financial bet.

It was a time to tread carefully, and for Evie to test tentatively what her parents were thinking about the proposal, and so she said, 'What do you two feel about this?'

She was relieved to learn that it wasn't going to be a quick decision either way, as Mrs Coyne was giving the Yeos first refusal and they had six months to think about it and to go back to Mrs Coyne with their decision.

Robert then went through the cons, which were quite big, being their lack of money (a very big con, actually), and the precarious nature of any financial venture a) while there was a war on, and b) deep in the moorland countryside where there wasn't a big population and therefore there could only be a limited number of patrons.

But the pros were more numerous, her father quickly went on to say, counting them off on his fingers: Susan knew what a solid profit the shop turned over each year, there was no other shop in Lymbridge and so there was something of a captive market, of course Susan knew all the suppliers and the clientele and how the business was run, and Susan had several ideas how the shop could be expanded in what it sold if she were in charge.

They had been up late the night before working out figures, and outgoings, profit and potential losses, Robert added.

What seemed to be exciting Robert and Susan particularly was that there was a possibility of growing it into something that truly could be described as a family business. Robert was wondering about maybe sinking a large tank for petrol storage into the ground beside the shop, with a pump above it, so that they could offer petrol too. Also, there was a derelict structure across the road directly opposite the village shop. It was a building where Switherns Farm had once stored hay and straw for their livestock, but for as long as Evie could remember it had been lying empty and slowly falling into disrepair, with waist-high stinging nettles springing up inside and at its front and sides every summer.

Robert thought Switherns might like a rental income if he and James set to repairing the building at no expense to the owners. And so he was wondering therefore if the maximum profit as far as the Yeos were concerned might lie in enlarging the business beyond just the shop, and then petrol, to include a garage workshop.

If they could make the sums work, and they believed they could get the business off the ground, then he'd be prepared to leave his current not particularly well-paid job, checking on production quotas at local farms and discouraging any black-marketeering, to work full-time alongside Susan.

As Robert explained to Evie, his and Susan's rationale was that to offer petrol as well as food and general supplies would lead to a growth in trade for the shop at the same time as a new amenity would be offered to the village, as currently locals had to go to Bramstone, the next village over the moor towards Plymouth, for their rationed fuel.

'I said all this to James just now, who was very dismissive; but I am thinking that with him the age he is and with the war not going to last for ever, surely, it wouldn't be long before I can train him as a mechanic, and later maybe Frank and Joseph too, so it can be a proper family business. Pattie told us this morning that she is going to be put to work on tractor engines too, and so it could be that after the war we'd even end up with one of the first women mechanics on the moor,' Robert explained, with a smile. 'And Susan thought that Julia might like to work with her in the shop as she won't want to be a postwoman for ever with all that cycling up hill and down dale to take the envelopes and chitties out to all those outlying farms hereabouts.'

Evie could see that her parents were very enthused by the unexpected proposal, and that there certainly was a lot for them all to think about.

But privately Evie felt that although it was an interesting scheme, it was destined to remain a pie in the sky dream as, with the best will in the world, the money needed to make it all happen was never going to materialise.

What a pity, and with that Evie tried to change the subject by asking if Marie's mother had been in touch to let them know how Marie and Catherine were settling back into living in Plymouth.

Half an hour later and Evie was hurrying home to Pemberley. Susan had been able to help with the ingredients needed for the biscuits, as long as Evie used a small biscuit cutter. She wanted to get them mixed and in the oven so that they would have a chance to cool on a rack before being wrapped in greaseproof paper and placed in a basket before she went to bed, ready to take to school tomorrow.

Evie was feeling now rather pleased with herself.

The cold had soon driven her sisters downstairs to the warm kitchen, and it wasn't long after that when Evie persuaded Julia to agree to organising the next meeting of the sewing circle. After their argument, Julia had been very conspicuous by her absence from the circle over the past couple of months and so this was Julia's opportunity to let everyone know that from now on normal service had been resumed between herself and Evie, and that she and Pattie would very possibly, if her public demanded it so, be resurrecting their party piece, the hilarious character of bossy but lovable know-it-all, Mrs Sew-and-Sew, that had on Mr Smith's aegis inspired the government's sewing tips in the how-to leaflets handed out to help novice seamstresses.

Minutes later Robert mentioned off his own bat that he would be happy to sort out the next meeting of the Spitfire fundraising committee for her; and then Pattie promised to think about speakers for the series of talks, saying that working outside on this farm or that meant she had a lot of time to ponder this sort of thing. Pattie said too that she thought she and Julia would be happy to take over liaising with the *Western Morning News* about this, and about the Spitfire cake, provided Evie made sure she sorted some other fundraising events in the run-up to Easter.

Evie leapt at Pattie's offer of help especially, as she'd been procrastinating so much over the talks and the damn Spitfire cake competition that she'd found herself rather frozen in inaction but unable to prevent a queasy tummy-sinking sensation every time she thought of them. To organise something different might re-energise her, with a bit of luck, Evie hoped.

Finally, Susan had come up trumps as regards a christening present that Evie could give to Hettie. She had bought Pattie a tiny sterling silver bracelet for her christening many years earlier, but had lost it before the big day, meaning that she had gone out and got Pattie another keepsake. (This had obviously happened in their more affluent days of running the garage, Evie surmised, as she could only ever remember her parents being thoroughly thrifty, and never replacing anything that had been simply lost, unless it was absolutely imperative that they do so.)

Anyway, a fortuitous few months before Christmas, Susan had been going through her old clothes, shoes and handbags, looking for items that could be updated at a meeting of the sewing circle in order to give her wardrobe a boost. And trapped between the lining and the inner side of the leather of the handbag she'd used at the time when Pattie was a newborn, Susan had discovered the bracelet – when she looked carefully, the stitching on one of the seams in the silk lining to the bag had parted, and so the bracelet, nestled inside a little drawstring silken pouch, must have worked itself through, slipping down to the flat bottom of the bag, being thoroughly hidden and laying undisturbed for at least eighteen years now.

Once the bracelet had been found, Susan had thought it would come in for a gift for her first granddaughter. But when Evie mentioned about needing something for Hettie, somehow that had instead seemed the perfect home for the piece of baby jewellery.

'I've been pleased with you, Evie, for the grace with which you have behaved as regards Timmy and Tricia, as this can't have been an easy time for you,' said Susan earnestly to her eldest daughter, 'and I think for you to give the bracelet to Hettie seems appropriate, and so please do have it for her, if you like it and feel it would suit.'

Evie was delighted as the bracelet was very pretty, and seemed perfect for what she wanted it for. She was also heartened to hear Susan's warm praise about her own behaviour as her mother wasn't one to bandy compliments about.

As she made her way back to Pemberley, Evie was just thinking about the delicate design that the silversmith who made the bracelet had etched into it when she noticed she was passing the village shop, and so she stopped.

She stood quietly and gazed at the familiar windows on either side of the shop doorway, with their triangles of tiered tinned goods displayed inside (Spam, and some sort of tinned fruit, it looked like in the night-time murk).

Evie tried to imagine what a new painted sign saying, perhaps, 'Yeo's Grocery' would look like above the windows, and then how it might be if there were a petrol pump to one side.

At this Evie turned her back on the store to stare across the road at the derelict barn directly on the other side. Evie was so used to seeing this dilapidated wooden structure opposite that she realised that she'd long since stopped really noticing it.

But actually Robert had a point: it was larger than it looked at first inspection, and in the perfect location. If tidied out and mended, it would make a very good garage workshop, that was obvious. Robert's previous garage, back when Evie was little more than a toddler and they had lived in another village about six or seven miles away, had had much less going for it than this, and until everybody's finances became strained in the wake of the stock market crash in the US at the end of the 1920s, Robert had had a thriving business running from it, despite the limitations of the building itself, as he was an excellent mechanic and had a pleasant way with his customers.

When she turned to continue back to Pemberley Evie was startled to see a car idling beside her.

It was Peter!

And he was winding down a window to ask Evie if she would get into the car and sit beside him.

'Peter Pipe... Peter. I'd like to be able to say, what a surprise!' Evie said to him in what she hoped was a cool and collected tone, although she did climb into the passenger's seat quite swiftly just in case either of them changed their minds before she could get in. 'But I learnt today from Timmy that your request to transfer had been denied, and so I presumed you were in the area still. Although I might not have known it from the silence, it seems you had never left. I was debating with myself whether it was worth it for me to come and see you at The Grange at some point. I hadn't decided either way, in case you were interested.'

Although her words might have sounded confi-

103

dent in tone, the reality was that Evie was uncomfortable and uncertain, and she guessed Peter would be able to intimate that, as she hadn't quite been able to say anything that made much sense.

Frustratingly she felt very much caught on the hop, and she couldn't really work out what she felt. She knew that she had more or less been saying anything, simply as a means of filling a potentially awkward silence. Her blood was racing, but it didn't feel as if it was doing so in any sort of particularly pleasurable way.

Evie realised that this unexpected moment with Peter was really just making her feel flummoxed.

She looked across at Peter, and he stared back at her. It felt significant, but it was dark now and so she couldn't see him properly, and Evie knew that she wanted from him something more clear-cut and less open to interpretation.

Peter pulled up his handbrake and quelled the engine.

They sat in silence and Evie could hear an odd noise that sounded like a clock ticking loudly and then she worked out that what she was listening to was the sound of the warm engine contracting in the chill January air.

Evie was confused as to how this was going. It looked like he wanted her to do the running, and she wasn't sure that she wanted to.

'Peter, are you going to say anything to me, or not?' said Evie.

He was a hopeless man, she thought, and she couldn't see why she felt about him the way she did. She decided that she would live with the silence, awkward as it was, and let him lead the conversation for a bit.

Peter looked down and fiddled with his jacket.

'Evie,' he began at last in a low and tentative voice as his long fingers started to beat out a soft pattern on the steering wheel, making his unruly hair quiver, 'do you think we should just get married and get it over and done with?' He sounded defeated, and not at all enamoured at the idea.

'What did you say?'

'I think you heard, Evie. I was asking you whether you thought we should take the plunge.'

And with that Evie punched him on the arm nearest to her without a hint of anything that might be described as playful, before, a second later, giving him quite a hard shove to the bit of his chest that was nearest to her. Evie heard Peter make a soft sort of 'ouff' sound. He hadn't attempted to push her away.

Evie hadn't wanted her first proposal of marriage from him to sound so lacklustre. She realised that to think of this as a 'first' proposal indicated that, somewhere deep inside of her, she secretly expected more than one from him, and that made her cross with herself too.

Not only was Peter hopeless, but so was she quite evidently.

Evie got out and thumped the car door shut with as much vigour as she could. She kicked the front tyre to the car. Then she wrenched the car door open again and flung herself down beside him once again.

'Happy now, Evie?' was all that Peter said.

'Peter, you have been the most infuriating person, really you have. Where were you driving just now? Not to see me, I'll bet. I daresay it was chance you saw me, and decided to stop.' Evie stared at Peter accusingly, and although he wouldn't be able to see the venom in Evie's eyes, the force of her stare meant that he shifted awkwardly on his seat. 'No, I didn't think you had meant to see me! Or to ask me to marry you! Do you honestly think I'm going to be thrilled when you spent a significant part of the autumn letting Fiona make snide digs at me, and then you decide you do care for me, but this is at the same time as you tell me that you have to, in effect, run away to avoid a difficult time with Fiona. And now you dare to talk to me of marriage, or "taking the plunge" as you call it, as if it's something you'd like least in the world to do? Is that the way into my heart, do you believe? Because if it is, Peter, I need to disabuse you of that notion right at this very moment.'

Evie glared accusingly in his direction.

He gathered himself and said dolefully, 'You're right, Evie, and you *should* be cross with me. I've tried to deny my feelings for you as the truth of it is that you make my life difficult. But living without you makes my life feel as if the colour has gone. And then I think of Fiona, and I feel I can't make things worse as far as she is concerned as she's not as strong as you are. I'm left feeling stuck, and unable to work out what to do for the best as far as we are all concerned.'

At this Evie gave what was virtually a snarl.

She wanted him to declare his love for her in a way that would make her feel special and desired, and not as if him giving in to the depth of his

106

emotion as regards her was something unpleasant. And certainly not in a way that managed simultaneously to be apologetic to Fiona either. Couldn't Peter see what she wanted him to do? It seemed very obvious as far as Evie was concerned: he should stand up and metaphorically fight for her like a red-blooded man.

But it was much less clear, apparently, for the forlorn dark shape beside her.

And so Evie leant across and made almost as if she was to give Peter a sound shaking. But then she remembered her fight with Julia, and her promise to herself never again to give in to this sort of violent physical expression, no matter how provoked she might feel. Evie thought it best she ignore the thump and the shove of a minute earlier. And the tyre-kicking. It was to be a clean slate for her from now on...

'What about *my* feelings?' Evie hissed. She had promised herself no violence, but she hadn't promised herself that that reining in of her emotions was also to include her speaking in a reasonable tone.

'It's all very well for you to go on about what *you* want, Peter. But to be honest I'm not interested, or at least not particularly, or this isn't how I expected it to be. I've got to think of myself, and frankly a half-hearted suitor with the feeblest suggestion of marriage known to womankind isn't what I've got in mind, and especially if the said suitor then mentions a former female companion in the same breath.' Evie's voice was growing louder, and so she fought to get a semblance of control. She could feel her curls quivering on

107

either side of her temples.

'I know, Evie, I know,' said Peter as Evie breathed rather heavily. 'I wish I were different, but I'm not. I worry what people think, and I think you're too much for me, and that Fiona needs consideration too. And I can't see what I need to do to make you happy.'

They sat quite still for several minutes, each deep in thought.

'Evie, might I kiss you?' ventured Peter quietly. 'When we kiss, it seems the time we get on best.'

Evie looked at him, uncertain as to what her response would be.

A shaft of moonlight was now making his face clearly visible, and in spite of everything it was a dear face to her. Evie took a slightly shuddery breath deep into her, and for a moment she imagined melting into him. He was weedy and academic-looking, she knew, but there was something about his silly hair, his keen intelligence (when not fumbling for words to describe his, or her, emotions, that was) and the way the light tended to catch the golden flecks in his eyes that made her want to give in to a wild abandon. The kisses they had shared, months ago now, damn it, were still the pinnacles of her life.

But then Evie thought of Fiona, and how easily Peter had considered moving away so as not to deal with her being upset about the fact that Peter cared for Evie instead of Fiona, no matter how unhappy Evie might have been at the situation or how much he himself wanted to be near Evie.

And she felt like a different Evie from the one who Peter had pressed up against the wall of the small sitting room in The Ritz, when they had last hungrily run their hands over each other's bodies. Now she was an Evie who had more backbone and less of a willingness to go with the moment.

'No, Peter, I don't think you can kiss me,' Evie declared, somewhat to her surprise, and to her consternation too, as this felt a formidable declaration no matter how riled at him she was.

And before she could change her mind Evie backed out of the car and was even able to close the car door gently, although she couldn't prevent tears brutally stinging her cold cheeks in the wind as she tramped home.

The next morning Evie felt headachy and flat. But she made herself rally as best she could, and she even remembered to pick up her packed lunch and then, after having made it as far as the front door, the basket back in the kitchen containing the biscuits, before heading off to the school. Somehow she had made the biscuits on her return to Pemberley, although as she was shoving the ingredients into the bowl in any old fashion as she followed Susan's hastily scribbled receipt, Evie couldn't have cared less whether the biscuits turned out to be tasty or not, with the result that some were a trifle undercooked while others had frayed and burnt edges.

Mrs Smith was standing in the playground deep in conversation with Mr Bassett when Evie arrived at the school. Evie tried, not terribly successfully, to smile in his direction, although she did manage to go up to him with her right hand outstretched, saying, 'Happy new year, Mr Bassett. I do hope you have a good term at the school; I'm sure the pupils who were taught by you last year will be glad to have you back.'

He shook her hand back more warmly than she expected, and said he hoped her infants wouldn't be put off their stride by having to be taught over in the village hall.

And then before they had to think of anything else to say to each other, mercifully Mrs Smith galloped to the rescue with various reminders of how they should go about welcoming the new pupils.

The plan was that all the new children would be delivered to the school on this first morning of the new regime, and there would be an assembly for everybody at the school which Mrs Smith would conduct, with pupils and teachers, and Mr Cawes too, all squeezed pell-mell into the juniors top classroom. Mrs Smith would explain to the pupils how the new system was all going to work, and then she was going to formally introduce Mr Bassett and Evie to the new children.

Evie would then take her class to the village hall, where she was going to play some games with them, and read them a story, until it was time to return to school for them all to eat their packed lunches together. Evie's infants would remain at the school in the afternoon for another session of games and fun competitions, and hopefully by the end of the day everyone, new and old, would feel a bona fide member of the forthcoming regime at Lymbridge Primary School.

Evie mentioned to Mrs Smith that she had made the biscuits, and the headmistress replied that Evie had been very thoughtful and, just this once, it wouldn't hurt if after assembly the pupils each had a drink of milk with their biscuits, as fortuitously the farmer from Switherns Farm, right opposite the school, had at Mrs Smith's request already dropped off a small churn that had come only that morning from his milkers.

'Oh my gosh,' said Evie, 'whatever are we going to use for beakers? We're never going to have enough for everyone to be able to have a drink at the same time.'

It turned out that Mrs Smith had thought of that too the previous Saturday morning, with the result that Mr Smith had been sent into Plymouth at Saturday lunchtime to buy extra drinking equipment and a couple of jugs. He'd been instructed to make sure there was enough for everyone who would be taught at the primary school, with extra to cover breakages and also for Evie to have a dozen or so beakers at the village hall in order that she could give the infants some water there when they were thirsty. Apparently what he had brought home with him had been a very motley collection of vessels, but it was the best he'd been able to find.

'Let's hope we don't have to let any of the parents see what their children will be drinking from,' said Mrs Smith. 'Some of the glassware is half-pint tankards, and I'm sure the more straight-laced of them wouldn't approve. But needs must – and I'd rather have a child drinking from a beer glass than being parched and uncomfortable.'

When Evie was ready to take her charges down to the village hall, Mr Cawes came with her, just

111

in case there were any last-minute hitches that would require two people to sort out.

But the children walked down the road two-by-two and then took to their new classroom like ducks to water. Evie was delighted with them, in fact, as there hadn't been any tears or mishaps. They'd enjoyed their milk and biscuits before leaving for the village hall, and actually Evie had been sneakily impressed with her own baking as the biscuits had turned out to be one of her better efforts – the biscuits were surprisingly tasty. She wasn't a natural cook by any stretch of the imagination, and so it was always pot luck as to the success of any of her creations. Mr Cawes chomped greedily the two large ones that she had made especially for him, at any rate, and Mrs Smith and Mr Bassett seemed to like theirs too. Biscuits were a treat these days, and so the pupils eagerly snaffled theirs up, and looked a bit crestfallen when Evie broke the news to them that a snack like this wasn't going to happen too often.

Once all the infants were ensconced at the village hall Evie's first task was to write a new register, to take account of the new children, and also of the loss from the class of Marie and Catherine. She made sure she knew who each of the fresh pupils were and where they were sitting, and that she felt confident in calling their names as she looked at them, without having to refer to the list that Mrs Smith had given her.

After everyone had answered, 'Here, miss,' when Evie called the register, even if only in the faintest of whispers, Evie wrote the newcomers' names on her painted wooden grid on which she awarded stars, Mr Cawes having painted out with white paint the names of the four pupils who had left the class since they broke for Christmas (there had been two other children who had been moved away, besides Marie and Catherine). As Evie filled in those recently vacated spaces with new names, she was pleased she'd had the foresight to ask for several extra lines when Sarah and Tina, the two WVS girls who'd used to lodge at Pemberley, had drawn up the chart for her in the dog days of summer before the start of the Michaelmas term.

Evie gave little Bobby Ayres, one of the more ebullient members of her class, the task of coming to the front of the hall to describe to the new-comers how the stars would be awarded, after which Evie awarded Bobby a star himself for doing the explanation so clearly, which he then stuck on the appropriate square of his row as a practical demonstration of the star awards system.

For the first game, Evie had rigged up a lamp so that its light shone on a blank piece of pale wall. She pulled the blinds to the windows to, and then, thanking heaven for James, as he had taught her how to do this, Evie was able to make a whole series of animal shapes on the wall by putting her hands in certain ways in front of the lamp's bulb. She asked the children to guess which animal she was making cavort around for their amusement on the wall, but she said she would only be listening to guesses that were made by an infant making the appropriate animal noises, and not by anyone calling out the word of what the animal was. The children cottoned on quickly, with the donkey proving particularly popular, although

113

personally Evie thought her duck to be the greatest triumph of her finger puppetry. She had had to admit to the children she was stumped when she did a rabbit, as she had no idea of what a rabbit's call might be like and so she suggested that they make the sound of a rabbit eating their favourite food, which was, of course, carrots, and this discussion led to Evie being able to talk through the different meanings of crunch, nibble, gnaw and chew, with the children being encouraged to attempt the appropriate noises for these different descriptions of eating.

Then the blinds were opened once again, and Evie made the class perform a simple counting game, using the children as counters, which was intended to be as much for her to gauge how well the new pupils already knew their numbers as for them to have fun with one another. After which it was time for a story, and so she read one that she had written the evening before as she sat up in bed that had jungle creatures in it, as well as farmyard animals, and again the infants were encouraged to make the animal noises when Evie held up some picture cards at the relevant parts of the tale, and to count out loud the number sequences she had built into the tale.

With all the moving around and shouting – and mooing, barking, neighing, baaing, growling, hissing and roaring – Evie hoped that the ice had well and truly been broken between the long-standing children in the class and the new arrivals.

Evie didn't know about the children, but by the time they were walking back to school for dinner time, she was feeling quite ready for her own packed lunch. She also discovered that getting her small charges into their coats on her own was much more time-consuming than it was when they were with older children, as then they tended to be keen to show what they could do to the bigger pupils, and so she thought she would have to adjust her lesson timings to take account of this.

Back at the primary school Leonard Bassett jumped up and insisted that Evie take his chair when she went to join him and Mrs Smith to eat her sandwich; and as Evie ate she thought she had certainly experienced quite a few less successful mornings over the past few months.

Chapter Seven

Timmy proved as good as his word.

When Evie returned home after school had ended (and it had seemed a long school day, Evie decided as she headed back to Pemberley, now there was the walking to and fro as she shepherded the infants between the primary school and the village hall, and so she thought the youngest ones would be plumb tuckered out), it was to discover two things.

The first was the PG empty-bed crisis looked to have been averted.

Mrs Worth was bursting with the news that the woman in charge of the administration department at the recuperation hospital, Miss Davis, had only that afternoon telephoned Pemberley about one of the vacant guest bedrooms. She was Sukie's superior, and so Evie was able to say to Mrs Worth that in general Sukie had had only pleasant things to say about her (and, thought Evie, she was very much the sort of person, being towards the upper end of the middle class, whom ideally Mrs Worth would want as a lodger at Pemberley).

And another caller had been Christopher Rolfe, a backroom person working partly for the airstrip, but also for the naval base at Plymouth. He had been promoted and was going to be one of the liaison people involved in building accommodation for servicemen in training, who would be feeding in to Lymbridge over the next month or two, and he'd be key too in organising various sorts of operational logistics and would have a variety of people reporting to him, both civilians and servicemen. Evie could remember him from the day of the point-to-point, and she thought he'd probably tired of living at The Grange, as everyone who wasn't a patient who slept there had to bed down on camp beds in one or other of the large attics and this couldn't be very comfortable long-term.

Then there had been a third telephone call too, this time from a woman called Miss Cornish, who nobody knew anything about other than she was a new friend of one of Timmy's nurses, and she also needed lodgings locally.

Mrs Worth was so delighted by the telephone calls that she had made a seed cake for the current PGs to enjoy after their teatime sardines on toast – seed cake was Mrs Worth's specialty, the PGs had quite often heard her say, although they probably enjoyed it a bit less (for it could be on the dry side) than she enjoyed the flourish with which she would bring it to the tea table on a special occasion.

None of the callers had yet been to see the rooms, but everyone who had previously enquired about lodgings had always gone on to stay as Pemberley was an obvious cut above the norm when it came to digs, and so Evie thought that this would be the case now.

'Evie, my dear,' said Mrs Worth, as Evie was saying that after tea she must get down to washing some clothes as she was behind on her laundry. 'If you want to move into one of the larger bedrooms, now is the time to stake your claim. Please don't feel that you must stay up in your eyrie if you'd prefer to move down into one of the lower and more spacious rooms. As you have been with us for such a long time, and I've become very fond of you, I would only expect the same rent that you are currently paying.'

'Thank you so much; that's very generous of you, and an extremely kind offer. But I think I'll stay where I am,' Evie replied after a pause, and then she popped the final piece of her slice of seed cake into her mouth and tried to have an expression that would suggest to her landlady that the cake was thoroughly delicious.

Indeed Evie had wondered briefly when Mrs Worth had been boasting about the telephone calls earlier whether she might indeed like to move into Peter's old room, the idea giving her a strange tickle deep in her groin. However, as she chewed now, the fond memories of her old attic room trumped the notion of Evie sleeping in Peter's former bed, the idea of Peter having previously lain (perhaps thinking of her) where she would be lying making her feel a bit fluttery, it had to be said.

A less good thing, however, was Evie's discovery ten minutes later, as she gathered her clothes that needed washing, that Keith and her kittens each had a heavy infestation of fleas, even though it was really the wrong time of year for this. To judge by Mrs Worth's silence on the matter, Evie guessed she hadn't noticed, and so Evie crossed her fingers in the hope that this would continue to be the case.

It was a problem that needed attending to quickly, though, as Mrs Worth would never forgive Keith, or Evie as her staunchest supporter, if a flea jumped onto the leg of a prospective PG who had come to view a room.

Evie presumed the infestation had occurred as Keith had started to hunt again now that her kittens were gaining a little independence, and so Evie thought a hedgehog might have been the host, as hedgehogs were known for being always riddled with fleas; perhaps Keith had found one hibernating and had thought it something to pat around and play with. Or maybe Keith had had a run-in with a fox, an animal which was most definitely active throughout the winter – it would only take an instant for fleas to jump from a red pelt to the cat's softer fur and then a new colony of the pest would be started. Or if these fleas could only live on cats, then Keith might have been cavorting with one of the tomcats across the lane at Switherns Farm.

Knowing how Mrs Worth only just about managed to tolerate Keith at the best of times, and although she was tired, Evie had no choice but to nip back to Bluebells for the family's dust comb that had done sterling work over the years with the family dog, Shady. On occasion it had also come in handy for any outbreak of head lice, which had been the scourge of Evie's own primary school years, and her sisters' too.

At Bluebells Evie found her patience severely tested by James and Robert egging each other on when they heard about the state of the cats' coats, each intent on outdoing the other with flea puns, such as 'You'd better hop to it, Evie', 'You'll be suggesting a flea circus then as part of the Spitfire fundraising', 'Time to flee home', and other such unamusing comments. Evie tried to give them the most withering gaze she could manage, but they were laughing too much to pay her any heed. As she was leaving, she heard Robert begin, 'A Cornishman, a Devonian and a flea walked into a bar...' and she had to smile in spite of herself, even though she had no idea what the punchline to the joke could be.

Once back at Pemberley, Evie had to tempt Keith and her kittens to come with her up to her nippy bedroom, using a feather tied to a length of wool – Keith looking at Evie as if she had taken leave of her senses, when there was obviously a much warmer kitchen they could all be sitting in downstairs. She then spent well over an hour combing all the pusses thoroughly, dropping the offending fleas she caught in the prongs of the comb into a jam jar that had a diluted half-inch of disinfectant in the bottom. It wasn't long before Keith and the kittens were revelling in the attention, and once they understood what Evie wanted they even went as far as lying on their backs with their legs in the air when she wanted to comb through their soft belly fuzz.

Depressingly, Evie got a hideously large haul of fleas, and she knew she'd have to comb the cats thoroughly every night for a couple of weeks until they'd be – more or less – flea free, as there were probably a much larger number of the varmints hiding in the carpets waiting for a passing feline to jump onto. Evie garnered a couple of nips from the fleas, who were understandably very peeved at what she was doing, which she didn't make a fuss about as she knew animal fleas couldn't survive on humans even though sometimes they would take a stray bite just to prove this to themselves. However, she was pretty certain that Mrs Worth wouldn't share the same philosophical view as she.

Evie was careful, therefore, not to let either Mr or Mrs Worth see the jam jar when she had finished, although Annabel Frome, one of the PGs, caught a glimpse as Evie headed off to empty it. Evie forced herself not to laugh when she saw just how horrified Annabel looked at the amount of tiny corpses she had collected and that were now clearly visible in their multitude swishing about in the cloudy disinfectant solution. Luckily Annabel nodded when Evie put a finger to her lips, in a silent plea for her not to say anything, as just at that moment Keith and her kittens skittered by the two women on the first-floor landing as they raced back to the warmth of downstairs.

Evie was made of steelier stuff, feeling that fleas were tiresome but a part of country life that couldn't really be avoided, and that Keith's loud purr and affectionate nature more than compensated, while the kittens were so sweet that she simply couldn't hear anything at all against them.

Once she was herself back in the kitchen, there was a familiar purrrp from her feet and Evie looked down to see with alarm that Keith had brought in a rat that she placed in front of Evie. That was quick work as Keith must have snuck out, immediately found the rat and then dragged it inside to present to Evie. Luckily, Keith had killed it already, rather than bringing it live into the warm kitchen to play with, or to give the kittens a lesson in hunting, by releasing it and encouraging them to give chase. Even so, Keith had more than a hint of self-congratulation about her, and she was now looking up at Evie with narrowed eyes as if she expected to be rewarded for hauling such a large beast inside.

Keith's marching orders would be signed immediately by Mrs Worth, should she catch sight of the rat, Evie knew, and so she steeled herself and picked the rodent up by its thick tail. She almost dropped it when she found that as it was such a recent kill its tail was still warm, as well as being of the oddest texture, with the skin sliding unsettlingly over the flexible and narrowing tailbone. The rat's lips were pulled back, showing its long yellowy teeth, and Evie couldn't prevent a shudder of revulsion at the sight of it.

Mrs Worth's footsteps were echoing down the hall sounding worryingly as if she were heading towards the kitchen, and so Evie only had time to pull shut swiftly the door to the cloakroom that had its window wedged several inches apart for Keith to come and go, and then open silently the back door and hurl the curled body as far away as she could, while she tried to keep Keith inside the kitchen with her leg. Keith might think it a game, Evie feared, and bring the rat straight back in again if she were able to get out into the garden again too soon.

As she bustled into the kitchen Mrs Worth looked suspiciously at Evie, who was now sitting at the kitchen table with an overly demure look on her face, but without any obvious reason for just why she should be sitting there at that particular moment, as the table was completely clear, it having only just been scrubbed after the washing-up had been completed by a woman from the village who came to Pemberley to assist with the evening meals. Mrs Worth had sounded so close that by the time she sat down Evie hadn't had time to grab so much as the daily newspaper in order to pretend that she was reading something particularly riveting.

Evie's eyes were shiny and she seemed as if she had been caught out in the act of something she shouldn't be doing, but although she looked to either side about her Mrs Worth couldn't notice anything untoward and so she decided to let matters drift for now.

What Evie could see, and fortunately Mrs Worth couldn't, was that Keith's tabby and white kitten (the largest and boldest of the three) was right behind their landlady, sitting almost upright, his haunches tucked under him, as he juggled and batted from front paw to front paw what was very probably his own first kill, a tiny grey mouse.

The next evening saw a meeting at Pemberley of the Lymbridge sewing circle. Julia took pride of place at the head of the table, and naturally everyone was much too polite to comment on her sudden reappearance after her equally abrupt absence of several months. Julia had been a very staunch member of the group when she had lodged at the guest house, being a founding member as well as someone who was always full of sound sewing advice, and she had been sadly missed when she had stopped attending the meetings in the wake of her and Evie's fracas. Julia was one of those people who made people feel happier when she was around. Her calm manner and warm personality always added to an occasion, and although she would never push herself to the forefront of any gathering, if she wasn't there, somehow it would feel as if a lamp or two had been turned off and the light shimmering around those left behind had quietly but most certainly dimmed.

The members of the sewing circle had just begun to work on their bits and pieces, and there was also a fair amount of knitting going on of socks, hats and scarves that were to be sent to the sailors at sea in answer to a call to knitting arms that had been made by the government at the start of the autumn. It was at this point that Pattie and Julia, in their old guise of Mrs Sew-and-Sew, began a skit that they had obviously worked on together, the object of which was to poke fun at Julia's absence. Evie didn't think what they said was particularly successful or funny, but she thought it quite a clever idea of her sisters' as it did help clear the air without either Julia or Evie actually having to say anything, or anyone there having to say anything to them either, on the subject.

As they worked, Evie found herself distracted by looking closely at a pattern for slacks that Annabel had loaned her, as she had decided to take the plunge into the trouser-wearing brigade.

This plan had been helped by Mrs Worth donating to Evie an old pair of Mr Worth's straw-coloured wool trousers that although now thin in the seat and the knees, she thought might nevertheless be suitable for Evie to adapt and cut down to fit her.

Pattie joked as an aside to Evie that just one of the legs of the trousers would make a pair for Evie, she was so much smaller than Mr Worth, but Evie frowned hard at Pattie as she didn't want Mrs Worth to hear in case she took offence, especially when she had been kind enough to make a present of them to Evie.

After a couple of moments Pattie looked for Evie's usual quick smile, but when none was forthcoming, to get on Evie's good side again Pattie told Evie that following a chance discussion she had had in The Haywain one evening with Mr Rogers, a Pemberley PG and its resident journalist, he was now helping her with speakers for the series of fundraising talks that she had taken off Evie's hands. Mr Rogers had dropped in to Bluebells the evening before to work out a plan of action, and the result was that Pattie and he had made some telephone calls that afternoon, and so the first six dates would be announced in the paper at the end of the week, as would the speakers.

The editor of the *Western Morning News* had agreed to speak (on local stories of interest), as had Robert (about the Home Guard), Mrs Smith ('witty stories about teaching in a village primary school apparently,' said Pattie, to which Evie raised an eyebrow), while Annabel Frome had also said she would speak (she hadn't quite decided what to talk about but it would be to do with clothes, and how to get the best from not very much, as before relocating to Devon and moving into Pemberley, she had worked as an upmarket seamstress, designing and then making many of her own clothes). Linda was going to talk about hot-metal work and the challenges of being a female farrier, while Sukie was going to get one of the doctors from the recuperation hospital involved too (he, they assumed, would be giving a practical demonstration of first aid – they were still waiting to hear which doctor it would be). The talks would take place in Plymouth and all monies taken on the door and for tea served would go to the Spitfire fund. The *Western Morning News* had already arranged additional talks by the sound department of BBC radio drama, and also (as Evie had suggested, remembering fondly how much she had enjoyed these when she was a kiddie) an afternoon of replayed BBC broadcasts for children from the 1930s of Grey Owl, who spoke of

125

conservation and the First Nations' way of life from his cabin, Beaverlodge, on the Ajawaan Lake in Canada. Altogether, this would take the series of guest events right up until Easter.

As Pattie finished speaking, Evie looked to be still deep in contemplation of Mr Worth's old trousers, and so Pattie reminded her eldest sister that their father had arranged a meeting for the fundraising committee the following week. And finally Pattie said that Mr Rogers had told her earlier that evening that Miss Farr, the home economics editor at the *Western Morning News*, would be taking over and launching the competition for the Spitfire cake.

Evie wasn't sure what to say to all of this, which wasn't quite the reaction from her that Pattie had expected.

The truth of it was that Pattie had been so efficient that Evie's nose now felt slightly out of joint, which wasn't a very laudable or a nice feeling, Evie was quick to admit to herself. It seemed that in just a day or two Pattie had got off the ground several things that Evie had been procrastinating over for weeks and weeks, and Evie could see that she really had been making far too much of a huff and a puff about it all.

Evie liked to believe herself to be the get-up-and-go one of the three Yeo girls, but now she thought Pattie rather looked to have stolen her crown with a startlingly efficient array of organisational skills that she'd previously kept well hidden. Evie still felt under par following her bout of influenza, and so it was good that things were happening without her, she knew. But all the

had such terrible second thoughts since.

For, when lying alone in bed in her garret room the previous evening, Evie realised she felt as if she had cut off her nose to spite her face, and perhaps if she'd been a little more sanguine there could have been a very different outcome to the meeting as Peter was, however awkward it had been, attempting at last to make some sort of overtures to her.

Chapter Eight

Evie was about to head over to Bluebells late in the afternoon the following day when she had a nasty shock.

She had finished tidying up an hour or so after school had ended and her pupils had been safely collected, and she was just locking up the door to the village hall at the same time as she was going through in her head her lessons for the next morning when a hand suddenly clutched her shoulder and swung her around to face the other way.

Evie gave a yelp of panic, thinking there must have been an invasion and that Lymbridge was under siege, and she was being attacked by a Jerry.

To her horror it felt – and this was definitely the case, in Evie's eyes, although she could see that another would think her trivial – to be a worse outcome than that dreadful thought.

It was Fiona.

And it was a truly livid-looking Fiona.

In fact, there seemed to be something strangely wild and unhinged about the obviously angry young woman standing before Evie: her hair was unruly, her coat was buttoned unevenly, and there were two vivid red spots the size of half-crowns on her cheeks. It was a shocking sight and a very long way indeed from the steadfastly proper and overly controlled Fiona that Evie was used to, with tightly crimped curls and a tendency to wear her left glove and always carry her right glove in her left hand, as Evie had heard tell was a rather posh thing to do. Where was the Fiona of well-cut, trim two-piece utility suits and hardly worn leather shoes, and a hideous but clearly expensive fox throw Evie had seen adorning her shoulders more than once?

The sight before Evie now was so out of character that she wondered whether Fiona might have had a swig of something strong for Dutch courage before coming to speak to her.

But whatever the story behind what was going on, Fiona was clearly on the warpath and in the mood for confrontation, with her shoulders thrust forward and her pointy chin stuck out. Evie could be in no doubt that Fiona intended to give her a piece of her mind.

In a flash Evie remembered Julia's assertion that Fiona was nothing more nor less than a common or garden bully, and so she decided to step in rather than waiting for Fiona to lead the way.

'Evie Yeo!' screeched Fiona.

At the same time Evie said firmly, but in a much more controlled and authoritative manner, 'Miss Buckley!' Then, just a little softer, 'Miss

Buckley. Miss Buckley, I don't think either of us want to make a show of ourselves out in the road, do we? I am going to unlock the door, and then we can go inside the village hall, and there, in private, you can say to me whatever it is that you have come here to say. I will listen to you, and let you say everything you care to. And then you can go home and leave me be.'

Evie turned and unlocked the door, listening to Fiona's ragged breaths alarmingly close to her ear. Sometimes being a school-teacher did pay dividends in the normal way of things; at any rate Evie could see that she was getting increasingly used to telling other people what to do, and having the pleasure of then watching them actually going on to do what it was that she had requested. Well, not Peter, of course; she had totally failed there.

Anyway, in this case there was the added advantage that Evie had been able to call forth in her moment of need some of Mrs Smith's imperious bossiness she had seen in action so often to bolster her own commanding words. Clearly there had been an unexpected benefit in hearing again and again her headmistress deal with recalcitrant pupils who didn't want to come in after playtime.

With a small frisson of self-congratulation, Evie discovered that she was rather impressed with her own coolness in the face of adversity.

Normally she would have indicated that Fiona should enter the room first in the way that good manners would dictate. But Evie wasn't feeling polite – far from it – and so she made sure that she went through the door first, flipping on one of the electric light switches as she did so with a hurried and temper-driven gesture.

With a sigh and shifting her weight equally over both legs, Evie turned to face Fiona, who had followed her in although her egress sounded as if she could have been stumbling slightly, which Evie put down to herself only having just turned the partial lighting on and the bulbs taking a little time to warm up.

Fiona was now before Evie, suddenly looking even more bedraggled and very much as if the wind had been punched from her sails. Without warning her fight seemed to have dissipated into nothing more than a whimper.

There was a silence, and to her surprise Evie saw Fiona's eyes start to well with tears and her lower lip tremble uncontrollably with her chin below dimpling peculiarly. This wasn't at all what Evie had expected, particularly when she noticed Fiona's shaky hands as she brought a gloved finger to her face to touch beneath her lower lashes.

'Fiona, please come and sit down over here,' Evie said much more gently, 'and I'll fetch you a glass of water.'

Evie indicated a sturdy wooden chair and after dashing to the hall's small kitchen to fetch Fiona a half-pint beer tankard with some icy cold water in it, she pulled another chair near so that they were sitting quite close together and facing each other.

Fiona seemed thoroughly dejected and unable to speak, and she had definitely had something alcoholic to drink, as Evie could smell the whiff of a spirit wafting in her direction.

'Why are you here, Fiona?' said Evie. Fiona glanced blearily towards her, and then looked down into the beer tankard. Evie continued even more soothingly, 'You do know there is nothing between Peter and me, don't you? Official or unofficial.'

There was still no answer. But Fiona's torso had slid down slightly against the back of the chair at the same time as it had tilted askew, making Fiona look for all the world as if she were collapsing in on herself, with one of her already angular hips jutting peculiarly outwards, her legs akimbo and her eyelids slowly drooping.

'You think that makes any difference?' muttered Fiona at last, in a low but still-snipey tone, as she jerked her head upright to peer in Evie's direction before allowing her chin to sink once more. 'He might not be betrothed to you in any official sense, but he is as good as.' Or at least this is what Evie thought Fiona was saying to her, as Fiona's normally strident voice had rapidly given way to the quietest of mumbles with her words running slurrily one into another.

Evie looked at the floor as she let out a long breath of incomprehension. She really would rather be anywhere but in the village hall just at that moment.

There was an unpleasant gulpy hiccupping noise from Fiona, and Evie looked across at her sharply.

All at once Evie felt worried rather than angry or put-upon.

Whatever was going on over on the other chair was happening very quickly and Evie could see that in what felt like an impossibly short space of time Fiona had gone from looking ready for a bust-up to the epitome of defeat.

And now that Evie stared at the woman before her anew, she saw that the situation had slithered down a further notch or two in just a very few seconds as Fiona appeared as if she were about to pass out.

Evie looked around the hall but couldn't see anything that she thought would help ease the situation.

But Fiona was now slumping most definitely, and very pale, and Evie could see she herself needed to take decisive action, and as quickly as possible, otherwise Fiona might hurt herself if she tipped from the chair and crashed to the ground. The beer glass slipped from her hands before Evie could get to her, but Fiona was too far gone to acknowledge the racket it made as the chunky tankard bounced on the wooden boards of the floor and splattered Evie's stockinged legs with glacial water, causing her to flinch at the un-expected damp chill.

Evie grabbed Fiona by the shoulders and sup-ported her while she edged her torso forward and away from the chair and eased her down until Fiona was lying full length and flat on her back on the floor. There was a draught blasting in towards them from under the outer door and it was freezing in the hall as Evie always turned the heater off when the class left to go to the primary school for lunch in order to save precious fuel, and she tried hard not to put it on again, allowing the children to wear their balaclavas and hats and scarves to keep warm when they returned to the village hall for the afternoon session.

Evie moved both chairs well away for safety in case Fiona lurched back into consciousness and joltingly staggered to her feet not knowing where she was and then blundered into them. Next, Evie placed her own coat over Fiona despite the grubby floor and it being Evie's only coat. Evie was sure that somebody like Fiona would have a wardrobe full of outer garments, and so it would hardly matter that Fiona was lying in the dust and grime of a floor where Evie's infants had been traipsing around all day in their muddy footwear. But for Evie this wasn't the case and normally she took great pains to take the best care she could of her garments in order that they would be faithful servants for as long as possible, and so her lips tightened at the sight of her coat looking so forlorn and ill-used. Fiona was so slender as to cause hardly a rise in the folds of the coat.

Evie had no idea what she should do in a situation like this. But Fiona's skin was deadly pale, and Evie thought she probably shouldn't get cold. Although she longed just to get up and walk out of the hall, close the door and leave Fiona to it as she headed off to Pemberley for a hot cup of tea, Evie knew that this wasn't an option as she couldn't leave the woman to chill right through to the bone and neither could she leave the village hall unlocked.

Blast. Damn. And double damn!

To hell with Peter. And to hell with Fiona, thought Evie.

She really didn't need this sort of thing to cope with at the end of a busy working day.

Evie didn't feel cool in the face of adversity any longer.

She gave Fiona's shoulders a little shake to see if she could get a response. There was none. Evie suddenly understood what was meant by the phrase 'the silence was deafening', as listening as hard as she could for some sort of reassurance from Fiona, all Evie could hear now was her own blood pounding in her ears.

'Fiona! Fiona? If you can hear me, I'm going for help,' Evie said loudly in the ear of the comatose woman as she crouched beside her.

There was no response to this either, although Evie noticed how Fiona's eyes weren't properly shut and that all she could see was white, meaning that her eyes had rolled upwards in their sockets. Whether this was a good or bad thing, Evie had no idea as she had never seen the like before, but her guess was that most probably it wasn't a sign that Fiona was doing well. Fiona's lips were slightly drawn back over her large teeth, and Evie was reminded uncomfortably of the dead rat Keith had brought in.

Evie ran from the village hall, uncertain of what would be the correct thing to do. She stopped in the middle of the road, but there was nobody about. Of course there wasn't – this was a midweek winter's afternoon in a small moorland village that was never heaving with people at the best of times, in the lull between school ending with parents milling around waiting to collect their offspring, and those who were working longer hours heading through the village on their way home to enjoy their own teas.

She looked over in the direction of Pemberley, but it seemed too far away, and it was quite a distance too to either Bluebells or Mrs Smith's. She faced one way, and then the other.

It seemed as if to head for the village store would be the best option as fortuitously, in line with what other shopkeepers were doing right across the country, this was the first week of extended opening hours for the shop, because the mid-afternoon closing time that had been forced on shopkeepers earlier in the war had been relaxed, and so closing time had now been shifted until two hours later to give those who were working more time to be able to get any supper fixings they needed. Susan had told Evie that many shop workers across the whole country were outraged as very often their wages remained the same as when they had worked the reduced hours.

Without ado Evie raced to the shop, and burst in through the door with its familiar bell jangling in protest as she frantically heaved it open, and let out a het-up cry of 'Mother!'

Susan looked up with an unnerved expression at Evie's uncharacteristic timbre; she knew instantly something was gravely wrong.

Susan was on one side of the counter, and Robert was standing opposite her on the customers' side of the counter, and they had some drawings spread out between them that Evie could see were to do with the derelict building opposite. Her parents looked as if they had been deep in discussion, and in spite of her anxiety, Evie thought they clearly were thinking seriously about developing the vehicle workshop.

'Fiona Buckley accosted me as I was locking up the village hall a few minutes ago,' Evie said urgently, her voice still high as she was finding it peculiarly difficult to catch her breath. 'Peter has ended their relationship because of me, even though nothing is going on any longer between us, and I think she wanted to tell me what she thought of me.' Evie could hear her own voice growing steadily squeakier.

Evie saw her parents glance towards each other in surprise. Clearly they had never suspected there might be anything between Peter and Evie.

She had been most careful the previous summer to keep her feelings for Peter under wraps, as the first time they had kissed she was technically engaged to Timmy, although by then Evie had known the secret that Tricia was pregnant and that correspondingly her and Timmy's engagement was all but over. Understandably, though, Evie hadn't wanted Susan and Robert to find out about Evie and Peter's stolen moments, or certainly not in quite such an abrupt way as this.

But the words had escaped her mouth before she'd been able to control them. Damn and blast again – what a nuisance, especially as she and Peter were all done and dusted, and in the past, and meanwhile Evie had only just rehabilitated herself in her parents' opinion following the falling-out with Julia.

Evie ploughed on, however, without stopping. 'But I think Fiona has been drinking, and almost the minute we got inside she passed out. She's in the village hall lying on the floor, and I can't get her to respond to me. I don't know what's to be done but I think that something needs to be as she doesn't seem right to me.'

The great thing about Robert and Susan, Evie thought fleetingly when she looked at Robert's calm face and without ado he buttoned his coat and pulled his scarf tighter ready to go outside with Evie, was that her parents could always be relied upon in a crisis. She was very lucky, she told herself. And so it proved to be.

Robert told Susan to stay where she was, as it was best that she didn't leave the shop.

He ran, side by side with Evie, back to the village hall.

Fiona was where Evie had left her, lying unmoving and oblivious on the floor, with Evie's coat over her. It didn't look as if she had shifted position in the few minutes since Evie had left to go and get help, although if anything the skin of her face looked an even frostier shade of alabaster.

Robert leant down and took off Fiona's glove in order that he could take her pulse, and then he sniffed her breath. After that he carefully lifted each eyelid to look underneath; in Evie's opinion, this was the most disturbing part of Fiona's condition as from where she was standing there was no sign at all of any coloured iris. Finally Robert stroked his finger over the soft skin of both of Fiona's wrists, and Evie thought he must be taking Fiona's pulse again.

'I don't like the look of her,' he said softly, as he carefully manoeuvred Fiona so that she was lying on her side, tilted slightly towards the floor but with her top knee bent and holding her in position on her side, and not on her back as Evie had left her. He took off and folded his coat and placed it under Fiona's head.

'Neither do I,' agreed Evie morosely, although almost certainly for quite different reasons to her father.

Robert said he would stay with Fiona if Evie could run over to Pemberley to see if somebody was there who could come and get them by car. His car was in the garage at Bluebells, but tiresomely was without any petrol in its engine.

Luckily, once at the guest house, Evie found that Mr Rogers had just returned from a day following up on a news story somewhere in Cornwall, and she was able to persuade him to drive down to the village hall to come to their rescue, hissing at him as she manoeuvred him adroitly down Pemberley's hallway to get him out of earshot of the Worths or the other PGs that she would very much appreciate it if Mr Rogers could keep all of this under his hat.

The young journalist raised a sceptical eyebrow in her direction, but then he nodded a prompt agreement when he saw that Evie was being serious and was not at all in the mood for larking about.

Back at the village hall Robert and Mr Rogers wrestled Fiona upright and then bundled her onto the back seat of Mr Rogers' car, and Evie climbed into the rear of the car too, thinking that this was an awful parody of several months earlier when Tricia had been in labour in the back of Peter's car and Evie had been crouching beside her, just as uncomfortably as now, as they'd then headed all-speed to hospital. This time the car journey took just a matter of seconds, though, as Bluebells was no more than a quarter of a mile away, and Evie felt angry and a little frightened, rather than excited in the way she had that earlier time.

Fiona was manhandled unceremoniously into the parlour by Robert and Mr Rogers, and deposited with a soft wumph onto her side on the uncomfortable sofa, with a rather threadbare old cushion slid under her head and Evie's coat over her being replaced by a woollen blanket Evie grabbed from Frank's bed. The room's empty coal scuttle was placed by Robert near to her head in case Fiona needed a receptacle.

Evie said she had never seen anyone in this condition, and even Mr Rogers agreed that Fiona seemed pretty far gone and that she needed to be looked after as if it was extreme alcohol consumption, it could cause fitting. Then he added that Fiona's body would treat what she had drunk as a poison to be eliminated, which would almost definitely cause her to be sick and could have even more embarrassing consequences.

Evie couldn't prevent a small shudder of distaste, and then she sent Mr Rogers back to Pemberley, with the stern reminder that this was to remain between them, please, with no one else at all in the know. If he valued Evie as any sort of friend, he wouldn't ask any questions at all as to what might have led to this state of affairs and he would remember too how important it was for a young woman to keep her good reputation intact. Mr Rogers raised another questioning eyebrow, but dropped it once more at Evie's pleading expression.

She saw Mr Rogers off on his way; he was dropping off Robert at the shop so that Susan could be brought up to speed as to Fiona's condition, and as Evie had watched from Bluebell's front porch, both men went to the car shaking their heads, presumably at the unexpectedness of Fiona's rash behaviour.

When she returned to the kitchen Evie tried to muster once again her schoolteacher's voice as she reiterated to Pattie and James, and Frank and Joseph too, that the fact that Fiona was unconscious in their parlour, now also with a large glass of water near to her too, was to remain firmly a secret between them all and it was a secret they were to go on keeping. She caught Pattie's eye, and Pattie shrugged her shoulders in response; Evie knew Pattie would reinforce the need to the younger Yeos that they must all hold schtum.

Fiona was an idiot, no doubt, but a young woman never deserved to have her name dragged through the mud if it could possibly be avoided, no matter how irksome her behaviour had been. Evie feared what had happened was the sort of thing Fiona might come to discover had scuppered her chances of making the best marriage she could, should it become public knowledge. Few men would want as a wife a woman who allowed herself to be drunk, Evie was sure.

Evie collected a second blanket, this time from Joseph's bed, and she went to sit with Fiona for a bit. After draping the blanket on top of her, Evie peered at her intently. Fiona's breathing was erratic, and she was quite unaware as to what was happening around her.

144

Evie could see, disconcertingly, that Fiona's eyes were still not quite shut but that now her eyeballs were sometimes moving, flickering the irises furiously at times from side to side, or up and down. It made Evie feel queasy to watch them. Evie was reminded of the music hall puppet acts, where a man would have a talking puppet sitting on his lap, and would manipulate the puppet's eyeballs around. Evie realised she was slightly scared of puppets; she felt similarly about Fiona right at this moment.

Although she and Fiona had met several times, these occasions had felt incredibly fraught as far as Evie was concerned, as Fiona always tried to have a dig at Evie, so much so that now Evie realised that up until this minute she hadn't really ever looked closely at her competitor for Peter's affections, finding retreat the better course of action.

Fiona was, Evie noted, very expensively dressed, which Evie would have expected as she was aware Fiona came from money – her family had land in Hertfordshire and also close to Torquay, Evie knew.

But Fiona was nervily thin with bony arms poking out of her jacket's sleeves, and although she wouldn't be more than in her early twenties, and was possibly younger, she already had quite deep frown lines etched on her forehead as well as sharper lines on either side of her nose that traced a cleft from each nostril down to the corner of her mouth. Her skin looked desiccated and even in repose she didn't look a naturally happy woman. She looked like she needed very

145

much a few good meals and some early nights.

Out of the blue Evie felt an unexpected flash of compassion, and she leant forward and laid a hand on Fiona's forearm.

Now she was so near to Fiona she could see several thin white lines across the inside of her wrist that was closest to Evie. Evie looked for a long time at the marks, pondering their possible meaning. With extreme caution, as she didn't want Fiona to come to and catch her in the act, Evie examined this wrist in extensive detail, and then very slowly drew the other wrist towards her. Fiona didn't stir. Her second wrist was a mirror image, with exactly the same lines. Evie thought it almost looked like little white ladders traced on the blue-veined skin.

Evie sat back in her chair and thought about what she had seen. She'd never come across this sort of thing before and, if she didn't know better as Fiona had always seemed to be the sort of rigid person who would go out of their way to be 100 per cent law-abiding at all times (and Peter was incredibly straight-laced too, and would have reinforced the sense of the straight and narrow in his companion, Evie thought), Evie's assumption would have been that Fiona had at some point made numerous slashes across her own wrists. Evie couldn't think of a rational explanation for how else those marks, which she now realised were rows of healed scar tissue, might have got there otherwise. Of course, suicide or, more accurately, attempted suicide was an offence punishable by law, and so Evie doubted Fiona would have risked prosecution. But what if Fiona had been so unhappy in the past she had harmed herself none-theless?

Evie didn't know what to make of it all, but at least none of the marks looked new. In fact, they were so well healed that it was very possible that if Fiona had been moving around in the normal way of things, then Evie would never have had her attention alerted to them.

It was very puzzling. As Evie mulled the matter over, her own brow clenched in a frown, she concluded that although her own background was modest in the extreme, without any sort of a financial cushion behind her, and she had to support herself by being a schoolteacher – she knew Fiona didn't have to work and could therefore enjoy a much more indolent life – it was she, Evie, who was perhaps better equipped to face life's challenges, very probably because she knew she *didn't* have a silver spoon in her mouth.

Evie felt her life compensated by being rich in other areas, with a loving family around her and an exceptionally close circle of friends. The impression she had always had of Fiona was of a rather isolated young woman whose family wasn't at all close, and that she was someone who didn't have the benefit either of many nice friends.

Certainly Evie couldn't imagine herself ever becoming so emaciated or so worried-looking as Fiona. And even if she were threatening to head down that route, it was likely that her family and friends would band together to do their utmost to prevent that happening.

The thought struck Evie that maybe losing Peter was more devastating to Fiona than it was to Evie.

She pondered it for a while, lulled by the sound of Fiona's deep but at last increasingly regular breathing, pausing in her ruminations only to make sure that both Fiona's icy hands were covered once again by the two wool blankets.

The parlour was chilly as there wasn't a fire in the grate; the Yeos used the room only very rarely, purely on high days and holidays, and so it was unusual for it to be warm at the best of times.

After a while the nip in the air drove Evie back to the kitchen, despite the fact that after a good shake to remove the dust from the floor of the village hall, she had slipped on her coat a good forty-five minutes earlier in an effort to keep warm.

Susan had finished her working day at the shop, and she had just come in (although Evie had been so wrapped up in thoughts of Fiona that she hadn't heard her mother open the front door to Bluebells) and she looked to be making herself busy sorting things out near the stove as she started to prepare an evening meal. But when Evie came into the kitchen she saw Susan toss her head upwards and then nod quickly in the direction of Robert, James and the boys, who took the hint and made themselves scarce.

'Evie, come and have a cup of tea with me,' said Susan once they had the kitchen to themselves, 'and tell me all about what's been going on.'

Evie sat beside her mother at the kitchen table and as they peeled a mound of potatoes and cut up some greens she slowly began to describe everything that had happened since the previous Easter, not bothering to hold anything back, or to

148

make herself, Timmy, Tricia, Peter or Fiona seem any better behaved than they had been. She even described the marks she had seen on Fiona's wrists, and at this, Susan got up and went to see for herself.

Afterwards, although she wasn't proud of any of their behaviour Evie felt such a huge sense of relief at the unburdening to her mother of what she had struggled to contain since the early summer in 1941, that she wished heartily that she had been brave enough to confide in Susan a long time earlier.

Susan had listened without comment and when Evie had finally run out of words, she urged Evie to think kindly of herself, and of the others concerned, saying they were still all young, and the process of growing up meant that everybody made mistakes and did things that afterwards they felt ashamed of. It didn't mean that anybody was a bad person as such, and it meant too that sometimes the seeds of good things would be sewn in the most unpromising of situations.

After a final cup of tea and another check on Fiona, who was still dead to the world but who now seemed to have the look and breathing of someone heavily asleep rather than a woman who was unconscious, Evie headed back to Pemberley. There was a call she needed to make, and Bluebells didn't have a telephone.

Before she had taken off her coat or hat, Evie dialled the operator and asked to be put through to The Grange. Once through, she asked to be transferred to the basement, and then had to be quite firm as whoever had answered the phone had clearly never put a call through to that particular part of the building. But Evie had spied a telephone on the lower level of the building on her visits to see Peter, and although that was probably for an outside line, she thought there was bound to be some sort of internal connection too.

'I need to speak to Mr Peter Pipe,' said Evie, when eventually a different woman's voice answered, presumably from deep within the bowels of the secret rooms underneath The Grange. 'Please tell him it is most urgent. My name is Miss Evie Yeo, and I really must speak to him. It's an emergency.'

If Peter had left for the day, Evie didn't know what she would do then, as she had no idea of where he was currently lodging; they'd never had that particular conversation since he had relocated in the autumn to Dartmoor from London. There had always seemed something else more important to talk about but Evie was surprised now that she hadn't been more curious. Honestly, she was feeble sometimes, she thought to herself.

There was quite a long delay before Evie could hear the sound of footsteps heading towards the telephone. Evie thought that she and Peter had never spoken to each other on the telephone before.

Evie realised that all of this was so indicative of their relationship; there were many things that they had never done together or said to each other, and thus, she supposed, it was only to be expected as although they had had their moments with each other, the reality was that their relationship was inherently lopsided and therefore always destined to flounder as it was too intense in some areas and totally non-existent in others.

Peter lifted the receiver to his mouth, and said a tentative hello.

'Peter, please don't ask me for details. But Fiona is intoxicated and lying dead to the world in my parents' parlour at Bluebells, and I was rather hoping that you could fetch her in your car and take her wherever she needs to be,' said Evie wearily. 'I think at the very least you owe that to her. And to my parents.'

There was a very long silence from the other end of the line as Peter thought over what Evie had just said to him.

Softly she replaced the handset back on the telephone without waiting any longer for him to grope for what he should say.

Of course Evie never breathed a word to Mrs Smith as to what had occurred at the village hall.

It had taken her a while to restore herself to Mrs Smith's good books following the argument with Julia, which had led immediately to Mr Bassett leaving his post with the result that Mrs Smith had had to leave Timmy's bedside to return to the school. This meant that Evie had no desire to let her headmistress know that she had once more been on the precipice of a full-blown showdown in the village hall, which was, rather a lot of the time, also a public place where Lymbridge residents could pop in and out of. It had been pure luck that Fiona had chosen to visit on the only afternoon during the week that the hall wasn't used for some sort of village meeting after

151

the school day was over and done with.

Evie was pretty certain that nobody who lived in Lymbridge had seen her and Fiona together, or had seen Mr Rogers and Robert heave Fiona into the car or lurch her out of it again. Evie hoped with all her heart that Fiona had arrived surreptitiously in the village just before she and Evie had had their contretemps, and that Fiona had gone straight to the village hall rather than doing anything rash such as wandering around on the village green while swigging openly from a bottle of spirits.

The next morning Evie had got up early to go to the village hall in order to search around on the ground outside. It was a hunch that paid off as it wasn't long before she found an empty bottle of brandy to the side of the hall, and she hid it at the bottom of the dustbin at the back door to the hall, underneath the rubbish from the classroom's waste paper bins that Evie would carefully empty every couple of days.

She kept her ear to the ground, as did Susan, and fortunately there didn't seem to be any untoward rumours swirling in the ether to do with Fiona's strange behaviour that they could discern.

Evie and Sukie and Linda had a drink over in Bramstone that evening and it was an outing during which their old, happy balance of friendship seemed to be restored to what it should be. Sukie seemed enamoured to be with them both, and Linda looked very much as if married life were suiting her. And Evie felt on surprisingly good form too as her new infants seemed to be settling in to the class, and they were all getting into a rhythm of trotting backwards and forwards between the primary school and the village hall.

It wasn't long before Evie decided that she didn't count her dear friends as people who shouldn't know any details about Fiona's indiscretion. And so Evie described, with only the occasional and slightest of exaggerations, all that had occurred – well, other than noticing the marks on Fiona's wrists, that was, as if she were to mention those, it definitely would have felt like she was taking a step too far in the befouling of her adversary. Her friends listened carefully as Evie described how helpless and panicked she had found herself to be as she watched Fiona's swift descent into deep unconsciousness. After the trio had gone over what had happened every which way, they all agreed it had been a very strange turn of events, but that Evie had (as Sukie and Linda would have expected) of course behaved in an exemplary manner. Evie wasn't so sure that she had, but it was nice of her pals to insist so, all the same.

When Evie arrived home from Bramstone, it was to discover a card addressed to her propped up on the hall table. It was made of luxury embossed paper with a pressed violet pasted under a thin gauze that was stuck behind the edges of an oval cut-out on the card's front, while the luxurious paper of the matching envelope was debossed with violet shapes; it was obviously a very pricy card.

Inside it simply said 'Sincere apologies, F'.

Immediately Evie felt a sharp pang of remorse at how gleefully she had so recently been describing Fiona's fall from grace.

This uncomfortable feeling was heightened when Pattie told her the next day that Fiona had also sent by messenger a similar card of apology to Robert and Susan, accompanied by a hamper of expensive titbits from Spooner's that had been especially delivered by the Plymouth store.

Pattie and Evie wondered how Fiona had swung this during the rationing and petrol shortages, but this wasn't enough to ease Evie's growing sense of disappointment with herself at having had, while not quite fun, a now-shaming level of enjoyment at Fiona's unexpected collapse of standards.

Evie felt unsettled, and she realised that Timmy was the person she wanted to see. He had the knack of making her laugh at herself, and he seemed to like her whatever she said or did, no matter how wanting Evie might have felt her own behaviour to be. This was probably the most appealing thing about him, Evie had thought several times.

After school, Evie borrowed Julia's heavy and cumbersome bicycle she used to do her rounds for the Post Office, and pedalled her way precariously over to the recuperation hospital, sliding a little on the ice settling on the road for the forthcoming night when she had to apply the brakes. Evie had never liked cycling much, and so she rather regretted not walking.

As she drew near, Peter was driving down the drive from The Grange and out into the road, heading away from Evie and towards the market town of Oldwell Abbott in the same direction as the cottage hospital that he and Evie had taken

Tricia to so that newborn baby Hettie could have the best medical attention a winter's Sunday afternoon on Dartmoor could provide.

Evie thought Peter might have spied her, although if he had, he hadn't made any acknowledgement.

'What's up, Evie? This is a surprise.' Timmy said in a cheerful tone several minutes later. 'You look odd, if I may say.'

'Thanks, Timmy, that's really helpful, and pleasant to hear.'

Irony was, as usual, wasted on Timmy, with the result that then Evie took a deep breath and decided to come clean about everything. Confiding all to Susan had shown her that perhaps her behaviour as regards Peter hadn't been so very bad after all. Of course, Timmy was her former fiancé but, Evie felt, he didn't have a leg to stand on as regards criticisms of poor behaviour, bearing in mind what he had got up to with Tricia while Evie had his engagement ring hanging on a filigree chain around her neck, nestled close to her décolletage.

As she unburdened herself to Timmy she thought that when a person hadn't got anything to lose, it was easier to be honest. There was nothing romantic any longer between her and Timmy, and so she could be frank. She couldn't imagine having quite the same degree of open honesty if she had been having a similar conversation with Peter, Evie realised, as she still would have wanted too badly for him to think well of her.

Haltingly at first but then picking up speed as she found herself lost in the memory of events past, her brow slightly furrowed in concentration, Evie told Timmy about how she and Peter had edged towards each other in the emotional sense around the same time Evie was wondering what she should do about Timmy and Tricia. Timmy did have the grace (or sense) to look a little contrite during this bit, but Evie didn't acknowledge this and went on quickly to describe how she had failed to tell Peter that she was engaged. She told of the shock it must have been for Peter when he learnt of her and Timmy's engagement, when a telegram announcing the grave injury Timmy had sustained arrived in the village and everyone was talking of Timmy as Evie's fiancé.

Taking a deep breath, Evie looked down as she described the two times she and Peter had kissed on the day of the summer Revels, which coincidentally had been earlier on the same day the dreadful telegram arrived to alter their lives for ever, and how very soon afterwards Peter had temporarily deserted the West Country, and, of course, Evie too, when he believed she was poised to marry Timmy.

And then Evie described how Peter hadn't left a forwarding address when she had raced back after Timmy had released her from their engagement as he lay poorly in bed in Stoke Mandeville Hospital, only to find that Peter had disappeared, and nobody knew exactly where he was. She mentioned the subsequent, unexpected kiss at The Ritz between her and Peter on the day Timmy married Tricia, and then she told of how horrified she'd been when Peter had returned to Dartmoor with Fiona by his side.

Timmy chipped in at this point to say in a jolly and helpful manner that he'd noticed Fiona well and truly staking her claim to Peter at the New Year's Eve dance and her demand that Evie back off from her man in no uncertain terms, and that on the small amount of Fiona that he had seen, frankly he didn't much like the cut of her jib.

Evie breathed out sharply at the memory of Fiona accosting her at the dance, and of Julia leaping to her big sister's defence.

'When we were counting the takings from the dance, downstairs in Peter's lair in the basement here at The Grange the morning afterwards, he told me that as he drove Fiona home after the dance he ended his relationship with her, and the conversation between them was uncomfortable and rancorous,' Evie went on dejectedly. 'Peter said to me as we sat either side of the table in the small mess room downstairs that he loved me, but that Fiona would make our lives untenable if we dared presume to have any sort of relationship together, and so he was going to go away. I should, apparently, make a new life; a life that's to be without him.

'He's not gone, as you know, Timmy, but he's not been in touch with me either, except for one silly time not long ago when he said in the most ridiculous way possible that maybe we should marry and get it over and done with, as if the idea was to him as unattractive as some dog dirt on the toe of his shoe, and without it being any sort of proper proposal. Of course, we argued, or more accurately I argued with him and he refused to argue back – and then I got out of his car and

157

slammed the door in his face. I've lost patience with him, Timmy, I really have.'

Timmy said Peter refusing to argue must have been irritating for Evie, and then he gave her hand a squeeze as he told her to buck up as worse things happen at sea. Evie exhaled a huff of air through her nose that could be interpreted in a variety of ways.

She went on, 'Just as bad was that this week Fiona turned up blotto to accost me after school, although she slipped unconscious before she could give me what for... Father thinks she may have drunk the best part of a bottle of spirits very quickly to buoy herself up to speak to me, without realising the consequences, and I found an empty bottle of brandy outside the village hall.'

There was an awkward pause as both Evie and Timmy realised this empty bottle may well have been lying right where baby Hettie had been conceived. Then Evie remembered that she had told herself within the last hour that Timmy didn't have a leg to stand on in the moral sense, considering his treatment of her, and immediately afterwards Evie berated herself for being crass as of course that was a very tasteless thought to have when poor Timmy couldn't stand up. Was there no end to the gamut of uncomfortable feelings Evie could experience?

Evie forced herself to rally, and she continued, 'And then later I found out something that makes me think that Fiona is fragile and vulnerable, and very difficult to predict as to what she might do. And tonight I'm pretty certain Peter saw me cycling here, but he just put his head down and drove the other way.'

Evie's voice was giving out a warning wobble, and so she closed her eyes and didn't say anything further. It would be too humiliating if she started to cry.

At this Timmy did his level best to cheer Evie up. He asked her if she had got everything off her chest.

Not daring to open her eyes yet, she nodded to indicate she had.

Phew, said Timmy, adding that he'd thought he was going to have to miss supper if Evie had gone on much longer.

Evie didn't smile at this quip, and so then he enquired whether she wanted to marry Peter – Evie shook her head in a resigned and (Timmy thought) regretful manner – or if she wanted Timmy to send Fiona another bottle of brandy, to which Evie was able to give something approaching a tiny smile of faint amusement as she ruefully shook her head, her curls giving a small bounce or two to offer a hint of their old abandon.

Timmy offered jokily to punch Fiona's lights out on Evie's behalf. Evie couldn't prevent a small snigger escaping, although then she felt she had to admonish Timmy for daring to think about a physical comeback of any sort, and especially in the case of him acting badly towards a woman.

Timmy rolled his eyes, and said he had only been trying to cheer Evie up a little, and of course being confined to his wheelchair or bed, he'd never thought Evie would take him seriously, even if only for a moment. Evie's expression hardened.

They frowned at each other, neither being quite

159

sure who Evie was cross with. She thought it was most probably herself.

In an attempt to get Evie smiling again, Timmy said, 'Well, in that case, Evie Yeo, there's only one thing for it. We need to find you a new man to fall in love with.'

Evie's expression didn't change.

Timmy added boldly, 'We can call sorting out your love life Project Evie's Victory of the Heart. Which would be P.E.V.O.T.H. Or maybe just P.E.V. – that's got a ring to it, hasn't it, and I'm less likely to get in a muddle with that. There is a further advantage too as only us two need know what we are talking about if either of us says "Pev". And so I will put my energies to finding you your Pev, don't you worry, Evie.'

Evie looked at him seriously. She thought Timmy has been reading too many adventure stories, and that personally she wasn't fond of acronyms. But, after a while, and very gravely, she nodded her head in agreement.

She hadn't been very good at finding happiness off her own bat – maybe Timmy would be able to help, as she didn't like the idea much of a future for herself where she remained a congenital spinster.

Sukie and Linda would think it odd, as would Julia and Pattie, but if there was a hope in hell that it would work, Evie was game. It wasn't as if, if it were to fail, that a joke or two at her expense about Pev would leave her in a worse position than now.

So the two old schoolfriends – one in bed and the other on a chair alongside, with a wheelchair

160

standing guard nearby – looked at each other, and slowly they smiled in collusion. It rather seemed as if they had just hatched a plan.

Chapter Nine

Early – very early – on Saturday morning Evie dragged herself out from under her warm eiderdown and, after a hurried cup of tea, clambered this time onto Mrs Worth's heavy bicycle to pedal laboriously over to Linda and Sam's farm.

It was still pitch black, so the three hunters Linda had borrowed the afternoon before and stabled overnight looked rather askance at Linda and Evie when they started to groom them just under where their saddles would go, and then tack them up. Two of the hunters were the ones that Sukie and Evie had fittened for the point-to-point in the autumn, although they had now been let down and Linda had had to shoe them quickly the previous day; the third was a quieter and older mare for Linda, who, despite being a farrier and used to being around horses, was a much more nervous rider than most people would assume. The coats of the horses were woolly and muddy in patches, as they hadn't been clipped out since hunting still hadn't returned to anything like what it had been pre-war, with the result that none of them were really being used much.

Linda and Evie left the horses tacked in their three stalls, with old blankets slung across their

161

haunches to stop them getting cold as they couldn't move much in the tight stalls, and the pals nipped inside the farmhouse where Sam's doting mother plied them with toast and tea, while they could hear Sam clanking about with metal buckets filled with feed for the animals in various outbuildings in the farmyard. Evie insisted she'd just have a small cup as else she'd want to spend a penny the moment they were out on the moor.

Then they got the hunters out, and mounted, with Sam giving Linda a leg-up, as he told her in a very quiet voice to be careful.

'Don't you worry, Sam,' said Evie cheerfully and much more loudly. 'I'll make sure she's back before lunchtime safe and sound.' She thought Sam looked ridiculously apprehensive, and so she smiled to reassure him.

The first few months of Linda's marriage, from the outside, looked to be going well, Evie thought, noticing the tenderness with which Sam then gave Linda's knee a gentle squeeze.

Evie led the horse for Sukie, which was the mount on which she'd won her race at the point-to-point; the stirrups were run up the leathers which had then been doubled back to stop the irons slipping down, and the horse's reins were over its head so that Evie could hold them, and they jogged over to collect Sukie just as dawn was breaking.

When Sukie came to the door at their knock, Evie laughed to see that she was wearing a dress as she thought the 'surprise' outing would be a jaunt to Plymouth.

'Don't be a daft maid,' said Linda, 'we're saving

up that treat for next Saturday, when it'll be the first of Pattie's talks for the Spitfire fund. This is to make you looked red of cheek and full of the joys of the country and all ready for Wesley, so go and slip into your breeches. And handsome is as handsome does, just you remember, Sukie.'

Grumbling she wouldn't have had her bath first thing if she'd known horses were involved as they were sweaty, dirty things, lovely as they were, Sukie sloped off to put on her jodhpurs and a warm tweed hacking jacket in an attractive shade of lovat.

They had a lovely ride. The horses were fresh but not silly, and although there had been a hint of frost the ground wasn't frozen hard below it, and so they were able to have a canter or three. It wasn't too long before the sun had popped out from behind some clouds and even in its mid-winter cloaking Dartmoor looked very impressive, with its dark tors thrown into ominous relief against the pale hues of the wintry sky and the shrinking white clouds dotted about. It was certainly the sort of morning to blow a few cobwebs away.

Sukie was right, though. They all got flecks of mud on their clothes and faces, thrown up by the horses' hooves on the sometimes splashy ground.

They turned to head for home, and then Linda said she had some news.

Evie looked at her, as did Sukie, and then at the sight of Linda's coy but thrilled expression, they started to laugh as they guessed immediately what Linda's news was.

She was going to have a baby.

'Oh my goodness,' said Evie. 'Congratulations, Linda lovey. But I feel terrible as I would never have suggested a ride if I had known.'

'Yes, I almost said something,' said Linda, 'but then I didn't. I'm not sure why, other than I'm not quite ready for my life to be totally different and turned upside down. I'm all too aware that very soon I'll have to give up work as I promised Sam I would, as he feels the risk of me getting kicked while shoeing is just too much, although I think even if I did get kicked I'd be unlikely to lose the baby as I am sure we are designed for them to hold fast inside, no matter what. And I've only just improved my mobile smithy, so I'll have to find a home for that, and someone to take over my customers for me. Anyway, today I've enjoyed every moment of this morning, which is great as it will probably be my last ride for quite a while.'

Sukie and Evie caught each other's eye. Horse riding could never be totally safe, and occasional falls were unavoidable for most riders. When the friends had been about twelve there had been a classmate whose pony had come down on top of her when it put a front foot down into a rabbit hole and the pair had tumbled off-kilter to the ground, and sadly the little girl had died from her injuries even though the accident had happened when horse and rider were only walking along on a generally even track; but Evie was determined not to remind anyone of this tragedy.

Evie was by nature a careful and often cautious person, and so she would never have tempted fate by suggesting Linda should accompany them on their ride if they had known Linda was pregnant.

164

She knew some women liked to keep horse riding when they were expecting but personally she thought the risk of something going wrong outweighed the pleasure. And now she understood why Sam had looked concerned at the prospect of their ride.

'Well, let's just walk slowly home while you can both tell me how best to beautify myself so that Wesley is completely bowled over,' Sukie chipped in, as an obvious attempt to keep the morning as pleasantly light-hearted as it had begun.

They walked on abreast with one another, chatting happily, with Sukie describing how much she was looking forward to seeing Wesley (a huge amount, it turned out), and Linda talking further about her regret about stopping work and wondering if she might be able to return to being a farrier after the baby was born. Linda added that she thoroughly loved getting a piece of random metal and turning it into something really useful or keeping workhorses shod so that they could be used to the full in food production, despite Sam always saying that if she wasn't farriering then she could be a wonderful boon to helping him around the farm on all the endless jobs that always needed doing.

The conversation moved to things to do with the intricacies of pregnancy, morning sickness and unusual cravings, and Evie and Sukie listened with wry amusement when Linda confessed to their squeals of disgust that she had now a piece of old stirrup leather that she was chewing away happily on every evening, while Sam's mother had told Linda that when she fell with Sam she had loved to lick a piece of coal now and again.

Evie and Sukie were fascinated by all Linda had to say on the matter as she was the first pregnant woman they felt close enough to that they could ask a host of intimate and revealing questions.

They were just skirting the far portion of the airstrip away from its Nissen huts, having been out for a couple of hours, with just the one stop so that that they could take turns to each have a quick piddle behind a large gorse bush, and they were right in the most inconvenient place when they noticed a small aeroplane taxiing near the far end of the runway, and then the pilot position the aeroplane as if he were about to turn to face them, presumably with the intention of hurtling down the length of the green in their direction as he prepared for take-off.

This wasn't good by any stretch of the imagination, thought Evie as she looked quickly around to check the terrain for the horses, who were likely to spook at the aeroplane. She then reminded herself that at least the horses weren't hunting fit and also that they would have had the edge of their freshness taken off, with the result they would be less skittish now than they would have been an hour or two earlier.

Still, there was no escaping the fact that the three riders were very exposed and in about the worst possible place they could be. They were at the lower end of the edge of the ground that had been levelled for the runway, having just come up quite a hilly track, with a stone wall to one side that prevented them simply trotting away with their backs to the airstrip.

The aeroplane's engine grew louder as the pilot turned the craft to face down the runway and then started to build up the revs of the engine needed to lift it into the air.

Evie continued to look anxiously about, and she could see that Sukie was doing the same. Yes, it was likely unavoidable that the horses would spook to some extent as they would never have seen anything like this at close quarters, and being herd animals, they would want to run together as far away as they could if left to their own devices, as the aeroplane would look to the horses like a beast hunting them for prey. If one of them went off like a cannon, the others would do their best to do likewise too.

Quickly Evie weighed up their options and concluded the safest was for them all to keep on walking briskly on tight reins in the direction they were facing as it was slightly uphill, even though this was a course that kept them closer to the aeroplane; but it had the advantage that they would have the benefit of a highish wall on one side to help prevent the horses from scattering that way if they did panic. Evie didn't think they should urge the horses into a trot as she wasn't sure Linda would be able then to hold her horse if it spooked. And to turn round wasn't a good option as to do so would suggest to the horses they should race down the hill and out on to the open moor, while the combination of going helter-skelter downhill and then out on to even rougher terrain would make it much more difficult for the riders to keep their seats. If the horses took off up the hill in the direction they were currently heading, at least that would make it easier for the riders to stay on board.

Sukie was obviously thinking the same thing, as she suggested that everybody shorten their reins and put their whips on the opposite side to where the aeroplane was going to come from as the horses would that way be less likely to swing towards the whip side; the riders should also incline the horses' heads very slightly towards the plane.

'Use lots of leg too, especially on the side nearest the wall, and try and stop any turning around,' Sukie commanded. She was by far the most experienced rider of the three, and so Evie was very happy to follow Sukie's instructions, and promptly she turned her horse into something like the shape of a banana, with both its nose and its quarters curved away from the wall.

Sukie added, 'I'll go first, and you tuck in behind me, Linda, and then Evie can bring up the rear.'

'Should I get off?' said Linda, her voice unable to disguise her apprehension.

'No, don't do that. I think you'll be safer on top,' said Sukie, who could see that the wall would be a struggle for Linda to climb over and so there could be either a risk of being mashed against the rocks from which it was constructed, or getting knocked over if Linda went to step onto the airstrip on foot if her riderless horse started to whirl around in fear. 'Remember what happened to you with Hector, when he took fright, and so you know how easy it is to get into a pickle when on the ground anywhere near to a terrified horse,' Sukie added.

Evie didn't think this was necessarily the wisest thing for Sukie to say to Linda.

This was because at the start of the previous summer Linda and a farmer had been leading two massive workhorses in from the fields for shoeing in the farmyard when they had been strafed by a lone German bomber who had caught them while they were still out and exposed in open country. The mare, Mabel, had taken a bullet to the head, her body slumping instantaneously stone dead to the ground with a reverberating crash, causing Hector, the gelding, to circle around wildly in distress and confusion, accidentally catching Linda on the chest with one of his enormous metal-clad hooves. Linda had had to spend several weeks in hospital recovering from a collapsed and punctured lung. Hector had redeemed himself a couple of months later by taking pride of place at Linda and Sam's wedding, with a lovely picture of him and Linda and Sam printed in the *Western Morning News* to prove it, but Evie knew it had been nonetheless a horrible experience for Linda and that she still mourned the loss of gentle giant Mabel, who'd been one of her favourites.

Linda looked incredibly tense, although she did as Sukie said and remained on board, despite not having taken such a tight hold of her mount as Sukie and Evie had done theirs.

Unfortunately, Evie thought, horses were such sensitive creatures that they could always tell when their rider was worried, with the result that this could be enough sometimes to cause a horse to respond with unpredictable behaviour simply through the fear of the unknown threat that was clearly concerning their rider. Linda's mare had rolling eyes, flickering ears and a clamped-down tail, and so had picked up on her rider's apprehension.

'Keep your reins short, but stroke her neck too with a finger to tell her to trust you,' Evie gently suggested to Linda in an attempt to bolster her confidence.

Ironically, Evie felt anything but plucky herself – she thought she knew what to do theoretically in the event of her mount panicking, but until it was actually put to the test she couldn't be sure. Still, although ordinarily Evie didn't approve of fibbing, she thought this was one time where a falsely cheery voice was the right thing to have, and so she added, 'And I'll keep very close to you – in fact, both Sukie and I will stay near the pair of you – to give her, and you, extra courage. Then she won't want to leave our two and strike out on her own.'

After what seemed to be an inordinate amount of engine-revving while stationary, the plane was heading towards them now and Sukie's horse began to prance and give half-rears in fright. But to the relief of everyone Linda and Evie's mounts remained calm, and aided by Sukie's firm but gentle handling as she leant forward for each rear and momentarily loosened the reins, her mount settled a little when he saw that the other horses didn't appear to be as upset as he was.

Still, the aeroplane was dangerously close to the end of the runway, and the riders, before it lugged itself into the air, and Evie could clearly see the concerned look on the pilot's face as he swept upwards only feet away from them. It was probable that the rickety control tower way over to the other side of the airstrip hadn't noticed them and had cleared the pilot for take-off, and that he had been concentrating too much on his control panel, with the consequence that he might have been well down the runway before he had seen them and at the point where it would have been too late to safely abort, especially bearing in mind there was the stone wall at the edge of the moorland to the fore of him.

The noise of the plane's engines throbbed through the air, but it wasn't loud enough for Evie to be unable to hear Linda's horse snort loudly, her nostrils opened wide. She swung her head sharply upwards to look at the plane. And then she dropped her nose almost to the ground and slid her front legs apart, exactly as if she was ducking out of the way. Linda was too frightened to slacken the reins slightly and so she was pulled forward and out of position by her shorter than normal reins until she was leaning towards the ground too.

It would have been comical if not potentially as dangerous as it was, as Linda was perched now in a most precarious position, with her body weight far too far forward and her bottom up in the air. Sukie and Evie had each adopted a safety seat, sitting quite far back in their saddles with the legs braced a little forward and the reins even shorter, and so were much less likely to be bolted with or to fall off, and Evie noticed that both she and Sukie had put their own reins into their whip hands to leave an arm free to grab at the bridle of Linda's horse if she suddenly went to shoot off, as sitting the way she was, Linda wouldn't be able to do much about that sort of behaviour.

But then the aeroplane, after seeming to judder and almost stop in its trajectory, had passed away over their heads and on upwards into the sky, and the moment of crisis was over.

Sukie and Evie's horses had proved stabilising, but the look on their riders' faces said it all – Linda would almost certainly have taken a crashing fall if her horse had chosen not to stay with the herd, as Linda had got into a vulnerable position, and that could have spelled disaster for her pregnancy.

Fortunately Linda's mare had proved to be a sensible beast, although also an opportunistic one as it turned out, as now that her nose was so close to the turf she was happily taking the opportunity for a cheeky mouthful even though the patchy winter sod was only providing slim pickings as the herds of wild Dartmoor ponies had already hoovered up most of the good stuff.

With a sigh and a wriggle Linda repositioned herself in the saddle, and pulled up the head of her greedy horse. The three of them rode up the track, all their hearts hammering wildly.

'Well, seeing Wesley is going to be quite the comedown after that surge of excitement,' was Sukie's only comment.

Linda was too rattled to speak.

And Evie thought that after what had gone on with Fiona, and what potentially might have happened if Linda had been thrown, and the resulting realisation that her own shaky knowledge on what she should do in the event of someone needing medical assistance in an emergency was more or less nil, as regards the series of Spitfire fundraising talks it might be a good idea if the one that was going to cover practical first aid happened sooner rather than later.

That afternoon, after a wash and brush-up that left the water in her large china abluting bowl in her bedroom very murky once she had cleaned every scrap of dirt off her muddy face, Evie got to meet the new PGs at Pemberley, who had all moved in and had completed their unpacking while Evie was out on the moors with the horses.

Mrs Worth decided to throw a little tea party of welcome so that everyone could be introduced to one another, and Mr Worth, Evie, Annabel and Mr Rogers had had their orders to make sure they were all present and correct in order to greet the newcomers. There were toasted teacakes, fish paste sandwiches and lots of tea. The best tea set was proudly on display, as were the heavily starched second-best linen napkins (they were the ones with the handmade lace worked around the edge).

Evie was relieved to discover that Miss Davis seemed very pleasant, the sort of woman who would be nice to have as a fellow PG. Miss Davis asked everyone to call her Lynn, please, as she didn't want to stand on ceremony as she had quite enough of that sort of thing at work. Evie mentioned to Lynn that Sukie was a very dear friend, and she was pleased to receive a big smile back – it looked like Lynn was a fan of Sukie too, and so Evie was sure that she and this new PG would get on.

Evie already knew Christopher Rolfe by sight, and although he'd always seemed pleasant enough and had looks that were quite easy on the eye, and despite Evie staring hard at him to see if she thought he might be the one or, as Timmy would undoubtedly say, the Pev to make her heart beat a little faster as a distraction to stop her thinking about Peter, Evie decided with a small surge of disappointment that sadly this was unlikely to be the case. He looked a trifle dull and he didn't appear to have much in the way of conversation after he'd told everybody to call him Chris, although this was possibly because he had appeared to be rather startled at the intensity of Evie's searching gaze.

Jane Cornish was the real surprise of the tea party as she was pretty and talkative, yet she only looked to be about fifteen years old. Evie was shocked when they came to speak as it wasn't long before Jane admitted to being positively ancient, at twenty-seven, and so was actually quite a bit older than Evie. She worked for one of the large art galleries in London as a picture restorer, and so had been relocated to the West Country in order to remain close to where some of the priceless artworks were being kept for the duration as the destruction of the blitz had led to galleries moving their treasures to outside of the cities. Jane had moved with a contingent of artworks to the West Country in order that she could keep an eye on things to make sure that the paintings weren't in danger of getting damaged by things like rising water or leaky roofs. Evie knew better than to ask where all the works of art had been sent to, but she guessed it couldn't be too far away. Jane had a car and a petrol allowance, and when Evie said how jealous she was of Jane's independence, the new PG instantly offered to let Evie have a go one day at driving.

Then the tea party took on an even jollier air with the arrival of four unexpected guests.

Two were Sukie and Wesley. Wesley was going to stay after all at Pemberley for the next two nights, and Sukie nodded at Evie to let her know that Evie's prudent words had struck a chord, and so this was the result.

Wesley beamed at everyone, and gave Evie a hug, although this was slightly awkward as Evie had gone to shake his hand. To make sure that he didn't notice her resulting pink cheeks Evie turned to get him a cup of tea, and she noticed that the three new PGs were taken aback by the sight of Wesley. They clearly weren't used to seeing a black person being treated as an honoured guest in the drawing room of a rather well to do house, and Evie remembered then how extremely surprised Pattie and she herself had been just a few weeks earlier when Sukie's booking of The Swingtimes for the New Year's Eve dance had yielded a dance band in which every single member was black. It had seemed very daring, and was terribly thrilling at the time, Evie recalled.

The potentially sticky moment that teatime was papered over reasonably quickly by Jane Cornish walking up to Wesley with a smile and an outstretched hand of welcome. Evie thought that Jane's previous life in London had presumably made her slightly less shockable than Lynn Davis or Chris Rolfe, who each kept shooting sly glances between Wesley's short black hair and Sukie's cascade of golden waves.

Then Lynn, who was Sukie's boss, collected herself first, and nodded hello to Wesley and asked Sukie in an unnaturally bright voice what they had planned for Wesley's visit.

Sukie looked slightly alarmed at this juncture, almost as if she wasn't sure what the best thing might be for her to say. Evie thought that Sukie had better wise up and think about this sort of social interaction, and quickly too, because if Sukie and Wesley were going to go on seeing each other, then lots of people would be asking questions, many of them probably seeming quite impertinent, and Sukie would need to have an array of answers ready and waiting so that there could be no hint of the apologetic concerning her and Wesley choosing to spend time together.

Mrs Worth came into her own, Evie was surprised to see, as hearing Wesley's distinctive lilting voice, she hurried into the drawing room bearing a refreshed pot of tea, saying how delighted she was to see Wesley again. 'I think I've only just about got my breath back after your wonderful playing on New Year's Eve,' she told him. 'I'm very much hoping that once again you and your wonderful friends in The Swingtimes will be showing us with your special panache how a really excellent dance band goes about things. Mr Worth and I have said several times since New Year that it was one of the best nights of dancing we have ever enjoyed.'

Thus their landlady made it clear, without

actually having to say a word to such effect, that Wesley was already a familiar acquaintance, and that the new PGs, while not necessarily having to like him (as who could ever demand that of anyone?), were expected nonetheless to accept he was a welcome guest at Pemberley and accordingly they must treat him with respect, however unusual and exotic he might seem on first impression. Evie thought it wasn't that the new PGs necessarily *wouldn't* treat him well if left to their own devices, but more that the fact he and Sukie being so blatantly there as an item was the potentially challenging social situation that could put some people on their back foot and make them unsure of how they should act in response.

Fortunately Wesley was used to dealing with white folks, and sunnily he acted as if the least interesting thing about him was the colour of his ebony skin, a tactic that made it increasingly difficult not to start agreeing with that supposition.

While everyone else remained transfixed on Wesley, who looked sneakily to be enjoying the attention, especially now the conversation had turned to the fact that he and his band were about to go to London to make their first recording, Sukie whispered to Evie that she had only phoned Mrs Worth about him staying an hour ago.

When they had got to The Grange, where Wesley had been going to bunk up for the weekend, it had turned out that some sort of night-time manoeuvres were planned for the next few days and these manoeuvres would require all of the able-bodied servicemen connected to the airfield who slept in the attic rooms to be working

177

during the night. And so she and Wesley had agreed that for the sake of reputation, Pemberley was going to be a much more sensible option for where Wesley should sleep as the resident PGs could be claimed to be chaperones if any villagers cared to spread unkind gossip about the pairing of Wesley and Sukie.

The other two unexpected guests at the tea party arrived soon afterwards: Tricia and a warmly wrapped-up Hettie. Tricia was now walking about Lymbridge most days as she pushed Hettie in the bulky perambulator for a daily airing, and so she had decided to call in on the off chance of seeing Evie. Tricia made everyone laugh when she said that hoicking the pram up the gravel drive to Pemberley was harder than it looked and so roll on the time that Hettie would be big enough to toddle up it under her own steam, although Mr Rogers rather cheekily pointed out at that juncture that it was a wonderful way of Tricia regaining her figure, or at least it would be if she had needed to, which of course she didn't, at which Tricia shot him a coquettish smile and batted her eyelashes, but didn't say anything. Mr Rogers looked well pleased at this, and Evie noticed he was smiling still as he held a match up to his unlit cigarette.

Evie didn't think either Mr Rogers or Tricia were flirting as such, but she noticed the ease of their brief interaction and she told herself that this was how people *practised* at being slightly flirty, and that Evie herself would do well to make more of this sort of casual opportunity to hone her own skills, which she knew were sadly lacking.

Sukie gave Evie a little nudge and obviously

batted her lengthy eyelashes, and Evie smiled in silent acknowledgement that all right, yes, that was how it was done and, yes, she had picked up a tip or two.

A space was made for Tricia close to the fire, and then Hettie was happy to be passed from lap to lap. She looked particularly adorable and seemed to have inherited Timmy's affable nature, thought Evie, and then she noticed that Hettie looked especially lovely as she had a delicately scalloped woollen bonnet on her head, with a sweet satin bow under her chin, holding it in place.

Evie had knitted the bonnet for Hettie, using the thinnest wool and the narrowest of knitting needles that she could find, but she didn't say anything, although she and Tricia shared a complicit smile as Evie chucked Hettie under her now rather plump chin while Tricia flicked her eyes significantly towards the bonnet and then towards Evie. Later, Annabel said she thought the cap looked like Evie's handiwork, and Evie had to agree that yes, it was, and didn't Hettie look a picture?

'Timmy wus talkin' abut yer t'day, an' 'e tells me you need a man. 'E says that useless streak of wind Peter is givin' you the run-round,' Tricia said when it was just she and Hettie and Evie left in the drawing room. 'Not sure why yu'd be keen to 'itch yornself jus' yet meself, when you can 'ave a fine time on yer lonesome, as ye're a maid that's earnin', an' you 'ave a nice place 'ere ter live that most wud gi' their eye-teeth fer. But still, Timmy says I mus' keep my eyes open fer you, as yer might not be up to it yornself.'

Evie stopped grinning down at Hettie, who was

now able to smile back at her. It looked now as if knowledge of her and Peter having had some sort of dalliance was moving from family and close friends into the arena of public gossip. Evie had positioned the baby flat on her back lying on her lap along the length of her legs, with her head at Evie's knees, and her little booteed feet held up in the air close to Evie's waist as she moved them up and down to make Hettie grin.

Hettie looked at Evie in confusion as Evie let go of her feet – it had been such a good game; how could Evie bear to stop it so soon? her little face seemed to be intimating.

As Evie considered the matter further, she turned towards Tricia with a grave look. 'Well, I'm not sure I'd put it quite like that. But I don't like to think that I may never marry,' she said with an air of resignation.

'Meself, I never paid much 'eed to marriage but I were rightly curious 'bout sex, an' I suppose this is wot it comes down to,' Tricia said as she gave a look of acknowledgement towards Hettie on Evie's lap, and then turned to stare into the embers of the log fire, her unexpected openness causing Evie to feel quite hot all of a sudden, although this was nothing to do with sitting a bit too close to the fireplace.

Other than that one conversation a few weeks previously when Julia had told her a little of what intercourse was like, Evie had never dared to talk to family or friends about the sexual act itself. Not even with Linda or Sukie, although now Evie wondered if this hadn't been taking politeness too far, and was a bit silly bearing in mind how many questions she and Sukie had been grilling Linda with over her pregnancy, which was of course the consequence of the coyly unacknowledged sexual congress.

There had been an incident a month or so back when Susan had discovered a copy of *The Naturist* in James's bedroom, hidden under his mattress, and Evie had heard Robert say to Susan that it was to be expected of a fifteen-year-old-lad, and Susan agreeing with her husband, but adding that she didn't want Frank and Joseph to be up to *that* sort of thing just yet. Evie had no idea what her parents were talking about, but she knew it must be something to do with sex as Robert and Susan were using the particular and slightly prudish tones they employed when talking to each other downstairs about matters that they considered should be confined to the bedroom. Later that same afternoon Evie had tried to probe James about the magazine, but he had gone beetroot red before literally running from the room in his flurried effort to avoid Evie's curious scrutiny.

A day or so after that in the hall of Bluebells Evie had come across the offending magazine stuffed far down in the kitchen's coal scuttle along with several copies of the *Western Morning News*, presumably all waiting to be ripped into spills that would be used to help light the fire or the range. Evie had leafed through *The Naturist* and was rather taken aback to see it contained photographs of naked women, taken as they carried out various ordinary-looking outside activities like walking or playing tennis. Evie thought there probably weren't many practising naturists on Dartmoor in the middle of winter as it looked a draughty way of going about things. There were a few pictures of naked men too in the magazine, but much fewer in number than the naked women. Annoyingly, both men and women seemed to have strategically placed bits of foliage between them and the lens of the photographer's camera in order to make sure that everybody's modesty was preserved.

Meanwhile Tricia ploughed on, 'Then I fell wi' 'Ettie, after no more than thirty seconds agin the wall behin' t' village 'all wi' Timmy, an' I think now that what's the fuss about? An' I'd better go on thinkin' that as I doubt I'll be doin' it again, seein' Timmy's condition.'

'Yes, I too wonder quite often, what's all the fuss about?' said Evie thoughtfully, caught up in her own thoughts as she stared across at the fire's orange and black embers.

The Naturist hadn't given away many clues as far as Evie was concerned, other than that women and men who liked to wander around without their clothes on tended to appear rather old and more often than not to be alarmingly flabby around their midriffs. Evie pressed her lips together in a mixture of bafflement and bemusement.

Then the two women looked anew towards each other, holding each other's gaze for a bit, before both bursting into laughter, with Hettie smiling her biggest smile yet at the sound of it and giving a series of strenuous kicks upwards in rhythm with the hoots erupting from Evie and her mother.

Chapter Ten

Later that evening Evie found herself the only one home at Pemberley. All the other PGs, and Mr and Mrs Worth too, had headed down to The Haywain for an early-evening tipple, with Sukie announcing that after she and Wesley had had one drink with everyone they were going to leave the party in order to go out dancing in Plymouth.

Evie had forced herself to go down to The Haywain with the group too, but after about fifteen minutes her ridiculously early start, hot on the heels of a busy teaching week, proved a real dampener on her spirits, and so she pleaded extreme tiredness and had slowly plodded on her own back to Pemberley.

Once she had taken off her coat, hat, scarf and gloves, she collected her latest book and made herself comfy in the high-backed armchair near the kitchen range as this was the warmest spot in the house. Within a few minutes Keith and the kittens were snuggling in too, all five of them curled up together in the chair, and almost immediately Evie found the ticking of the clock on the mantelpiece and the sound of the occasional shifting of the tamped-down fuel burning in the range to have a distinctly soporific effect, with the result that she simply couldn't keep her eyes open. The book remained as resolutely closed as when Evie had picked it up in her bedroom.

Keith and the kittens scattered when the telephone in the hall unexpectedly jangled into life twenty minutes later, the prick of their sharp claws on Evie's thighs as they sought purchase to jump to the floor forcing her awake with a real start. She grabbed a blanket folded over the back of the chair as the hall was polar in temperature and flung it over her shoulders as she went to answer the ring.

'Lymbridge 316,' said Evie in her best telephone voice, although it was one she hoped didn't make her sound silly or fraudulent, or as if she had been caught napping only seconds before. She only used a telephone two or three times a year and so she never got to the point where she felt natural talking into the handset.

'Ah,' said the caller, and then there was a pause.

'Good evening,' said Evie cautiously. She hadn't been able to tell if the caller was male or female. 'How may I help you?'

'Is that you, Evie?'

Evie's heart lurched uncomfortably, and she had a dipping sensation deep within her ribcage. It sounded very much like Peter. 'Yes, it is,' she replied, with her voice pitched unintentionally a notch or two higher all of a sudden.

'It's Peter. If I were to drive to Pemberley now, might you be prepared to see me, just for a little while?' he said without preamble, Evie noticing that his stutter seemed to be plaguing him a little more than usual. There had been a time when she had thought it virtually gone, but recently it seemed to have been making a resurgence.

Evie wasn't sure what to say to Peter. They had

to see each other at some point, she knew, but she wasn't sure she felt in quite the right frame of mind to cope just at the minute if, as would probably happen, the conversation turned awkward. She was trying so hard to keep her life moving forward and to think positively, and the horse ride that morning had definitely helped her throw a sense of perspective onto what had been going on, and somehow at the moment interactions with Peter always seemed to conspire to make her feel worse. And anyway, why did Peter want to speak with her? It wasn't as if things weren't pretty awkward between them already, and shouldn't he be thinking anyway of conserving his fuel and not making an unneeded car journey?

However, to make a telephone call like this was most unlike Peter, while the rapid pulse of Evie's blood coursing round her body suggested to her that even though she had found him wanting in so many ways, she still had what felt like an almost animal reaction to the mere sound of him speaking that was incredibly hard not to respond to.

Somewhat against her better judgement, Evie heard herself saying therefore that she would be waiting for him in fifteen minutes at the gates to Pemberley, and they could talk in his car, to which he agreed with alacrity. She had suggested the vehicle as a meeting place because she didn't want to have to answer any awkward questions or, at best, to put up with the curious glances of her fellow PGs, if they returned from The Haywain to find Peter sitting somewhere within Pemberley alongside Evie, although she knew the Worths wouldn't mind him as a visitor as of course he had been himself a PG at Pemberley the previous year.

Evie raced up to the first-floor bathroom and inspected herself in the mirror. She sighed, as she was wearing only very run-of-the-mill clothes that paid virtually no heed to current fashions. And when she peered closely at her face in the mirror it was to see a visage that was distinctly heavy-eyed, with puffy lids from her nap, and thus she didn't appear (in her view, at least) to be in any way enticing, although quite why this should matter when she kept insisting to herself there was no chance for her and Peter was something of a moot point.

Evie pinched her cheeks quite hard in an attempt to inject a bit of colour into them, and then she tipped her head upside down to fluff up her hair a little as she thought it looked dowdy, being too flat after wearing her headscarf tightly knotted under her chin when riding earlier. Wishing she had a little lipstick to hand – a forlorn hope as she had loaned Pattie both of her lipsticks the previous afternoon for a night out with John, who helped out Barkeep Joss behind the bar at The Haywain, and they hadn't made their way back over to Pemberley yet – Evie bit her lips both top and bottom as she thought that might make them redder. She supposed she would have to do, although she did regret her laziness in not making any attempt to sluice through her hair after she had changed out of her jodhpurs. She tipped her head downwards to fluff it up a second time, and wished she had a little perfume.

After waiting for a very tedious ten minutes she put on her coat, having given it another hearty shake as she was convinced it remained dusty after its sojourn on the floor of the village hall along with Fiona, but she decided not to wear hat, scarf or gloves as she thought they might make it seem as if she had prepared herself for a long meeting with Peter. Instead she wanted to give him the impression that when he telephoned it was to interrupt her from doing Something Very Important, and so she had made the time to nip out momentarily to have a word with him, but it was nothing more to Evie than a scant moment or two of brief punctuation during her hectic evening.

As she walked hastily down the drive, with her heart pounding erratically, accompanied by Keith trotting along at her side, although not the kittens as they had resumed their snooze only now in their wooden crate by the kitchen range, Evie told herself to get a grip – one of Peter's strengths was that he was an acutely observant chap, and this meant she knew he would see right through any false posturing on her part.

Already his car was by the gate with its engine running, and Evie ran around the bonnet and slid onto the passenger seat with a curt hello. Peter grunted as he slipped the car into gear and drove slowly a couple of hundred yards down the road in the direction of the deep moorland away from the village. Then he pulled over and parked in a passing space, designed so that a car could back into it if another vehicle was coming in the opposite direction as the lane was too narrow for two cars to pass each other without some awkward positioning on the part of the drivers.

'Peter, I was very surprised to get your call,'

said Evie in an attempt to get the ball rolling when it looked like Peter was having difficulty in saying whatever he wanted to tell her.

'I realised that I would be seeing you this week at the meeting of the Spitfire fundraising committee, but that the meeting wouldn't be an appropriate place for me to say to you what I need to.' Peter started well enough, Evie supposed, but then all too soon he ground once again to a halt. What a frustrating man he was.

'Right,' said Evie surprisingly calmly. 'What is it that you want to say to me?'

'Well, firstly that I am sorry about the other evening, when Fiona wasn't on the best form.'

'That's to put it mildly! She really came gunning for me,' cried Evie.

And then she remembered the silvery marks on Fiona's wrists, and immediately she felt more conciliatory. 'Well, it's all in the past now, and I do hope your Fiona is feeling much more like her usual self. She sent me a very decent card by way of apology, incidentally, although with no sender's address and so I've not been able to write back to her and say that I hope she is feeling better now, which sincerely I do, and so you may care to pass on my acknowledgements to her. She also contacted my parents, who were of course very appreciative as well.'

Evie hadn't been able to resist slipping in the word 'your' when talking about Fiona; she wanted Peter to be in no doubt that Evie still aligned the both of them together. It was a dart – a small one, but a dart all the same – that she thought had very probably found its mark.

Peter caught his breath in something that sounded rather like a gulp, and then he told Evie that he knew it must have been a testing experience for her, and that he and Fiona appreciated her prompt actions, and then her discretion afterwards.

At this Evie felt a twinge of shame, and tried not to dwell on how she had experienced a feeling that was too close for comfort to glee when she had gone over the incident at indecent length with Sukie and Linda on their night out at the public house in Bramstone.

Evie decided it might be wise to steer the conversation to arguably less contentious matters. She wanted too to be a bit bolder with Peter than ordinarily she was. 'Actually, Peter, it's been a horrible few months all told, and so really what happened with Fiona was just a little bit more of the same. You probably should know that Fiona looked desperately unhappy, although I don't get the sense she is naturally a sunny person, and although in comparison I felt happier than she on the night she came to see me, the reality is that I'm feeling low and pretty fed up too.'

Evie didn't dare look towards Peter, although she was acutely aware of the sound of him breathing as he sat in the driver's seat beside her, and the fact that he was nervously playing with the steering wheel.

She grasped the bull by the horns, and continued in a quiet but resigned voice, 'I just wish you had hung around at Pemberley when I went to see Timmy at Stoke Mandeville last summer, as then it would all have been so much simpler.

But I lied by omission and I handled things badly with you, while you were too jumpy for your own good and leapt ship without even trying to discover what I felt about you or whether I really was about to marry; and then you picked up with indecent haste with Fiona simply to make yourself feel better. And now Fiona is making it clear how upset she is, while I can't see that either you or I are dancing around with joy either.'

'That's about the sum of it, Evie,' agreed Peter. 'It's a mess, but I must point out I didn't start seeing Fiona merely to make myself feel happy. And I have said as gently to Fiona as I could think how to that it's best if she gets used to the idea that she and I are not going to continue with our relationship, although I'm not sure if it's sunk in with her yet. And I suspect depressingly that there is no possibility that she won't make life difficult for us in the future, even though I have been very clear to her that there is nothing going on between you and me.' Peter sounded doleful.

'I said much the same thing to her as well,' said Evie, 'I mean, about us not being attached, although I'm not sure if she heard me. Actually, I am not sure why I am sitting here with you, Peter, seeing as you and I keeping telling each other we are not involved with each other.'

Evie was a little frustrated that she had started to become vague again with Peter, but she decided not to try and clarify things as she thought that the likelihood was that she would just be filling a silence with empty wittering. She didn't really know what she wanted to say, or actually what it was she wanted. She knew she was thinking more about what she was saying (or not), though, rather than anything Peter might say back to her. And she was starting to regret that she hadn't worn her scarf and gloves as the temperature in the car was plummeting, and her fingers were cold.

Peter seemed to intuit the last part of what she was thinking about as, turning slightly towards Evie, he took hold of both of her hands in his.

It was pitch black outside and Evie couldn't see Peter's face properly as there were just a few stars visible and only fleeting snatches of a slim moon, and she was aware that neither could he see hers.

Somehow it was better that they couldn't look at each other's faces. Peter's hands were warm and they felt very strong as they enveloped Evie's.

Despite the fact that their hands being linked made something of a mockery of all that they had just said to each other, Evie found it comforting to have her hands clasped thus, there was no doubt. And somehow Peter's gentle touch seemed to be more eloquent that anything he could bring himself to speak.

But when her thoughts turned to how pleasant it might be if she and Peter were to wriggle a little closer together so that he could slip his arm around her, Evie had to remind herself abruptly that if anything happened between them before Peter were wholly free of Fiona – and that was certainly not the case at the moment, and didn't look likely to be for the foreseeable future, and very probably not for all time – or before Evie herself felt a whole lot less skittish about Peter, it could only be a disaster.

And so with a determined but downhearted squaring of her shoulders Evie shuffled her bottom a little further away from Peter as she removed her hands from his and laid them in her lap, and suggested that it was time for Peter to turn the car around and drop her back at the gates of Pemberley.

She heard him hold his breath for a beat or two, and Evie realised she was keeping hers in too.

Keith had stayed in her position of watch-keeper at the bottom of the driveway, and Evie saw the cat's eyes turn mother of pearl in the reduced-angled lighting of Peter's dim headlights as his vehicle drew near.

Still without much of an idea as to why Peter had wanted to see her (in fact, she didn't really believe that he had any idea of why he had telephoned her, either), Evie got out of the car, and began to trudge up the drive with Keith beside her.

She supposed it didn't matter really precisely what it was that Peter had wanted with her as they seemed stuck together in a strange and dis-satisfying no-man's-land of emotions where they were unable to go forward, but weren't quite able to go backwards either. It was a hard feeling to define, being better than totally dejected at the thought of Peter's absence, but not a feeling that was giving her any proper sense of satisfaction or happiness either.

Evie halted and turned quickly to catch a last glimpse of Peter before he drove away. She could just about pick out the outline of his face in the velvety darkness, although she couldn't tell from the cast of his head if he looked pleased or disappointed in how their meeting had gone, or even quite if he were looking at her at all still.

Maybe he was relieved he didn't seem to have managed to say to her anything much at all; while in some ways most disappointing, it was arguably a pretty non-contentious outcome at the same time, and so perhaps there was some comfort to be drawn from that, although not very much it had to be said.

What a disheartening Saturday evening, Evie sighed as she and Keith turned as one to start up the drive once again. It was one that had answered no questions, but had just posed a couple more. What was she doing? She had no idea, if truth be told. Evie thought she wanted a bit more certainty and purpose.

And above all she wanted to quash her own hankering for Peter. Or at least quite a large bit of her did.

There was another part of her, though, that wanted them to be alone somewhere together, in the warm but with subdued lighting, and with no chance of interruption so that they could kiss and begin to explore each other's bodies.

This realisation led to an even deeper sigh, a sigh that seemed somehow to echo with a clench deep in Evie's groin.

Maybe Timmy's idea of Pev was something she needed to embrace wholeheartedly. Perhaps thoughts of Peter would only be cast asunder by the romantic attentions of a new person.

As she opened the front door Evie could hear people talking in the sitting room and so evidently the Worths and the PGs had come back from The

Haywain while she and Peter had been parked outside the village. Presumably they thought she had already retired to bed, but at the sound of the chatter her heart bumped a little lower.

Stealthily Evie crept past the living room door and on up to her bedroom – she couldn't face talking to anyone until she felt more sanguine, and that was likely to be Sunday morning, she suspected.

Sukie arrived at Pemberley in time for breakfast the next morning, and she and Wesley greeted each other ebulliently. Indeed they seemed tiresomely chirpy, Evie thought, and although Sukie had had a late night as well as a fearsomely early start the day before, it would be impossible to guess by her shining eyes, smooth, unblemished complexion and lustrous hair. Life wasn't very fair sometimes. To drive this home to Evie, it seemed as if Sukie and Wesley had had a wonderful time in Plymouth the previous evening.

Evie tried to be happy for her best friend, but she couldn't quite summon up her usual smile for long. She caught Sukie scrutinising her once or twice with quite a piercing look, but fortunately the lure of Wesley was too strong and Sukie was easily diverted back to laughing with him.

Lynn came and joined the breakfast party, and Evie found it much easier to chat to her about this and that than to try to fudge things with Sukie. Then Jane and Annabel came down too, and the conversation moved to what the Lymbridge sewing circle were up to (still mainly knitting jumpers and socks for the merchant seamen), and Pattie's

194

roster of talks (the first being confirmed as Mrs Smith's 'Tales from the home front of a moorland primary school'). This gave Evie the opportunity to describe the Spitfire fund in more detail to the new PGs, and then she added that there was a fundraising meeting at The Grange on Tuesday, to which the two new PGs at breakfast said they would come, and they thought Chris Rolfe would be persuaded to join them too.

Evie was just going to go and get ready for church when the telephone rang, and Mr Worth called her to the hall. Her heart flipped – what on earth was Peter going to say to her now?

But instead of Peter's familiar, slightly stuttery voice, it was Leonard Bassett on the end of the line, a much less welcome outcome, Evie realised, and she almost had to sit down as her legs had gone wobbly, such was the slither of her disappointment that it wasn't Peter after all who had summoned her into the cold hall.

Leonard was ringing to see if Evie could meet him over at Mrs Smith's later in the morning, so that the three of them could consider how the latest system at the primary school was working following the merging of the schools, and whether there were any improvements they needed to make, after which they could discuss how the new pupils were settling in. Evie felt she had no option but to agree to meet with him and Mrs Smith, although really she felt she'd rather be going back to bed to catch up on her beauty sleep, which had been woefully lacking during the restless and broken night following the unexpected few minutes she and Peter had snatched the evening before.

An hour or so later Evie left church the moment she could (and actually before Rev. Painter had made it out to the porch to shake everybody's hands and to say good morning – she had never dared to do that before), and she trotted briskly straight over to the other side of Lymbridge.

On the way she saw Mr Smith standing on the patch of scrub ground alongside a younger man decked out in a heavy tweed coat and a grey homburg hat. Even though it was Sunday they were engrossed in the large folded sheets of white paper they were holding between them, with their breath coming in little huffs of cloud in the cold air as they stood together with their backs to the road and their heads quite close together, looking downwards. Evie guessed these were the plans for Timmy and Tricia's new home, and so this man would very probably be either the architect or the project manager for when the house was ready to be built. She waved generally in Mr Smith's direction in case he could see her from the corner of his eye but she kept on walking without waiting for or expecting a response as the pair looked so engrossed in what they were doing.

As she drew close to Mrs Smith's cottage Evie could hear what sounded suspiciously like hammering coming from away in the distance across the picturesque valley that dropped behind the end of the orchard reaching back behind the dwelling, and when she got inside Mrs Smith told Evie to nip up onto the landing and to look out of the window in the general direction of The Grange.

Evie could barely believe her eyes. In the space of only a couple of days up had sprung a large cluster of Nissen huts erected in geometric-looking rows across some of the outlying fields that belonged to Switherns Farm. She went downstairs feeling quite agog at the number of servicemen the accommodation looked to be going to house, as well as marvelling at how quickly the rows of huts had been constructed.

Mrs Smith said that she had heard the rumour from the dinner queue that there were going to be hundreds, if not more than a thousand, of servicemen moved in within the next week or two. Apparently Lymbridge was a good location for training as the moors offered a variety of terrains, there was the new airstrip, plus the coast wasn't too far away, and so it could cater for a range of trial scenarios for those about to leave to fight, be it with army, navy or air force.

'Goodness, I never heard a thing about all these huts until just now. And the new PG, Mr Rolfe, is something to do with organising this, I believe, and he's not breathed a word. I know he only moved in yesterday, but still... I mean, Timmy said something about an influx of servicemen coming to the area, and I think Sukie might have mentioned it too, but I don't think I was really paying attention,' said Evie, who didn't knowingly like to be caught on the back foot when something was happening locally without her say-so.

'Anyway, I daresay Mother and Father will be sorry they haven't been able to raise the finance for their purchase of the village shop, as these new people in the area will be a veritable gold

197

mine. Barkeep Joss at The Haywain must be delighted, though – he'll be laughing all the way to the bank, I don't doubt.'

Mrs Smith agreed that The Haywain would definitely be a winner in this new scenario for Lymbridge, and she suggested then that Evie had better have a cup of tea to get over her surprise at all the Nissen huts that had snuck up when she wasn't looking.

Mrs Smith was, possibly, making a joke, thought Evie, but she gave only the most fleeting of smiles in response as it was, after all, a jest at her expense, and in any case she wasn't in the best mood for being teased, no matter how gently.

Tricia and Hettie came into the kitchen to say hello, and Mrs Smith managed to find some ginger cake in the cake tin and so they all sat around the kitchen table with tea and a small slice each as they waited for Leonard Bassett to arrive. There was an enticing aroma of a Sunday roast lunch with the occasional pop of sizzling fat as it cooked in the hot range, and there was a moment when Evie had to nip in swiftly to make sure she got Hettie to cuddle before Mrs Smith did.

Before too long there was the sound of the front door opening, and footsteps coming down the hall to the kitchen, and then Mr Smith and the man in the tweed coat walked in. Evie noticed the guest had a pronounced limp, and as she had noticed the distinctive gait which with some of Timmy's fellow patients moved if they could manage without a wheelchair, she wondered if he had a prosthetic leg.

'Ah, I'm glad to see you both here,' said Mr

Smith, and he went on to introduce Tricia and Evie to his companion, who was indeed the architect of Timmy and Tricia's new house.

He was called Mr Drake, and when Evie went to shake his hand she noticed he was much younger than she had assumed. Up close he didn't look more than thirty at the very most, although he could well have been a fair bit less than that. He had floppy brown hair that hung askew across his forehead (just a little like Peter's cowlick, although Peter's hair had much redder hues to this man's duller colours) and a pleasantly ready smile. And when Mr Drake and Mr Smith started to pore over the plans again, talking about the implications of wheelchair access and the need for no steps inside the dwelling and a ramp outside, Evie saw that the young architect had a rather nicely proportioned face and broad, manly shoulders.

As Evie went to pick up her teacup again, she couldn't fail to notice Tricia's significant look in Evie's direction that was indicating that she had noticed these attributes too. With an alarming lack of subtlety Tricia was now glancing repeatedly from Evie to Mr Drake, and back again, with the occasional miniscule nod towards the third finger of Mr Drake's left hand, which was without a wedding band.

Luckily both men had their heads bent over the plans and were deep in deliberations. They seemed oblivious as to what was occurring on the other side of the table.

Evie felt herself colour slightly, and then the blush on her cheeks deepen rapidly. Mrs Smith had caught wind of what was being telegraphed between Tricia and Evie, and she had given a conspiratorial nod and made sure that she too caught Evie's eye and then gave a pantomime look towards Mr Drake's ring finger.

Evie tried to give the smallest of head shakes to say that she wasn't at all interested in Mr Drake, and so would they both please stop it, and if they couldn't, would they remember that only a minority of married men wore wedding rings.

But with a characteristic look directed back at her from her headmistress that left Evie in no doubt she was being told not to be such a ninny, Mrs Smith crinkled her brow for a moment in concentration as to the best way forward for her to nudge Evie's marriage prospects along, just in case he was unmarried.

The result was that Mrs Smith poured two cups of tea, and then pushed one towards her husband and the other towards the architect, saying, 'I might be able to find you a tiny bit of sugar, if you wanted, Mr Drake.' He looked at Mrs Smith with an affable expression, and said no thank you, he was very happy to have his tea just as it came. And before he could immerse himself in the plans once again, Mrs Smith added in a casual-seeming voice, 'Did you have to come far, Mr Drake? Will you have to hurry home for Sunday lunch, or will your wife be able to keep it hot for you?'

'Oh, both my office and my digs are in Oldwell Abbott, so not far really. And sadly my landlady's Sunday lunches aren't worth writing home about as she isn't much of a cook and so I'm not too worried as to what state my food will be in when I get home as it will probably all taste pretty much the same, whatever time I get back. In fact, I'm going to see if The Haywain can rustle me up a sandwich, seeing as we want to fetch Timmy this afternoon to look at the plot,' he said in an easy but unassuming manner.

Mr Smith was now looking at his wife with a benignly curious expression as this exchange wasn't the sort of thing she normally would ask so blatantly of someone she didn't know well.

'In that case,' replied Mrs Smith with such a hint of firmness in her voice that Evie gave a small involuntary shudder as it was suddenly obvious to her what was about to happen. Sure enough, Mrs Smith steam-rollered on just as Evie had anticipated, by saying, 'we'd love to have you join us for lunch, Mr Drake. We're having roast chicken – one of our own that was killed only yesterday – and Tricia here' – Mrs Smith gestured vaguely in the broadly smiling Tricia's direction – 'always helps me peel an absolute torrent of potatoes, as we use the leftovers for bubble and squeak to-morrow. They are already roasting and we can easily stretch to feeding another. And we have stewed apples for pudding from our own apple trees in the orchard. In fact, Evie, you must join us too as time is running away with us and we've still got lots to talk about; Evie has come around, Mr Drake, so that we can talk over some business to do with Lymbridge Primary School, where we both teach.'

And before Evie could think, Golly gosh, but how this is awkward, she noticed Mr Smith give a complicit look towards his wife, having finally cottoned on to what was afoot.

There was a brief kerfuffle as at that moment Leonard Bassett arrived, and in almost the same breath and before he'd had time to even loosen his woolly scarf, Mrs Smith asked – or commanded really – that he stay to have lunch with them as well, which Evie took to be Mrs Smith's slightly clumsy attempt at disguising her crude match-making.

Mr Drake, Leonard Bassett and Evie looked from one to another. It was a look that seemed to say Mrs Smith's insistent invitation might be a bit odd, but it was probably easier to go along with her suggestion than to broker an alternative.

Tricia stood up so that she could lift Hettie from Evie's lap and plop her down in a drawer that was on top of the widest portion of the dresser and that had been made up inside with what looked like some folded blankets to make a comfy spot for baby to have a doze, and she placed a cut-down thin eiderdown over her in the hope that she would catch forty winks.

'Come on, Evie, you can help me do some more veg while Mr Bassett removes 'is coat. I wan' a word wi' you,' Tricia said firmly, a glint in her eye shining unmistakeably in Evie's direction.

Evie pursed her lips in the direction of both Tricia and Mrs Smith to indicate she knew what they were up to. She even gave a miniscule frown in Mr Smith's direction, although unhelpfully he pretended not to notice.

Mr Bassett looked slightly perplexed as he hadn't expected Evie to be whisked away quite like this or so abruptly when they were still to discuss school matters, and Evie made sure she didn't catch his eye as that would be just too disconcerting for either of them, she was sure.

Out in the scullery as they sorted through some carrots and turnips, and set a massive cauli to one side, in a stage whisper Tricia made Evie very aware that Mr Drake seemed to be presentable and – a tremendous bonus – as if he could well be single. She told Evie that she should smile at him a lot, and ask him questions about himself.

'Yes, I can see that is a plan. Men do seem to enjoy talking about themselves,' Evie whispered back, and then she found herself breaking into what felt like her first genuine smile in ages, at which point Tricia shushed back, 'And don' you dare forget it!', before she shooed Evie out of the scullery and back into the kitchen so that Evie and Mr Bassett and Mrs Smith could get the 'borin' ol' school stuff', as Tricia described it, out of the way before they ate.

Much to Evie's surprise it ended up being rather a convivial meal and not at all awkward. In fact, Evie would have been hard pressed to say when she had last enjoyed herself quite so much.

Even though it was only lunchtime, Mr Smith opened a bottle of red wine, and then a second 'just in case', which was left unobtrusively on the dresser near to the drawer that Hettie was in, to let the wine breathe and start coming up to room temperature, and once they sat down to eat Evie soon found herself feeling a little squiffy as she wasn't used either to wine or to drinking alcohol at lunchtime, and she told herself that she mustn't pick up Hettie afterwards in case she dropped her. She had never been drunk (or even merry) in her life before, and so she reminded herself that she didn't know her limits and that it would be very wise to constrain herself to just the one glass. Dealing with Fiona after she had quaffed the brandy had proved to be very sobering, Evie discovered.

Both Mr Bassett and Mr Drake acted as if they were very appreciative of the wine, which seemed in Evie's opinion to be simultaneously sophisticated and also extravagant to have with an ordinary Sunday lunch. To Evie one wine bottle looked just like another, and even though Mr Smith was at great pains to point out that really a dish like roast chicken should be accompanied by white wine, but that this particular Sunday it would have to be red as that was all he'd brought back to Lymbridge from his wine cellar in London, each of the male guests seemed to know a little bit about wine, or at any rate they pretended to, and so there were declarations of what a very fine choice this particular wine was, and what a treat they were all in for. Evie knew that Mr Smith kept a very refined wine cellar, and so she was in little doubt that what they were drinking would be top quality. She wasn't really certain she liked the taste of wine herself, though; in her humble opinion this all seemed rather a lot of fuss about what was ultimately not very much.

As the dining room was unheated and cold, it had been decreed by Mrs Smith that they would slum it and eat in the kitchen. Tricia had set the table with efficiency, once Mrs Smith made the men put the plans for the new house away. Evie noticed that Tricia got out a clean tablecloth, and there was no hesitation of what size knife and folk and spoon should go where, and so Evie assumed that Mrs Smith had given her a lesson or two in matters of table-setting etiquette. Tricia's background was very modest, Evie knew, and Tricia had been the first to acknowledge that when she moved into the cottage she knew nothing about this sort of thing.

Everyone – well, excluding Mr Bassett and Mr Drake; and Evie too, of course – conspired in making sure that Evie and Mr Drake were seated next to each other, and it was unavoidable that everybody had to sit closely with one another as it was quite a squeeze to get the six of them around the kitchen table.

Evie tried to act demurely, which felt peculiar as the unexpected turn of events over the lunchtime all felt a bit strange and very much out of her hands. But after a while she decided that her best course of action would be just to go with the flow of things.

Luckily Mr Drake turned out to be incredibly easy to find things to say to, although Evie felt shamefully out of practice at talking with a man she wasn't already familiar with. Still, it wasn't long before she found out that his first name was Thomas, although he much preferred Tom, and so would Evie please call him that, at which point Evie responded by saying that she found Miss Yeo to be too formal and so could he reciprocate by calling her Evie, her preferred diminutive of Evelyn. And so on. By the time the stewed apples were making their appearance Evie and Tom had been able to establish that they were both single, that they were both extraordinarily fond of cats, and that they each very much enjoyed going to the pictures.

But before that revelation grew into any sort of significant moment with the potential for turning awkward, Evie broadened the conversation to ask Tricia and Mrs Smith what they thought of the plans for the new house, and she added that Timmy must be very pleased too that things were moving on in this respect. Mrs Smith and Tricia said they had all had lots to think about, such as low windowsills so that Timmy would get a sense of space and be able to see the garden easily from his wheelchair, and Tricia was very excited that it looked like there were going to be two lavatories in the house, which she considered to be the height of luxury, and Evie found herself thinking that actually she rather agreed with Tricia about this.

Mr Smith added that after lunch they were going over to The Grange to collect Timmy, and then Mr and Mrs Smith, and Timmy and Tricia, and Mr Drake were going to meet on the site to discuss the final details of the plans. And if everything were agreed that afternoon, the plans would be put forward to the planning committee in Plymouth within the week, which hopefully would mean the build would start in the spring, with Timmy and Tricia and Hettie being able to move in by the late summer.

Evie noticed that Mrs Smith's smile was very slightly fixed when Tricia and Hettie moving out was mentioned, and she knew that Mrs Smith had been hoping that Timmy would either move back into the family house when he left the hospital, or that the new home for him would be built in her orchard just behind the cottage. Evie could see that it would be a real wrench too for the older woman to have Hettie moving out; Mrs Smith looked to be in her element when she dandled the baby on her lap. Evie smiled at her headmistress in acknowledgement that she understood Mrs Smith would have very mixed feelings, and that she sympathised.

Mrs Smith looked back at Evie, and her eyes took on a polished cast for a minute or two, but then her hand was patted by Mr Smith, who had noticed too his wife's slightly bereft look. And before long Mrs Smith was able to say to Mr Drake in what would sound to anyone who didn't know her well to be a perfectly normal voice that she was very much looking forward to watching Timmy's reaction to seeing the plans while they were meeting later, as they would all be standing (or, in Timmy's case, sitting) in situ where his new home would be built and so she thought it would all suddenly feel very real to him.

Evie had a brainwave that she thought might help her headmistress adjust in a tiny way as to the changes that were going to come. Mrs Smith would miss having Hettie around, and nothing would be able to fill that void, of course. But perhaps the presence of one of Keith's kittens would, although in no way a replacement, be something to love that might make things feel a little more bearable. All the kittens were well handled, and were very affectionate.

'Mrs Smith, Keith's kittens are going to need good homes soon. Do you think you and Mr

Smith might like one? I'm sure a kitten would make Hettie laugh when she comes back to visit you, as they really do get up to some funny antics,' said Evie.

Mrs Smith looked a little taken aback, but she said she would think about it, although this was uttered in a manner as if she had already made her mind up to the contrary. But Tricia manfully picked up the baton, saying, 'Go on, Mrs S., yer know there's mice up in t' thatch, and so yer need a gud mouser.' And Mr Smith added that he thought a kitten would be a very welcome addition to the family as he had a soft spot for cats.

Mrs Smith stared sternly at her husband and Tricia, and looked then at Evie in a resigned manner that let Evie know one of the kittens had a home to go to.

Tricia said then that she'd be willing to have one for the new house too, if that was a help, and so maybe two of the kittens could come to Mrs Smith's cottage for the time being, and then one of them could be moved to the new house once Timmy, Hettie and herself had settled in.

Evie said how wonderful, and she thought immediately afterwards that if there were just one kitten left, then perhaps Mrs Worth might be persuaded that it should stay on at Pemberley along with Keith.

After getting Evie to describe the kittens and then a debate during which Mrs Smith and Tricia declared they'd have the two black and white kittens, they fell to talking about names. They decided they'd name them after either bomber planes, or maybe naval ships, but that they'd get the kittens back to Mrs Smith's cottage to see what their personalities were like before naming them definitively.

Evie was secretly glad the tabby and white hadn't been chosen. It was her favourite and she knew she wanted to keep it.

Leonard Bassett had remained fairly quiet while all of this was going on. But after Evie had offered to stay at the cottage while Timmy was collected and they then had their discussion where the new house would be, saying she'd be happy to keep an eye on Hettie in the warm kitchen if that were helpful, as long as Tricia gave her a feed first, and Tom had added that after the meeting he would come back to the cottage to pick up Evie to run her back to Pemberley, Evie saw Leonard looking between herself and Tom with a slow dawning of recognition at what was afoot.

Promptly Evie busied herself stacking the used crockery on the table so that she didn't have to endure the pointed smirks from Mrs Smith and Tricia at Tom's offer of a lift home.

As Evie snuggled down in bed that night, rather than thinking of Peter as she usually did, instead she planned what she would wear the following evening.

Tom was going to be taking her to the pictures.

And the evening after that it very much looked as if he would be at the fundraising meeting for the Spitfire that was going to take place over at The Grange, and Evie would have a chance then to compare both him and Peter as they sat near to one another.

With that thought still fresh in her mind, Evie

smiled to herself at the idea of Timmy being there too, as she knew he would be unable to resist making some reference or other to Pev and the fact that it looked as if pretty speedily Evie was doing something about her miserable lack of a romantic life. Peter would be there too but Evie wasn't going to give a damn what he thought, was she?

Chapter Eleven

By ten to seven on the Tuesday evening a large upstairs room at The Grange was packed with people ready for the next meeting of the Spitfire fund. There were quite a lot of new faces there, with people such as Pemberley's recent PG arrivals swelling the ranks, and so before the meeting got underway there was a flurry of people introducing themselves one to another.

And of course Tom was there for the very first time, sitting directly across the table from Evie. This was giving Evie a distinct sense of electricity. Every time she lifted her head from her notebook, it seemed as if it was only to see him smiling back over the table at her. It wasn't the sort of smile that most people would notice, but although they had only been on the one evening out together, there was something undemanding and seemingly uncomplicated about him that made Evie feel that she knew him well enough already to detect a slight uplifting of the corners of his mouth. She felt as if she trusted him to notice her eyes were twinkling back at him in return, even if she was too decorous to keep grinning in his direction back over the wooden trestle.

They had enjoyed a very pleasant evening the day before. Tom had collected Evie from Pemberley before five o'clock, and Evie had noticed that Mrs Worth and Annabel hadn't been able to resist the temptation of coming to the front door under the guise of seeing her off, although Evie knew this was merely a ruse so that they could catch a glimpse of what he looked like. She admonished them with a little wag of a finger that she hoped Tom couldn't see as he held the car door open for her. They beamed back at her and promptly proceeded not to make themselves scarce in the slightest.

Tom had then speedily whisked Evie to Oldwell Abbott, and asked her if she fancied a teatime snack. Evie was always hungry, as were most people since rationing had come in, and so she said how wonderful. And then, after they had eaten some toasted teacakes, he had taken her – joy! – to see *Casablanca* at the Odeon, splashing out on the best seats in the house.

Evie felt rather spoilt as it was nearly a year since she had been to the cinema with a gentleman friend. The last time had been with Timmy, and he had made her sit through a Charlie Chaplin film that he thought hilarious and she found only mildly amusing. Evie didn't understand what it was about Charlie Chaplin that made some people cry with hilarity; she thought his movies tended to be mawkish and too openly sentimental. She couldn't remember that Timmy had actually asked

211

her what she wanted to see, but she thought he had most probably instead assumed that if he liked it, then Evie would too. Looking back as she settled herself into her seat with Tom beside her just as the Pathé news broadcast began to open the evening's programme, she did remember a feeling of being slightly put out at the time by Timmy's assumption, and that she'd told herself that when she was married to him she would have to make sure that she put her foot down a little more firmly.

It was a different story with Tom. As Evie had devoured the biggest toasted teacake she had ever seen, he told her that they could watch whatever she wanted – there were three cinemas in Oldwell Abbott, and so they had a choice. The cinemas were all very popular even though Oldwell Abbott was only a modestly sized market town, and Evie had mused that it was odd how busy they were considering there was a war on and how tight money was these days. However, she supposed then that people wanted cheering up from the glum account of Britain's progress (or not) against Hitler, and the cinema was a relatively cheap night out while the darkness inside meant it was a safe and warm place for a couple to canoodle if they felt so inclined. Then she thought about what she might do if Tom wanted to smooch with her but was unable to guess what her reaction might be.

Linda and Sam had already been to see *Casablanca,* and Linda had praised it highly when they had been out riding together that Saturday on the moors.

Evie suggested it to Tom, but she added immediately that if he didn't fancy it, then it wasn't a problem in the slightest as they could easily see something else. Tom, however, declared *Casablanca* a perfect choice, and added he had been looking forward to seeing it. She wasn't quite sure she believed him, but it was nice to hear such an enthusiastic declaration all the same.

Evie loved *Casablanca.* She didn't think she'd ever seen such a romantic film, and she had found herself so swept up in the story that there was only a little bit in the middle when she was distracted temporarily by thoughts of Peter. On the way back to Lymbridge, as the car bounced along over the country lanes, she and Tom enjoyed a spirited conversation about whether Humphrey Bogart's character, Rick, or Victor Laszlo, played by Paul Henreid, was the best choice for Ilsa. Evie rather surprised herself in the heat of discussion by suggesting as a throwaway comment that perhaps Ingrid Bergman's character should have considered being on her own as an option, rather than having to assume that she could only go on with one of the two men. Tom thought about this for a moment, and then he bellowed with laughter, calling Evie 'a card', before pointing out that if Ilsa had stayed in Casablanca with Rick, it was very possible that he might not have let their relationship take off once more, or that Ilsa would have tired of being with him pretty quickly. Evie disagreed with the last part of Tom's comment, saying she didn't think a woman would ever tire of being on the arm of either Rick or Victor, although the appeal would be different with each of them.

Naturally Mrs Worth and Annabel were waiting

for Evie in the kitchen when she got in – there had been no smooching in the cinema, or after, and Tom had very obviously offered his hand for Evie to shake when he stopped the car outside Pemberley's front door so that there could be no confusion as to whether he would lean over in her direction, or not – and Evie teased the two women by only talking about the film as she stroked the tabby and white kitten who had jumped up onto her lap while she was sipping her cocoa.

Evie took a deep breath, and looked towards Mrs Worth then, as she went on to explain that she'd found homes for the black and white kittens, but this poor little mite was sadly without a home to go to. His coat was looking smooth and glossy from all the rigorous combing that Evie was doing every evening to remove any errant fleas, and she thought he looked at his very best.

'Wouldn't Laszlo make a wonderful name for this one?' she added, as she lifted him so that he could nestle under her chin as Evie waved one of his little white paws at her landlady. Evie knew he would be looking butter-wouldn't-melt adorable. 'If we were going to keep him to do some mousing, that is.'

Mrs Worth changed the subject very quickly, but not before she looked at the kitten with quite an audible tut.

Annabel and Evie smiled at each other – this was round one in Evie's offensive of making the kitten a permanent PG at Pemberley, and they both recognised it as such.

Mrs Worth thought she was going to have her way, of course, with Keith and the tabby kitten soon to be banished back to the primary school where Keith had lived previously, once the kitten was just a little bigger and the nights weren't quite so frosty. Evie was pretty certain meanwhile that the tiny sweetie would prove to be more than a match for her landlady. Evie decided on a second line of offence: tomorrow she would start making sure that the softer touch, Mr Worth, noticed how lovable little Laszlo was.

Evie's newly cheerful mood lasted throughout the following day.

Even by the time of the Spitfire fundraising meeting that evening, Evie definitely felt quite smiley still. She had had a good day at the school as the recently arrived pupils seemed to be amalgamating themselves well into their new classroom and routine.

Evie thought too that going to the pictures had been good for her as she had noticed a distinct fillip to her low spirits that had kept her cheerful the whole day, despite one of her new pupils not quite being able to make the lavatories in time.

When she thought about it, Evie couldn't say that she was wildly attracted to Tom, although she thought perhaps she could be, given time. She reminded herself that for quite some weeks after they had met she hadn't noticed Peter in the slightest as a romantic possibility, and look how he had made her pulse gallop since then, following his bold move that resulted in their secret kisses behind the Nissen hut on the school playing field as they captured the runaway piglet at the village's summer Revels. What she did know right now was that Tom was certainly very nice to be around

215

nonetheless, and seemed to be unusually go-getting, manly, well-kempt and good-mannered, a combination Evie found most beguiling.

She had even dared to ask about his limp during their snack before the cinema, and sure enough, as she had suspected, it turned out that he did have a prosthetic lower leg, following an injury sustained fighting in 1940 that had infected and eventually caused the loss of a foot. But Tom didn't appear to be the slightest bit embarrassed by what had happened or to be particularly hampered by it as he seemed able to drive an adapted car with no problem, with the result that Evie didn't feel awkward or embarrassed either. Indeed Tom seemed happy to talk about it and answer whatever questions on the subject that Evie might care to ask, not that Evie wanted to press him for details as she wanted to keep their night out at a jolly level.

He'd gone on to say that although he was happy to work on drawing up the plans for any sort of building, his own disability had led since his return to Civvy Street to a special interest in designing property for people in wheelchairs or who might be bedridden, and that he had been recommended to Mr Smith as the ideal architect for Timmy's new home because of this.

Evie was not so naive as to be unaware that Tom was bound to be making a little light of something that had, even if only for a time, felt completely devastating to him in the personal sense. No young man would choose to lose a foot, or would automatically assume that a potential partner might not feel at least a little peculiar about it. But Evie tried to show that she appreciated Tom's seemingly open and frank attitude by responding in an equally calm manner, and giving him the courtesy of really listening to what he had to say on the subject.

And then she thought that although stupidly she had always assumed that she would marry an able-bodied person, and this was in spite of seeing Timmy lying sick and close to death in his hospital bed whilst they were still engaged in the technical sense, while she and Tom were talking Evie realised that if she were in love (with Tom, or with another man with a heinous injury), then it really wouldn't matter to her at all what physical problems her husband might have. If a man had struggled to a personal victory over something grave that had deeply affected him – and actually Evie also included Peter and his awful stutter in this category – then, if love came calling, Evie would make it her objective to search for the positivity in the defeat and overcoming of something traumatic, rather than looking for the downside in what it could go on to mean in the practical sense, she promised herself.

Of course, somebody who had been as badly injured as Timmy might not be able to live to make old bones. But that didn't mean that he couldn't still become a very suitable husband in the meantime, and Evie realised she felt a growing respect for Tricia, who seemed to have embraced with equanimity the injured Timmy exactly as he was. Tricia was a down-to-earth sort, and she didn't seem to be paying much mind to what had happened to Timmy's body. Instead she seemed to be treating him pretty much as an able-bodied

217

man, albeit one who had to sit in a chair for everything. Tricia had told Evie when they were sitting by the fire at Pemberley the other night that she was sure Hettie would think of Timmy exactly as she would if he had been able to walk around with her – he was her daddy, and he loved her, and that would be all that mattered to Hettie.

Trying not to look at Tom, Evie felt the meeting for the Spitfire fund sink back into the hinterland, her eyes misting as she thought anew of little Hettie and Timmy together, and the growing bond between father and daughter. She had a vision of Hettie as a toddler supporting herself by holding the arm of Timmy's wheelchair as she gazed up at him and he looked down at her. They wouldn't be looking at each other with any sense of failure or encumbrance, but simply with adoration. At least that was how Evie hoped fervently it would be.

Evie busied herself folding her coat onto the back of her chair to give herself a chance to regain her composure just as Timmy wheeled himself into the meeting and, with a loud American-style 'Howdy' and a flamboyant swivel of his wheelchair, took a place at the table right beside Tom, and turned immediately to shake his hand.

Timmy's cheeky expression instantly told Evie that Timmy knew all about Tom and Evie, and the sortie the previous evening to Oldwell Abbott. Clearly, Tricia had primed him as to the matchmaking of the Sunday lunchtime, and although Evie gave a small groan inwardly as Timmy wasn't utterly to be trusted not to make a show of her, or not to have a bit of fun at her expense, she supposed that was only to be expected.

As Evie pretended to be fascinated by Sukie taking a seat beside her, she had to endure all the while Timmy making some silly faces in her direction to which she tried to respond by frowning, although without looking at him directly and in the probably vain hope that it was the sort of frown that would stop Timmy in his tracks but that would be disguised as an amiable look that wouldn't alert Tom, who was now saying good evening to Mr Worth and Mr Rogers, to what Timmy was up to.

There was no sign whatsoever of Peter, and as the meeting was called to order by Mr Rogers, who was the chair, when he tapped his pen against a glass of water, Evie assumed that Peter must have had second thoughts or else he was caught up with something to do with work that he couldn't leave. She wasn't quite sure whether to be pleased or not.

Then the door opened and Peter hurried in with a look on his face that managed to be both flurried and anxious, and – horror! – he had to slide onto the seat next to Tom, but on the other side of Tom to which Timmy was sitting, as this was the only seat remaining free at the table (which was actually three long trestles lined up together lengthwise in order to make enough room for everybody, such was the number of people who now wanted to be involved in organising various events for the Spitfire fundraising).

Of course, the upshot was that Evie could now see the three most important men in her romantic life sitting in a line. Sukie had, obviously, noticed this too, and was pushing her heel down on Evie's foot, with a whispered, 'See No Evil, Do No Evil, Hear No Evil; or at least it would be if Timmy weren't one of the trio, don't you think, Evie-Rose?' out of the corner of her mouth in her friend's direction.

Evie responded to this by looking towards Mr Rogers with a guileless expression but nonetheless jabbing her pencil into the part of Sukie's thigh that was closest to her. Sukie gave a peep of surprise – the tip of the pencil having found its mark with a little more force than Evie had intended – and this meant that fleetingly everyone glanced over towards the pair of them, at which Evie put her foot on top of Sukie's in admonishment, and received an answering poke in her posterior from Sukie's own pencil.

Biting back her own sharp intake of breath at the sharp prick of the pencil's lead in her buttock, and as she felt three pairs of eyes scrutinise her from across the table, Evie decided her best option would be to keep her eyes turned firmly and innocently downward in the direction of her notebook for the duration of the whole meeting.

The last thing Evie saw before she looked down, though, was Timmy rolling his eyes dramatically at the sight of Tom and Peter sitting next to each other, and then swiftly crossing his eyes so that the pupils pointed to one another over his own nose (Timmy's ability to cross his eyes so dramatically was his party piece, and he once had confessed to Evie that it had taken daily practice over the whole school summer holidays of the year he turned fourteen to hone this particular skill), while both Tom and Peter looked vaguely puzzled at the rather peculiar colour Evie had suddenly flushed.

Evie did her best to concentrate on what was being talked about in the fundraising committee. It was, however, intensely dull looking without respite at her blank sheet of paper in her reporter's notebook, and Evie doubted she'd be able to last the length of the meeting in this way, no matter how much she tried to entertain herself by doodling pictures of Keith's kittens.

The news that the various members of the committee were reporting to the meeting was most heartening, though, as the fund had made a very promising start and stood already in excess of £750. A whole network of local businesses were now getting involved and so the cash raised was starting to tot up most encouragingly, and there was a real web of fundraising events taking place over the four West Country counties of Cornwell, Devon, Somerset and Dorset.

Clearly Evie's idea that they should band together to raise the £6,000 needed to buy a Spitfire that could be donated to the war effort had come along at precisely the right time, and for the first time Evie was able to dare think that although the sum needed to buy the fighter was so large, there might be a chance that they could actually achieve their objective.

People's imaginations seemed to have been ignited by the fund at any rate, and although she was fighting very hard not to feel just a trifle smug, Evie found it very gratifying nonetheless to see how excited people appeared to be by the whole endeavour. She suspected that to some extent this was probably not so much to do with her having had a brilliant idea (even though she did rather think she had excelled herself in this respect), but more that everyone working together to a single good cause was a consequence of well over two years of being at war. Many local folks now yearned to be able to reinforce the old sense of community spirit during a time when the war was continuing to cast long shadows over them all and insistently wafting towards them the sense of the irretrievable loss of the nostalgic Britain that everyone could easily remember from the 1930s.

Evie was relieved to hear that the Spitfire cake competition was being organised now in its entirety by the *Western Morning News;* with her energies directed towards her new pupils, she'd actually more or less forgotten about the dratted cake. And the daily local newspaper was also publicising in each issue the series of talks that had been Evie's idea originally but that fortunately Pattie and Mr Rogers were now making such a huge success of organising.

The crewmen on the airfield were turning up trumps too, as they had quite a lot of good ideas about how to harness interest in the fundraising amongst the new recruits who were about to enter the area who would presumably be keen to be involved.

Most of the familiar faces – Mr Smith, Robert, Mr Worth, Mr Rogers, Leonard Bassett, Julia, Susan, Mrs Smith, and of course Timmy and Peter – were soon voted onto or co-opted onto various projects. Even the normally painfully shy and awkward Sam Torrence offered to run a skittles championship between several local public houses, and a little cheer went up after he had described his idea in a halting and diminutive voice that everyone had to strain to hear, and so Evie suspected quite a lot of the men present would be eager to form a team or two. Then the air crews said why didn't they also run a special darts tournament in tandem, as that way most people would pay to enter both competitions? They could run a round-robin knockout tournament to take place on different dates at various local public houses that had skittles alleys (every pub having a darts board), and to have the two events running together would attract people from further away to support the cause.

But there was no particular project that Evie was in charge of, or contributing to, and this felt a bit strange as she knew that normally she was first in the queue to put her name forward for this sort of thing.

Evie continued to hold back from volunteering for anything, although she hoped that nobody would notice or would be inclined to hold her newfound apathy against her. She had just had an idea for a project that felt equally as important, although it wasn't anything to do with the Spitfire fund. She wanted to speak with Mr Smith about the practicalities before she breathed a word about this idea to anyone else.

And the truth of it was too that even though she had felt more positive over the last twenty-four hours, Evie still felt jaded and rather weighed down with January blues. She supposed she probably hadn't quite regained her normal *joie de vivre* following her bout of nasty influenza, while her longer working days and having to write lessons for a term she hadn't taught before were still rather taking it out of her, with the result that she felt in general rather like many of today's motor cars: running on empty.

Peter hadn't said anything either, other than to read out loud the running total of the money raised, and to explain how he was keeping any recently raised cash in the safe downstairs, but was regularly banking the proceeds in the special bank account for the fund that he and Mr Worth had set up.

Eventually Evie decided that she did have one suggestion to make, which was that although the days were still very short and in fact the worst of the winter weather was probably about to descend, they should already be remembering that Easter would follow soon afterwards, and May Day not too long after that, and so it probably wasn't too early for anybody to be thinking of fundraising events for the springtime that could perhaps be tied in to these pertinent times of the year. She was wondering, for instance, about something to celebrate May Day, possibly something such as an inter-school maypole dancing celebration?

There were nods of agreement to Evie's general reminder, with several people saying they'd put their thinking caps on as to special themed events, and then the meeting moved on to other things, which was good as Evie had realised once again that she had drawn the attention of the three sets of eyes opposite back to her, which hadn't been her intention at all. But this wasn't before a chuckle united the meeting when a smart aleck from the air crew called out, 'I've got it: skittles and darts, as we dance the maypole.' Evie had to work quite hard not to give the jester a stern look.

Sukie was sitting next to Evie and a minute or so later there was the sound of a fold of paper skittering across the table, which Sukie deftly fielded. She nudged Evie and passed it to her. It had Evie's name scrawled on the front, and when she opened it she saw a cartoonish line drawing of the popular Chad, only in this case saying 'Wot! Do I spy Pev beside me?!' It was rather well done.

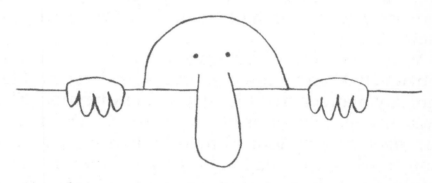

Wot! Do I spy Pev besides me?!

Evie didn't need to be told the note was from Timmy, and she found it had caught her funny bone much more than the maypole quip had done. Her resulting silently quaking shoulders and fluttering curls as she stared doggedly towards the piece of paper she was holding in her lap caused a quietish eruption from Timmy's chair that Evie could tell was amusement, although she thought most of the other attendees would put it down to a cough or something maybe a bit more rude in polite company. Either way, it had the fortunate effect of luckily diverting attention away from Evie who now was in real danger of laughing out loud, which would have been absolutely unforgiveable seeing as the discussion had now turned to memorials for the fallen.

All in all, it was a relief when the meeting ended.

As people started to stand up Sukie sidled up to Tom to give him, Evie suspected, a bit of a grilling. Tom looked slightly shaken to be the obvious focus of Sukie's stunning looks and quick intelligence. Evie was in no doubt that before the evening was out Sukie would be reporting back to her precisely what she had made of Evie's potential new beau.

With Tom otherwise engaged, Timmy was all too obviously keen to catch a word with Evie, and he quickly manoeuvred his chair in her direction. She was immensely pleased to see how very much stronger he now looked than he had in comparison to when they had held the inaugural meeting of the fundraising committee back in the previous November. Then, sitting up in his wheelchair for a meeting that had lasted for less than an hour (and this one had gone on for nearly two) had left Timmy pasty-faced, exhausted and clearly in pain, and Peter had been very solicitous in making sure he got back to his ward as soon as he could. Evie could remember how deeply touched she had felt when she saw the care and compassion with which Peter unobtrusively pushed a dog-tired Timmy out of the meeting to ensure that he could get back to his ward and hospital bed as quickly as possible but without alerting people to the fact that Timmy was clean tuckered out.

Now, Timmy looked quite impish and full of beans, even though this meeting had lasted for what felt to Evie like a very long time as the agenda had been pretty packed, and many people had wanted to speak about contributions to the goings on.

'Whatever you are about to say, don't you dare, Timmy Bowes!' said Evie quietly but firmly when he was close enough, giving her former fiancé a stern and appraising look. Out of the corner of her eye she could see Tom being interrogated by Sukie, and Peter hovering but lurking further back in the room, clearly undecided as to whether he should come over and say something to Evie. She realised she wasn't in the mood to help Peter out, especially as with her luck the minute he came over would be the precise second that Tom's attention was no longer being diverted by Sukie.

Instead Evie crouched down so that she could whisper in Timmy's ear, 'Chad says, Mind your own business, Timmy Bowes!'

This had the desired effect and Evie felt gratified when Timmy's resulting bark of mirth could be heard right across the room, causing Mrs Smith instantly to cast an unanswered questioning look at Evie and her son.

With a tap of dismissal on Timmy's shoulder Evie ignored them all, and straightened up so that she could cross the room to speak to Robert and Susan, who were standing with Julia and Leonard Bassett. As they spoke Evie could see that Leonard appeared to be jotting something down on what looked like the back of an old envelope.

227

What a strange old life it is, Evie mulled as she drew near to her family. It's only a few months back that Julia and Leonard were daggers drawn with her, with Susan and Robert not knowing which daughter to disapprove of most following the fracas at The Haywain; and now here they all were, standing around making small talk as if everything had always been sweetness and light between them. And of course less than a year ago Mrs Smith had been horrified at the thought of Timmy impregnating Tricia, then a lowly dairy parlour maid, and now the two women appeared to be growing close, to judge by how relaxed the pair of them had looked together over their joint preparation of the Sunday lunch at Mrs Smith's cottage.

As Evie mused, she cast an appraising look around the room and saw Peter heading for the door. He stopped, just for a fraction of a second, and glanced over to where she was, before he pulled the door open and stepped out to the landing beyond, closing the door firmly behind him. Evie felt a pang that was followed immediately by a momentary desire to follow him down to his lair in the basement of the grand house.

But it didn't last more than the merest instant, and by the time Evie had gathered her thoughts once more, a debonair Tom was at her shoulder ready to tell her what an impressively lively meeting it had been, and wasn't she a clever old thing to have thought of fundraising to buy a Spitfire in the first place.

Evie smiled at Tom, and seamlessly turned to introduce him to her family without allowing herself the luxury of another thought about Peter.

The next day was a lovely sunny winter's morning, and so Mrs Smith said that they should grab the opportunity the unusually clement weather offered, and take the whole school for a walk together. Mrs Smith had told Evie previously that she thought school outings with everyone involved were generally quite a positive thing to do, as the little ones could learn from the older pupils, while having the small children present would hopefully begin to instil the first feelings of responsibility for those less able to look after themselves in the minds of the older and more able children.

Evie thought that was a good idea too as often in winter the moors could be decidedly inhospitable and frequently misty, and so this would be the perfect opportunity for all the children to let off a little steam, as everybody could go a little stir-crazy if they had to be confined to the classroom for weeks on end. Personally, Evie thought, as long as their winter coats were warm enough, the pupils benefited by being outside as much as possible – it certainly made everyone a bit less tetchy when doing sums or writing, if they had been allowed to run about a bit first.

The teachers decided, though, that they would stay quite close to Lymbridge, just in case the weather changed abruptly. Moors were notorious for their quickly altering weather, and Evie didn't fancy them all being stuck a long way from school if a fog came down.

They started by heading down to the old village green, which was now the location of a whole variety of pens and runs for stock, so that the children could look at the animals housed there. The chickens were scratching around in their runs, and there were some ducks making quite a racket too as they paddled about in some blackly muddy water in several old tin baths that had been placed in their enclosure. Some of Evie's little ones remembered the geese that had taken up residence on the village green after Tavistock's Goosey Fair in October, the school's previous outing, but Evie had to explain that probably all of the geese had been for the Christmas lunch table, and so were sadly no more. The children nodded wisely at this as being country children, they were used to the idea that animals kept for food might not be around too long.

There was also a discussion on what a predator was. Mrs Smith told the children that foxes were a good example of a predator, and soon the children were asking if wolves and tigers were predators too. Evie described how foxes were intelligent and wily, and that they would try to target poultry and fowl kept in pens, and then little Bobby Ayres made even the oldest juniors top children laugh by suggesting that the villagers should install some searchlights and barrage balloons to keep the foxes away from the village green.

There were several porkers busily rooting in their muddy enclosures, and two goats penned up but looking rather indignant about their captivity. Their expressions were so silly, with their unruly beards shaking about below their chins, that they made everybody giggle, and at the sound of this both goats stood on their hind legs with their

230

forked hooves on the top of the fence around their enclosure, and made their strange bleating noises that sounded like a scary mixture of an oddly human bellow, cry and groan, presumably meant by the goats as an encouragement that the fastening on their enclosure should be loosened so that they could escape their confinement.

Evie told everyone to ignore the sounds the goats were making and then she pointed out the curious shape of their rectangular pupils in their topaz eyes clearly on display as they looked down on the schoolchildren with their hooves still balanced on the top of their fence. Evie asked the students to look into each other's eyes and call out the shape of the pupils that humans had. Bobby Ayres caused the teachers to chuckle by insisting that April Smith's pupils were like a parallelogram, and so the children laughed along too even though many of them could have had no idea as to what they were laughing at. Where an earth had Bobby picked up that word from? Evie thought with a shake of her head, as she hadn't covered that in her mathematics lessons.

Then there was a discussion over the two uses of the same word, in this case, pupils; one meaning of course being to do with the description of the schoolchildren themselves as attendees of Lymbridge Primary School, and the other meaning to do with eyes. Mr Bassett asked for examples of other words that had more than one meaning. Parallelogram made another appearance, naturally, and there was quite a lively moment or two as this was debated, before Mr Bassett asked for other examples.

The children got quite animated and began fiercely to try to outdo each other, and the goats appeared to be rather fascinated too by the vehemence with which the children were now shouting each other down, with Mrs Smith saying eventually that she thought that the pupils' audience of the two four-legged animals who had each remained intent on standing on their two hind legs had improved the school's repertoire of words that could be used to mean more than one thing. All in all, the members of Lymbridge Primary School had excelled themselves with coming up with such an excellent range of words with more than one meaning, and the goats were clearly very impressed, Mrs Smith added.

The goats turned out to be sisters who were called Elizabeth and Margaret, and they had been named after the two princesses seeing the war out in Buckingham Palace in London. Elizabeth was caramel coloured, while Margaret was more of a soft straw shade, but they both had matching backwards-facing short horns, impressively hairy beards and pristine white bibs running from under their chins right down their chests.

The pair were owned by school caretaker Mr Cawes, who had taken the opportunity of everyone being out of the school to pop down to give them the bitter outside leaves of some greens, and he made everyone smile by saying he'd taken the goats to his back garden over the weekend for a little grazing, whereupon within five minutes of him removing their rope halters so that they could wander freely in the walled space, they had nibbled the bottoms off all the tea towels that his wife Bessie had pegged out on the washing line first thing that morning. The nibbling had reached as far as the goats could stretch their necks upwards, with the result that all the tea towels had been shortened to a uniform new length.

'And as for what Elizabeth and Margaret did to my Bessie's bloomers that were just washed an' on t' line besides t' tea towels, I really don't care t' mention, as it don't bear thinkin' of!' finished Mr Cawes, and Evie found herself sharing a smile with Leonard Bassett, and she thought that was the first time they had ever done such a thing as share a moment of complicity. Who'd have thought that her and Leonard's first time of true bonding would have been over Bessie Cawes' bloomers?

Each class was given some tasks to do. Evie kept a careful ear out for oncoming traffic as the little ones were sent to the side of the road to pick some grass for the chickens and ducks, Mr Bassett's juniors middles were allowed to help count eggs into boxes to be stacked ready for market the next day, while Mrs Smith's juniors top were told to look closely at the fencing of every enclosure and to write a list of any spots, and where they were, that might look in need of repairs in order for Mr Cawes to attend to later (although Robert and James would periodically help him with this responsibility, it was Mr Cawes who tended to make sure that the fencing was robust for all the villagers' animals and fowl).

After about twenty minutes or so, the children were told to say goodbye to Elizabeth and Margaret, and the porkers (who had been a bit disappointing as far as the children were concerned as they had refused to lift their snouts from hunting through the churned mud at their feet), and then the whole of Lymbridge Primary School was walked in the other direction through the village to go to Switherns Farm to see if anything was going on in the farmyard.

As it turned out, Linda was present in the yard as she was just about to trim the feet of the milking cows, and so she gave an impromptu demonstration to the children of how this was done, and then she described the various tools she had with her, and showed everyone the different shape of a horseshoe nail when compared to an ordinary nail for something like a fence. And when Joseph asked Linda if she ever trimmed the feet of Elizabeth and Margaret, she said she did but that to do this she would use a smaller set of hoof nippers than she would use on the bigger and chunkier feet of a large animal like a cow or horse, although quite often these days she'd use a special curved knife for cows as that was quicker now that she'd developed her own knack for it.

Evie indicated to Linda not to go into too many specifics on the intricacies of foot trimming, as the finer technicalities would be lost on the young audience, adding, 'I know you're wanting to practise some of your talk on farriering in Plymouth, but I think that really you'll be wasting your breath if you go into very much greater detail this morning.' Linda looked intently at the children, and then told Evie that she saw what Evie meant, and she'd just get back to work if that was all right with the teachers, although she had been tempted to spend a little time on why herd animals had hooves while predators had soft pads and claws to their feet.

The farmer who owned Switherns allowed the children a drink of fresh milk, and a visit to the outside privy to one side of the farmyard for those who wanted, before they were taken to the village churchyard to look at the many different sorts of lichen growing over the slate or granite gravestones. Mrs Smith told everyone that such a variety of lichen was an indication of how pure the air was in Lymbridge, which was quite a height above sea level.

Once 'sea level' had been explained, she then pointed out the dark green yew trees in the churchyard, telling the children in a very grave manner that yew trees were very poisonous and so they must never touch them or eat any of the evergreen foliage or any berries; and if they were ever to touch the trees, they must make sure to wash their hands before eating.

Again the children were given tasks. Evie's infants had to count the gravestones on the portion of grass to the front of the church, and write the answer on a piece of paper on which they would also have written their name; Mr Bassett's had to take it in turns to read the notices out loud on the public noticeboard in the generous church porch, which wasn't as easy as it sounded as some of the notices were handwritten and most of the children were only used to seeing words in a book or in a schoolteacher's cursive script on a blackboard; while Mrs Smith's were allowed to collect dead plants from any water containers on the grave-

235

stones and take them to the compost heap. Evie pointed out to her own youngsters that many of the water containers were actually part of the headstone, and some had a metal contraption covering where the water went, that had holes in it so that the flowers could be artfully arranged, but she told her infants that the older children in the juniors top would pick out any dead plants from the containers and so their job was still just to count and then total the number of gravestones.

The outing ended with the teachers counting all of the pupils to make sure no one had gone, and then everyone going back to the primary school, where after the three teachers had quickly moved the chairs and tables to the sides of the room, all the pupils were told to sit cross-legged on the floor in the larger of the two classrooms in the space that had been made in the middle, and draw their favourite thing of the morning. It was no surprise to Evie that Elizabeth and Margaret proved by far to be the most popular choice for the children's pictures, although Linda featured in at least a couple of them, wielding a massive pair of nippers. There had to be a joke in that, Evie thought to herself, but for the moment she wasn't quite sure what it might be.

Chapter Twelve

After school that afternoon fortuitously Evie was able to flag down Mr Smith when she spied him driving through Lymbridge. He was just about to set off for London, where he would be working for the next week.

After joking as to whether he was going to bring some white wine back with him this time, or only the red, he joshed back that Mrs Smith had suggested that by the look on Tom's face when sitting across from Evie at the meeting on Monday, perhaps Mr Smith ought to collect some champagne that they could put aside 'just in case' for any special announcement that might be made in a month or two.

Pointedly, Evie ignored these latter comments and said instead that she was glad to catch him, as she wanted to ask his advice.

She told Mr Smith about Mrs Coyne no longer wanting to go on as the owner of the village shop, and that Susan and Robert were interested in taking it over, but also in developing a motor business alongside, but that their well-laid plans as to the long-term viability of such a project had apparently stumbled over the finance.

'Mother and Father are dears, but I can't help wondering if they are quite up to exhausting all the possibilities as to potential ways of raising the money they need,' said Evie. 'Of course, it's really important that they don't saddle themselves with unrealistic mountains of debt, but all the same, I feel that there must be a way for them to do this. Father is a wonderful mechanic, while Mother has more or less been running the shop for years, which means that if they can raise some money, there is scope for this plan to become a real family business. And the fact that it looks as if there's a lot of various people about to pour into the area means surely that this must be good for the shop as those newcomers are going to need somewhere to go to buy their bits of this and that, even if they aren't going to be on Dartmoor for long.

'I know Father had a word with the bank manager, but I don't think the outcome was good news as at the Spitfire meeting he seemed a bit down in the mouth, I thought, while Mother looked unusually lacklustre too. I just wondered if you might have any thoughts as to other avenues they could explore.'

Mr Smith nodded in sympathy, and said he would have a think as he drove up to London.

Evie waved him on his way, and then was surprised when almost straightaway a car horn tooted behind her, as she hadn't realised that another vehicle had driven up. She was sure she had made the driver smile as she had given, she suspected, a rather obvious jump at the unexpected sound of the car horn.

As she turned to look at the car better she saw that its driver was Tom, who wound down his driver's window to tell her he was taking Timmy back to The Grange, and then Timmy craned his head in her direction from the front passenger seat and gave Evie a jaunty wave. They'd been off to see a house that Tom had designed on another part of Dartmoor that had dealt with some of the issues that Timmy's prospective home was facing, as Tom had wanted Timmy to see how the solving of some of the accommodation and day-to-day living problems faced by wheelchair users worked in practice.

'Why don't you hop into the car too, and come down to The Grange with us just for the ride? We could do with the company of a nice young lady in order to keep us on the straight and narrow,' said Timmy in a cheerful manner, although Evie suspected that this was Timmy's way of throwing her and Tom in each other's paths. Timmy was by nature an opportunistic person – indeed when he'd been called up to fight, Evie told him that she supposed it was either that or else he would become an out and out spiv dealing in the black market, an assertion to which he'd happily agreed – and so she knew that Timmy would be reluctant to let the gift of a chance meeting between Evie and a suitable young man go to waste without a fight.

In fact, once she was seated in the back of the car, Evie saw that Timmy was so chipper that she guessed the two of them had had a good time out together and that they may well have included a stop-off at a moorland public house along the way. Although Evie didn't approve of alcohol consumed the wrong side of the yard arm, she was pleased in this case, as she felt that it must be hard for Timmy to have to get used to such a different future for himself than he would have been imagining at this time the previous year, and it would be good for him to make some new friends since his injury and to spend some time doing the sort of ordinary things most people didn't really think much about, such as having a pint in a pub when they fancied it.

A lot of people were having to come to terms with serious injuries, she knew, but the rakish Timmy of old had always seemed so especially bursting with vitality, that not being able to move about as he had done previously must have often felt to him to be a very high price to pay. And Tom, with his artificial foot, was a good example for Timmy, Evie hoped, as although Tom had been much less severely injured than Timmy, he was still a walking, talking example of how a young man with an injury could make a very good stab at living a full and rewarding life upon leaving hospital.

Tom had given Evie a friendly grin as she had got into the car, to which Evie found herself answering with an equally effusive smile. As they drove along Tom said that he was going to take Timmy and Tricia over to Plymouth on the Saturday for the first in the Spitfire fundraising talks, which was due to be Timmy's mother's talk as it turned out, and so why didn't Evie come with them too, and they could make up a foursome?

Timmy added that a friend of Tricia's had said she'd mind Hettie for the morning, if Tricia wanted, but apparently Tricia was going to bring Hettie with her, and so technically it would be a fivesome.

Evie thought Hettie would probably find a talk

very dull, but she said how lovely for Tricia and Hettie, and what a good idea. And yes, she'd love to join them all on the outing.

Evie didn't stay with Tom and Timmy once they'd arrived at The Grange, though. Instead she headed to the rooms towards the back of the building on the ground floor where the administration department had their offices, and from the corridor she waved through the glass of a wide door until Sukie looked up, and then came out to see her.

'I just wanted to say hello,' said Evie. 'I didn't expect to be here, but now I've been talked into it, I feel a bit at a loose end to be frank although it's only a flying visit, and so I thought I'd waste a little of your time as well as my own.'

Sukie laughed, and then said that much as she'd like to stand in idle chit-chat with Evie she had to get back to work as she still had an hour or so to go until she would be able to knock off and there were quite a lot of letters she still needed to type. But she'd see Evie soon, and meanwhile it might cheer Evie to know that Tom had her seal of approval as a suitable companion for her to spend a little time with.

Evie shook her head at Sukie for being a little cheeky, and then she retraced her footsteps and peeped around the door into Timmy's ward, where she saw that Timmy was now back in bed, and he and Tom looked to be deep in concentration while they sketched out something or other, their heads angled towards each other as they stared with concentration at the paper before them.

Feeling restless and uncharacteristically fidgety, Evie went to the front door of the hospital as she wondered if there might be lots of stars shining brightly in the sky above her, and suddenly she felt as if it were only the sounds and the smells of the surrounding moorland in the velvety darkness that would soothe the jangling fibres of her being.

She closed the heavy outer door quietly behind her and stood on the broad and wide stone top step to the grand sweep of the front of the house, looking high above her head.

Evie didn't think she'd ever found the evening sky looking so huge and as unfathomable as it did just then, domed spectacularly and reaching far out into the cosmos. At first it seemed to be a uniform sooty colour, but the longer Evie gazed into the heavens, the more she could see that actually the dense darkness was giving way here and there instead to a whole range of deep colours, with patches of starry black dotted amongst the glowering clouds of very slightly lighter metallic tones.

It was a panorama that conspired to be simultaneously mysterious and divine, as if designed to make anyone looking up towards it feel diminutive and as though the problems faced on earth were insignificant against the context of the massive endlessness stretching overhead.

'It makes one feel a mere dot in a mystifying tapestry, I always think. Would you agree?' said Peter quietly from somewhere behind her. Evie felt a quickening of her heart and she decided that he must have snuck out of the building in order to stand now on the steps with her.

Not for the first time Evie thought that Peter

had a knack of seeking her out and then knowing what she was thinking, although without her having to set it out for him. Well, unless she was silently hoping for him to declare his undying love for her, that is; for some reason, that was the one area where Peter didn't seem to share the same compulsion to lay voice to his thoughts, despite the fact that Evie had so longed for him to do so at times. Still, in spite of this inexcusable oversight on Peter's part, she doubted that she would ever meet anybody who seemed quite so attuned to the same things as she was.

'Yes, it does. Very small indeed,' Evie murmured back to Peter in a dreamy tone.

They remained near to each other in the chill night air, standing on the top step to The Grange as they gazed far above them and out on to something that felt crucial but that neither of them could quite focus on or encapsulate.

They felt caught still, trapped at the base of an immense whirlpool, as if atoms and electrons were bouncing from one of them to the other, and instantly back, merely in order to do it all over again.

The hairs on Evie's arms and legs lifted as if by sorcery.

And then she felt Peter's fingers slip with a feather-light touch down the length of her spine on top of her coat. It made her aware of her petticoat, and her dress and her cardigan beneath the coat. And then his delectably inching fingers made her aware of her whole body poised goose-bumpy and now thrilled beneath her clothes.

Evie sighed softly, and closed her eyes as they stood wordless in the huge silence of the massive

243

moors and let the deep hush of the night wrap around them.

A fox barked, and Evie thought it sounded as if it were coming from a tremendous distance away; it sounded a yelp of ecstasy. It seemed Peter and she were spinning off into their own cushioned vortex.

It was as if every cell of her being had shrunk into the path being so delicately traced along the length of her back. It was a rare and exquisite sensation, and Evie felt it heightened by a soft breeze of a caress on her exposed neck as she inclined her neck slightly towards her shoulder.

She felt so full suddenly of something – she wasn't sure what – that she almost cried out, although she bit it back so that the only sound that escaped her lips was that of a deeply shuddering breath.

Peter's breath sounded quicker and more urgent than normal, as if it were pressing against something bigger than him.

There didn't seem any words that could add anything to the intensity of the moment.

'Evie! Evie – where are you?' From somewhere deep within The Grange Tom's voice broke across their reverie. It sounded very mundane.

In an instant the erotic charge of the moment that Evie and Peter had shared had cast into a million miniature fragments.

Evie's whole body felt spent, as if she'd been taken to the edge of a precipice and had plunged over it into an unknown but vital void.

Peter shrank back into the darkness from whence he'd come, just as Tom opened the front door to The Grange and stepped out to join her. Certainly Evie couldn't see any sign of Peter in the dim light that momentarily shafted across the step.

'I'd better take you home,' Tom said in a voice that sounded so normal and ordinary that for an instant Evie thought she might weep.

As she tried to muster a smile for Tom with what felt like pulsating and swollen lips, she wondered if she looked any different to him from the Evie who had walked at his side into The Grange only a little while before.

Although what had just occurred couldn't be easily described – in fact, Evie didn't really understand it at all – she felt completely altered and transported, as if she had experienced true desire and then satisfaction for the very first time, but she didn't want Tom to be aware that she might be any different.

It felt too intimate and private a feeling for that, and she certainly didn't know him well enough to describe something that had felt so dangerously arousing of all of her senses and across her whole body. Indeed she was still aware of her hardened nipples touching the silk of her petty.

As Evie looked back at the recuperation hospital as she positioned herself in the front seat of Tom's car, she double-checked, and she wasn't surprised that she could see no sign of Peter.

It was as if he'd never been there at all. As if she had conjured him simply from her imagination.

There had felt something incredibly potent about the dark night and the sense of a tremendous otherness somewhere in the ether above them, and so maybe she had conjured Peter up just for that instant, thought Evie as she tried to make herself listen to what Tom was telling her about something or other to do with Timmy and Tricia's house.

She didn't know if she had, but if she could feel like this perhaps just using her imagination, then what might she be capable of experiencing while openly in the company of a man she trusted and loved? she wondered.

It was a desperately intoxicating thought and Evie could barely wait for Tom to deliver her back to Pemberley so that she could think about it further while cocooned alone in the sanctuary of her bedroom under the eaves.

On the Saturday morning Tom and Evie, and Timmy and Tricia (and Hettie too), squeezed into Tom's car for the trip to Plymouth.

This was after Evie had squashed herself into the pair of slacks she had made herself from Mr Worth's old trousers. She thought they were perhaps a little on the snug side to be flattering, and the waistband was definitely too tight, Evie had thought with a grimace as she had fought with the button. How can I be probably the only person in Lymbridge who's putting on weight during all this food rationing, Evie had wondered, and while I'm continually feeling peckish too, which should mean I'm not eating very much? But she'd not been able to wrangle the material another way to make the fit more generous, as she had donated a large part of one leg to something that Annabel had been making, and so in an adventurous moment she decided to wear the trousers anyway, just to be daring.

And when she caught Tom looking at her haunches in what she took to be an appreciative manner as she climbed into the car once they had manhandled Timmy's chair into the boot and had looped the boot door shut with a sturdy leather belt (with Tom saying that there must be a way of making a wheelchair that could fold economically for reasons of space, and he might have a think about how this could be done when he had a spare moment), Evie was rather glad she had worn the slacks.

Once they had parked the car in Plymouth, and Evie had persuaded Tricia to let her carry Hettie for a little, the perambulator having been too big for the boot in Tom's car with Timmy's chair having already bagged the space, they headed for the teahouse where they were to have a morning chicory coffee with Linda and Sam, who were bringing Sukie over to Plymouth with them. When they arrived, Sam was feeling chuffed as he had been able to drop off some livestock at a friend's farm, which he'd been meaning to do for a while, and Sukie was pleased too because, as she confided to Evie, she was missing Wesley and needed something to take her mind off him as it would be a couple of weeks until he was down again.

Evie didn't say anything, but although Hettie wasn't a particularly big baby, she was a surprisingly weighty thing to carry far, and so she was relieved to deposit her back into Tricia's arms once Tricia was sitting down. Tricia smiled at Evie to indicate she knew how heavy Hettie was and that it was nice to have had someone else carry her for a while.

Linda was a little green around the gills after the journey, though, and so Evie told her cheerfully that Susan had always claimed to her that a lot of morning sickness showed how fighting fit the baby growing inside was, and Linda's queasiness was therefore likely to be a good thing rather than a bad one. Evie thought she wouldn't mention just for the moment how heavy Hettie had felt; Linda looked as if she needed to find nice things to think about regarding her and Sam's coming little one, and so how a small baby could still feel incredibly hefty probably wasn't quite going to fit this bill.

In any case Linda looked back at Evie with a disbelieving expression, as if to say that it was as may be with the morning sickness, but she felt grim all the same. And then before she could say anything Linda had to stand up abruptly in order to make a hasty dash to the lavatory.

While she was gone, Evie suggested to the others that at the talk they should ensure that they sat as near as they could to the door and had already pointed out where the lavatories were to Linda and the quickest route for her to take if she were caught short. And that they should make sure too that Linda had the seat at the end of the row so that any more unscheduled dashes wouldn't be too obvious to everyone else if they occurred slap bang in the middle of the talk.

Timmy and Tricia told everyone they now had a date for Hettie's christening, several Sundays away; they'd put it back a little from when they had first wanted it to be just in case a snowy snap came in.

Evie and Sukie then had the inevitable discussion about what they would wear to the christening, the consensus being that if they could find some material they might just have time to make new outfits for the occasion, or at least to gussy up some old garments so that they would feel like new ones.

Once they were at the venue for the Spitfire fundraising talk, Tom seemed to know quite a lot of people who were there, which surprised Evie a little, as she always assumed that *she* was the person with the largest number of acquaintances at any gathering. In fact, her wide circle of people whom she knew was something she'd always prided herself on, but now it looked as if Tom was stealing her thunder as he nodded hellos towards members of the aircrew, the local council bigwigs and so forth who were present.

Tom had the good manners, though, to ask Evie if it would be all right if he just went to say hello to the odd audience member or two. She waved him away with what she hoped was a gracious smile, although her cheeks felt just a little stiff and unresponsive.

As far as Evie could tell, it looked like the great and the good in Plymouth had made a real effort to attend, and the room was fast filling up, which had to be very good news indeed for the coffers of the Spitfire fund.

Tom's popularity was especially irksome, Evie contemplated as she settled herself into her own seat, when it was taken into consideration too that it was Evie's headmistress Mrs Smith who was going to be the opener to the series of talks, and what she was going to talk about would be based around Evie's stomping ground of Lymbridge Primary School. In Evie's opinion it was to be expected therefore that she herself should know the larger proportion of the people who would turn out in support of Timmy's mother, although this didn't look at all to be the case.

Sukie laughed at Evie's slightly miffed look, and Evie had to smile back as she knew Sukie had rumbled her. Tom was 'very nice', in Sukie's expert opinion, she reminded Evie; and this wide acquaintance of his just went to prove that Evie didn't know as much, in quite a lot of ways, as she thought she did.

'I know!' said Evie, in a manner that could have meant she was agreeing with either of Sukie's assertions, and then in a different tone and after a pause, she went on in a somewhat deflated way, 'I'm not sure Tom is the one for me, though, Sukes.'

'Seriously, Evie-Rose, give the poor man a chance, as well as a little more time,' Sukie told her in a wise and yet quite firm manner that made Evie listen to her with all seriousness. 'It's easy to let something wonderful go for a whole host of silly reasons, and I've done that in the past and it's not done me any good. Which means that now I've met Wesley, I'm reluctant to let him slip away from me too easily as he does seem special to me. With Tom, it's as obvious as the nose on your face that he likes you very much indeed; and I think you like him too, at least a little. So think about taking my advice, and don't you write him off too easily without thinking it through, simply because he's not Peter. It could, after all, even turn out that he's better for you than Peter is.'

Evie knew Sukie was talking sound sense, and so she promised that she would think as kindly as she could of Tom.

It was a slightly sobering thought, Evie realised, that if she and Tom were to start walking out in the official sense, then she might have already had her very last experience of being alone with Peter.

While Peter and she had insisted (several times at least) that they 'could never be' as a couple, Evie still found the thought of things not altering between them to be too jarring to countenance.

But before she could ruminate further on this, Mr Rogers stood up on the dais at the front of the hall in order to introduce Mrs Smith as the speaker for the morning, and to talk a little bit about the Spitfire fund and how actively the *Western Morning News* was behind the fundraising campaign.

Suddenly Evie noticed Sukie stiffen as Mr Rogers fiddled with her lectern. Then her friend turned towards Evie with dramatically widened eyes.

Evie tipped her head back a little in order that she could look over her shoulder to see what had ruffled Sukie's feathers.

It was Fiona!

She was taking a seat at the rear of the room and was accompanied by a smartly dressed woman

251

who looked just like her, although a Fiona who was perhaps twenty-five years into the future. Evie supposed that Fiona's mother had asked her daughter to accompany her to the talk.

This was a surprise, and not an especially welcome one.

Tricia had spied Fiona too. 'Evie, look at what t' cat's dragged in,' she said none too quietly, making Timmy then look sharply in Fiona's direction, and Tom also, even though he was caught midway through taking off his warm jacket, although to judge by the questioning cast to his face clearly he had no idea who Fiona was.

In fact, Evie wasn't really sure what Tom did know of her romantic background. She hadn't mentioned anything to him – their night out and the short sojourn to The Grange hadn't brought them yet to that confessional sort of conversation. But of course Tom had spent time with Timmy, who may well have told him about his and Evie's broken engagement, and possibly Timmy would have gone on then to mention Peter and Fiona.

Evie felt wrong-footed all the way around, and she frowned sternly at Tricia to make sure that she didn't say anything else. Evie also gave a hard look in Timmy's direction, just to give his reins a half-halt too.

Oh, for Pete's sake, and for crying out loud, what a damn nuisance!

'We only need Peter to turn up now to make it *really* awkward,' Sukie whispered in Evie's ear.

'Don't, Sukie. Don't!' Evie muttered back, just as Timmy shot her the sort of maddening look that let Evie know that he was thinking exactly the same thing.

Luckily Mrs Smith started speaking then, with her plummy voice booming across the audience, and so nobody in their row dared to peer back over their shoulders at Fiona again. And Peter had the good grace to be otherwise engaged that morning.

After about forty-five minutes the talk ended and then there were questions, and following that Mr Rogers stood up to say that tea was going to be served and so nobody must feel in a rush to hurry off.

Evie had paid virtually no attention to what Mrs Smith was saying, although she was dimly aware that a lot of people around had laughed at various times and so she assumed the talk was going down well. As Mrs Smith had begun speaking, very quickly Evie had concluded that she had heard many of these stories already, and so she had pasted an attentive look on her face, but behind that she allowed herself to give in to her intruding thoughts in an effort to decide what she should do about Fiona.

After a while Evie thought of something that felt thrillingly audacious, and she wondered whether she could dare to see it through. Evie realised she must have moved or sighed as she noticed then that Sukie was looking at her with an inquisitive half-closed eye, and so Evie had to shake her head at her friend.

It was a thought that actually had been provoked by an innocent comment that Tom had made when they were driving back from Oldwell Abbott after the cinema at the start of the week, when they were deep in discussion about *Casablanca* and the whys and wherefores of how Rick had seemed happy to allow some Nazi officers into his club.

'I suppose he was following the Machiavellian edict of "keep your friends close and your enemies closer",' Tom had commented casually, causing Evie to frown in concentration as she started to think this concept through as she'd not heard this saying before (and actually nor had she heard of Machiavelli, and so she had had to look him up in Mr Worth's large encyclopaedia when she got back to Pemberley). But she had understood the gist of what Tom was driving at, although at first it felt very much an alien concept to her.

Previously Evie had always thought it clearly black or white as to how one might deal with both friends and enemies, but with Tom's few words he had lit the way to a suggestion that managed to be more complex and less obvious, although perhaps ultimately to be a more successful possibility.

Just as vice-admirals and generals might plan an offensive, Evie wondered in the days following if it might be possible to use a fighting strategy to apply to a problem she faced in ordinary life. It certainly was an idea worthy of further consideration, she decided.

As Mrs Smith wrapped up her answer to the final question, Evie replayed once more in her mind the conversation she and Tom had had in the car, and what the implications might mean as far as she was concerned to do with keeping her own enemies close.

The result of these ruminations was that the moment the clapping of thanks to Mrs Smith and chair Mr Rogers had drifted to the hum of people starting to gather their possessions, and they could all stand up, Evie leant over to whisper in Tom's ear that she would be back in a minute as there was somebody she simply must speak to, but it wouldn't take her long at all and she'd be back before he knew it.

Without so much as a look or a word in Sukie's direction, in case her friend countenanced a different course of action, Evie brushed closely past Tom, causing him to take a step back, and then also Sam, who was in the seat next to Tom (Linda having made another dash to the lavatory).

With a defiant straightening of her shoulders, Evie marched straight up to Fiona and Fiona's mother, who looked to be discussing whether or not they would go to the café at Spooner's for lunch, with Fiona so deliberately not looking in the direction of Evie or her friends with such a stance of determination that Evie was convinced that Fiona was really acutely aware of where each and every one of them was standing or sitting.

'Good morning, Miss Buckley, and Mrs Buckley,' said Evie to Fiona and her mother in what she tried to make a reasonably friendly voice. She could feel Sukie's eyes boring into her back as she stood there with the Buckleys, as were Timmy and Tricia's too. 'How refreshing to see so many people out in support on such a sharply cold morning. The Spitfire fund needs all the help we can give it, though, don't you agree?' Evie went on in what now felt to be a slightly dogged fashion.

Fiona looked nothing so much as terrified at what Evie might be about to say in case it was

255

anything to do with her scandalous kicking over of the traces in the village hall, and Evie couldn't help but think that poor Fiona appeared rather as if she were a rabbit caught in the pre-war full-on headlights of a motor car.

Up close meanwhile Fiona's mother appeared to be rather snooty, but at least she was looking towards Evie and not in the direction of her petrified daughter. Evie could see from where Fiona had inherited her sometimes supercilious attitude.

She turned towards the older woman, but before Evie could say anything to Mrs Buckley, Fiona took a small step forward that Evie thought was designed to slow Evie down a bit.

'Mummy, allow me, please, to introduce you to Miss Evie Yeo – she is, er, er, Miss Yeo is a primary schoolteacher over at Lymbridge, a village out on the moor,' Fiona said quickly and with an anxious chirrup that cut into her normally petulantly strident voice.

Evie nodded politely to Mrs Buckley, and asked if she had enjoyed the talk. Not much of an answer was forthcoming – and possibly this was because Mrs Buckley appeared to be intent at staring at Evie down the length of her thin and rather lengthy nose, her gaze transfixed on Evie's trousers – and so Evie thought it safe to assume that the answer was no.

Evie turned to Fiona, and said, 'Miss Buckley, or Fiona if I may, I was wondering if you might care to meet me in Plymouth one Saturday, and perhaps we could go for coffee? I don't feel we know each other well enough, but perhaps it might

256

be pleasant for us get acquainted with each other a little better; and a coffee together, or tea if you would prefer, one afternoon, could go some way to rectifying that situation.'

Fiona's mother looked as if the slacks-wearing Evie was categorically rather a long way away from the sort of young woman that she hoped her daughter would associate with, but with eyes pleading that if she were to agree then would Evie please leave them pronto to rejoin her friends, an obviously thunderstruck Fiona managed to squeeze out a strangled, 'What a nice idea, Miss Yeo, er ... Evie. Do let me ring you to arrange an appointment when I have my diary to hand.'

Evie nodded, and said that the telephone number for Pemberley was listed under Worth and that she was looking forward to hearing from Fiona, and then after a perfunctory 'goodbye' and with a turn on her heel, she promptly made herself scarce.

She thought Fiona might have agreed to meet her purely in an effort to end the conversation in front of her mother as quickly as possible.

But even if that had indeed been the case, Evie hoped that Fiona would telephone her all the same, and that they would go on to meet up.

It might help clear the air between them (quite in what way Evie didn't care to delve into too deeply, although she had had the tiniest day-dream that maybe Fiona would say she was going to return to Hertfordshire and try to put the doomed relationship with Peter behind her), but Evie thought that whatever the outcome was, it was very unlikely to make a bad situation worse.

And Evie certainly didn't want to live the rest of her life out in abject dread of the unexpected arrival of Fiona at any public event, and so to face this fear head-on may well reduce its power from being so discombobulating as far as she was concerned.

As she headed back to where she had been sitting Evie discovered that Timmy, Tricia and Sukie were still staring at her intently while all trying to pretend that they weren't really doing so, clearly eager to find out what she and Fiona had said to each other.

Tom was looking at Evie too, although without the intensity of her old friends, but she could see that he was very curious as to who Fiona might be as he had obviously picked up on the charged response of the others and so had worked out for himself that Fiona must be somebody of significance or consequence. Evie had noticed that Tom had flicked his eyes curiously in the direction of the Buckleys more than once.

With a slightly teasing toss of her head in their direction, Evie strode right by her friend without a word. She'd had enough of her morning commandeered by thoughts of Fiona, and so now she was going to collect Pattie, who was standing across the room with her beau, John (who worked with Barkeep Joss at The Haywain), and also Mr Rogers, so that Tom could be introduced to all and sundry.

Evie's brother James was standing with Pattie and John too, although lurking behind them in a way that meant that Evie hadn't realised he was there. She noticed that he kept glancing over towards Jane Cornish, who was several rows back where she had been sitting alongside the Worths.

'Out of your league, Jamie boy,' intoned Evie into her little brother's ear in passing, 'she's twenty-seven, and she would have you for breakfast.'

'I should be so lucky,' said James, but very quietly as he didn't want Robert to catch him making a risqué comment in public. Susan was working in the village shop that morning, and Evie knew that James would never have dared to mutter what he had just said to her if Susan had been in the same room as he. Susan was renowned in the Yeo household for having the hearing of an owl, a bird which could pick up the sound of a mouse moving from hundreds of feet high in the sky above.

Although she didn't want to encourage her little brother to be coarse, Evie found herself smiling along with James. And then she noticed that Tom had followed her across the hall, and so she made James and then Pattie say hello to him.

Later Tom drove Evie, and Timmy, Tricia and Hettie, on a circuitous route home so that they could enjoy the Dartmoor scenery. There was a lot of laughter and joking, and when Evie got back to Pemberley after Timmy and then Tricia and Hettie had been dropped off, she realised that despite the unexpected presence of Fiona, it had been a most pleasant way of spending a Saturday. Tom obviously had a natural way with people, she thought as she shook his hand goodbye, and Evie decided that this was a quality with which she could be impressed.

Chapter Thirteen

The next few weeks passed in a flurry of activity for Evie.

Sukie, Linda, Pattie and Julia pooled bits of this and that, and so Evie, with the help of Annabel Frome, was able to rustle up a spiffing dress to wear for Hettie's christening. Handily Jane Cornish had the same-sized feet as Evie, even though Evie was rather taller, and so Evie was able to borrow a pair of very fashionable shoes Jane had bought in London just before relocating to the West Country.

Evie also decided to go ahead definitely with the inter-school maypole dancing competition, which hopefully would take place on the first day of May, or a day or two either side of that, depending on what else was going to be happening locally.

Of course, the maypole dancing competition turned out to be a lot more extra work than Evie had expected – wasn't it always? – as in order to get other local schools involved too, she had to write notes for a story to publicise it in the *Western Morning News.* Mr Rogers took Evie's notes with him into work one day for one of the journalists to work up into copy for the paper, to be published alongside a truly hilarious photograph that he had snapped of Evie, Pattie, Julia, Annabel, Jane, Tricia and, of course, Sukie and Linda all practising maypole moves with pieces of string attached to an old broom handle held aloft by a long-suffering Mr Worth in the sitting room at Pemberley, with Mrs Worth also in the picture as she was reading to them the moves from a book of maypole dance instructions, and with the furniture pushed back to the edge of the room.

Mr Rogers had actually delivered a selection of photographs to the paper but in the one they decided to publish, Evie had an expression of abject terror on her face, Sukie looked as if she wanted to murder somebody (most probably Evie, claimed Linda, once she'd stopped laughing when she saw the picture), while poor Julia came off the worst of them all, as she had been caught in a pose with her eyes shut and looking for all the world as if her knees were buckling under her and she were in the process of fainting.

At the end of their one and only practice session the conclusion of the adult dancers in the photograph had been that maypole dancing was much more difficult to master than it looked. And if Evie could get her schoolchildren dancing 'The Gypsies' Tent' – an open plait of ribbons from the top of the maypole forming the tent bursting out from the pole as the dancers dipped and weaved, with the tent being then equally seamlessly unravelled as the dancers continued to prance back on their steps of weaving – as she intended, with no awful slip-ups, then Evie would deserve a medal, had been the general inference.

Evie had worked out a very simple plaiting dance for the younger children, but ignoring her friends' ribald comments to the contrary, she remained determined the older ones would do 'The

Gypsies' Tent' perfectly, and so she was making them practise hard, sometimes to stifled guffaws from Leonard Bassett and Mrs Smith when it went spectacularly wrong. Which it did quite often, unfortunately, although luckily nobody got strangled by tangled pieces of string.

The biggest problem, thought Evie, was not so much that the schoolchildren were without the necessary skill or experience in what was undeniably a tricky dance to perform, although that was without doubt the case, but that they lacked the ribbons for what was required, as none of the shops in Oldwell Abbott or Plymouth had what she needed. Pieces of string just weren't quite cutting the mustard as replacement ribbons and so it wasn't the dancers' faults when it went wrong, Evie would snap back when she heard her colleagues chortle or when her dancers were staring at her with perplexity. She had to stare stonily at Joseph for a moment or two when she heard him grunting, 'A bad workman blames his tools.'

Then Tricia told Evie that Timmy had had a brainwave – Evie should speak to the commander of the airstrip as perhaps there were some torn parachutes that she could have to cut up in order to have real silk ribbons.

There were indeed some camouflage-green parachutes with salvageable sections to them that were ideal to piece together for what Evie needed, and so she told herself that although khaki wasn't really the right colour, being more utilitarian than the sugar-almond colours she would have preferred for the ribbons as a celebration of spring, it would remind everyone of the war and the need to raise money for the Spitfire.

And so Mr Rogers was able to take a second picture, this time of the very pretty Jane Cornish demurely cutting the silk that would be hemmed and joined into ribbons that, once Evie had selected the best ribbons for her own dancers – there had to be some perks surely? – other schools wanting to enter Evie's competition could be allocated.

A few days after the *Western Morning News* ran this second story Susan confided to Evie that James had cut the picture of Jane out of the paper, and pasted it onto the wall beside his bed. Evie didn't think she'd share that with Jane.

Another thing that happened was that hundreds of soldiers, and RAF and Navy recruits, were ferried with a fair amount of hullaballoo into the area to be billeted in all the new huts that had been put up, and the moors became awash with the sight and sounds of men practising various manoeuvres and fighting tactics, and Evie had to take extra care walking her infants between the primary school and the village hall as the amount of traffic in the village had increased exponentially with the influx of recruits.

Despite a vicious snowy front that swept across the moorland, making the impressive tors seem a forbidding black, for several weekends a scarved and gloved trio of James, Frank and Joseph became avid fans of a rickety climbing frame that had been erected on the edge of the airfield, as this had various levels of platforms for the servicemen to practise leaping from and then landing safely in order to prepare them for parachuting from aeroplanes flying over France, Holland or Germany, and so the three lads would cycle to the airstrip and spend hours watching the men jump.

Timmy told Evie when she visited him that the doctors at the recuperation hospital were having to do quite a lot of patching up of sore shins, deep bruising and the occasional broken bone from the men who were using this contraption.

Pattie mentioned then to Evie that John had heard during his serving stints at The Haywain that some of the recent recruits to the area were townies who were very unused to the unfamiliar sounds of the moor. One bright spark had turned the lighting in his Nissen hut low, and had proceeded to read out loud over several evenings instalments of *The Hound of the Baskervilles,* which had a large part of the story set in the West Country, to a hut crammed with men billeted from across the campsite, after which quite a lot of the men had apparently been very disturbed by odd screaming noises coming at strange and unpredictable hours from the heart of Lymbridge village.

The sisters wondered what on earth it was that was alarming those new to the area so.

Then Evie and Pattie had to hold their sides as they laughed so much their tummies hurt when they realised these noises must be the peculiar bellows that the goats Elizabeth and Margaret were prone to making when they were hungry or bored, both of which they were quite a lot of the time, to the point where the village locals barely noticed the racket they made any longer.

Evie found that the fact the town lads hadn't

been able to recognise the noise that goats made really touched her tickle bone. She could see why this had happened, though, as goats were very vocal and if one were upset by something it was almost inevitable that the other one would be set off too, until they were both making a right old din, which could, if one thought about it for long enough, sound very much like a human scream-ing.

She wondered if there was something here that might make a good picture story for Mr Rogers, and he agreed.

In the end Mr Rogers made a few calls, the result of which was a school outing one morning as Mr Cawes, helped by Evie, Mrs Smith and Leonard Bassett, and all of the warmly dressed pupils at the school, walked Margaret and Elizabeth over to where the servicemen were billeted so that the goats could be photographed in front of a group of recruits in uniform standing in front of their huts.

When they got there, Mr Cawes was asked by the site's commander if the goats could be tempor-ary mascots for the men, and Mr Cawes mumbled back that such an honour would make him proud, Evie noting that there was a teary gleam in the old man's eye as he nodded his agreement.

In a trice little banners were placed on each of the goats' backs, in order for Mr Smith to take another photograph. And then he took a photo-graph with all the school pupils and their teachers standing with Mr Cawes and the goats wearing their banners, Mrs Smith and Evie caught right at the moment they were sharing a humorous com-ment about the peckish cast to the goats' faces at the sight of these banners, which after their chomping of the tea towels and Mrs Cawes' bloomers probably looked to them like another tempting snack just waiting for them to nibble.

Mr Cawes was asked if he could get Elizabeth and Margaret to make their goaty noise, but despite his and Evie's best efforts the goats remained resolutely closed-mouthed and silent. This was a first, and Evie said they must be starstruck as she had never heard them so quiet before, at which point Elizabeth screamed loudly right in Evie's ear just to show Evie what a dimwit she was. And when the recruits laughed Margaret gave a corresponding guffaw, much to the amusement of recruits and pupils alike.

The recruits took the pupils into one of the huts and they showed the children how they made up their beds each morning with the neatly tucked corners in the blankets, and sheets pulled tightly just so, and how they looked after their kit. The older boys asked if they could hold some weapons, ideally guns although bayonets would do, but Leonard Bassett stepped in quickly at that point to say pupils holding weapons wasn't appropriate, but what was, in his opinion, was that he had heard that the recruits were very keen on seeing how quickly the pupils of Lymbridge Primary School could complete part of the assault course that had just been constructed. Leonard added that after they had attempted the assault, with one of the recruits timing them against each other with a stopwatch, the pupils had been invited to have some lunch sitting alongside the men. And the children would be sharing the very same meat stew from little square metal tubs, using a spoon, as the soldiers would be too from their own containers. Thus a sticky moment over the weaponry was neatly swerved by Leonard.

By the time Elizabeth and Margaret were back in their pen, and the children were sitting once more in their classrooms, everybody was tired and muddy. It had been an outing unlike any other the school had been on, and the pupils and teachers had enjoyed themselves, as had the goats who definitely jogged along with something of a swagger as they were led home. Evie hoped though that the pupils' parents wouldn't be too peeved about how dirty and dishevelled many of them had got, or too cross their packed lunches hadn't been eaten.

She had been persuaded to swing from a rope across a dry ditch, and so had Mrs Smith – they hadn't been brave and they hadn't been elegant, but they had indeed lurched their way from one low platform over to another. Evie thought she would remember that for quite some time to come, and she was rather sorry that Timmy hadn't been there to see his mother bowl through the air, with Joseph's cheeky comment of 'Watch out everyone; here comes Tarzan!' making everyone laugh.

Evie had promised one of the sergeants that if he or the commander could choose fifty of the men billeted who would be free on Sunday afternoon, then she and her sisters would give them high tea in the church hall. She added that she'd love to be able to provide tea for all the men on the new site, but she simply wouldn't be able to scavenge the provisions for the number required. The sergeant replied that he perfectly understood the situation and that sure enough Evie would have fifty men at the village hall at precisely three o'clock on the Sunday.

Over the next couple of days Mrs Smith took it upon herself to rustle up donations of food for the recruits' tea party, and she and Tricia went to the hall on the Sunday morning just before lunch to get it ready and to light the heater, as well as leave the food they'd gathered ready for Evie and Julia and Pattie to make into sandwiches and so forth.

When the three Yeo sisters arrived not long after Mrs Smith and Tricia had departed it was to find the village hall door swinging open, and that a wild Dartmoor pony stallion had wandered in. He was now happily standing in the hall's small kitchen as he inspected the reconstituted egg that had been made up in a large mushroom-coloured pottery mixing bowl ready to be made into sandwiches, snaffling down as much as he could get his chops around.

Evie tried to shoo him from the kitchen, but the little beggar closed his eyes and pushed his nose firmly in the bowl to take a mouthful, his only response being to raise his tail and deposit a large pile of dung on the floor.

'Well done, Evie,' teased Pattie, 'that worked brilliantly.' Julia tried flapping a tea towel at him, but he didn't even angle an ear in her direction.

'I'm sure I'll get kicked,' said Evie, 'but I'm going to have to go into the kitchen with him.'

Julia warned her to be careful, not that Evie really needed this saying to her.

The Spitfire fundraising talk the previous day had been the one on first aid, and nobody wanted just yet to have to put into practice what they had been taught, as some of the injuries that had been talked about had sounded most unappetising.

What had been most revelatory about the talk had been unexpected, though, as the doctor had talked openly about venereal disease, which he shortened to calling V.D., and its symptoms and treatments. Evie had never heard of such a thing as V.D., and although she couldn't prevent herself squirming with embarrassment a little, she had been intrigued by what the doctor was saying.

However, apparently the *Western Morning News* had received during the afternoon a flurry of complaints about the explicit and unexpected material that the lecture had contained.

It had actually only constituted a small part of the talk as the bulk of it was to do with stopping bleeding and what to do in the event of injuries that were typical for civilians in bombed-out properties.

But as they had been making their way to the hall to prepare the Sunday afternoon tea as arranged, Evie and her sisters agreed it was a good thing that the doctor had been so daring as to mention VD., as ignorance would obviously provide no protection at all against something that was evidently very nasty. It was obvious that some people were feeling liberated enough by the shifting times of war to dare to have more than one sexual partner, whether they were married or

269

not, and so one couldn't pretend that venereal disease was something for other parts of Britain but not Dartmoor.

With another look at the stallion Evie tried not to think of injuries a moorland pony could inflict with a well-placed kick or bite as she gently talked to him and then eased past, attempting to move steadily so as not to spook him, but also trying to make sure that she moved around him in a confident enough manner so that he would be less likely to turn aggressively towards her.

Rather to Evie's surprise the small stallion let her put her arms around his neck and gently manhandle him backwards out of the kitchen, and then amazingly, as he really was unnaturally placid for a wild pony who wouldn't be used to being handled, he allowed Evie to guide him all the way across the hall and at last out of the door.

Once standing in the area outside the door to the village hall, the cheeky chappie turned to stand looking imploringly at Evie, his hairy brown ears pricked so far forward that their delicate black tips were almost touching. He'd obviously enjoyed his impromptu snack.

But Evie hardened her heart against his pretty face, bushy mane and woolly coat that was making him look like a cuddly teddy bear, and she retreated back inside and firmly closed the door on him. A deep whicker from the pony told her what a mistake she was making.

She went back to the kitchen to find that actually the pony hadn't eaten too much of the egg, although he had left rather a generous portion of grass shavings nestled amongst the egg mixture that he must have had already in his mouth when he came into the kitchen. Evie and her sisters picked out what they could, and then made the sandwiches up anyway even though they couldn't remove every piece of grass or provide replacement egg as it wouldn't be long before the men would be arriving and in any case they didn't have any more egg they could make up.

As Pattie put a Vera Lynn record on the gramophone that Robert had driven over earlier, Evie discovered it was her job to pick the pony's dung up, and to give that bit of the floor a perfunctory rinse with a mop. She had only just finished and given her hands a quick wash when they heard the sound of soldiers marching to signal the arrival of their guests.

Later, one of the men asked Julia what herb was it that they had put in the egg sandwiches as they were delicious.

'Cress,' chipped in Julia in a cheery voice without missing a beat.

Evie and Pattie caught each other's eye, but they didn't allow themselves to smile. This was harder to do when they then noticed the stallion watching them all through one of the windows, looking for all the world as he angled his head this way and that, and pricked his ears even more intently, as if he was checking to see if there was going to be just a smidgen of eggy mixture left for him.

Pattie selected the smallest sandwich that was left and pressed it into Evie's hand with a 'For your new boyfriend', and so Evie went outside to give it to the little stallion, after which the pony seemed quite content to wander off back to his mares and his foals (who would be yearlings soon), who she could spy gathered waiting for him on the edge of the moorland.

The other thing that was keeping Evie busy was that Jane Cornish was teaching her to drive. Evie and Tom had fallen into the pattern of seeing each other one or twice a week, but although Tom seemed keenish on her in the romantic sense, on the one and only time when he weakened and allowed Evie to have a go behind the wheel in the driving seat of his car, he had only lasted about ten minutes before he said that perhaps it was time for him to take over the driving again.

Jane was much more patient and generous.

Unfortunately it was soon clear to all that Evie was a simply dreadful driver, and that she absolutely couldn't get the hang of double declutching or the theory of which gear should be used and when.

Robert watched her rackety progress through the village one day, and told her later that if she could stay in first gear and make sure she never had to do a hill start, then she'd probably be fine after about a year or so of daily practice. Evie tried to summon up a look that would take the wind out of her father's sails, but she failed abysmally as Jane had told her pretty much the same thing only an hour or two earlier following a near miss with Peter when he was driving through Lymbridge in the opposite direction.

Evie decided she didn't want to test her new friendship with Jane too much, and so maybe it was sensible therefore if she let the driving lessons lapse for a while. Maybe when the sunny weather came as spring gave way to summer in a few months, a miracle would happen and Evie would mysteriously transform herself into an able driver.

A more serious bout of snowy weather announced itself with an arctic blast, making the previous snow seem nothing more than a mere flurry, and so this put paid to driving or school outings in any case.

But Pattie reported John saying that The Haywain was doing a roaring business each evening as the recruits billeted in the huts had realised the public house was the warmest place for miles around, with the enticement of the roaring fire that Barkeep Joss would light in the grate each evening, and so the ladies' bar was now suspended, meaning that unaccompanied men could drink for the first time on either side of the horseshoe-shaped bar.

Evie got her hopes up when Mr Smith telephoned her at Pemberley one evening to speak to her about Robert and Susan's financial problems as regards Mrs Coyne's shop, but sadly his call was only to deliver the miserable news that he had had a word with several of his friends in the know of banking procedures, and tragically it didn't look as if Susan and Robert would be able to borrow the money needed for the shop and garage, and that was even if they used their equity in Bluebells as surety for the debt. The banks deemed them and the idea of expanding the business in such a remote hillside village during the straightened times forced on everybody because of the war to be too

273

great a financial risk.

Mr Smith went on to say that ordinarily he'd have been happy to buy into the venture himself, thus helping out Evie's parents at the same time as giving himself a new business opportunity, but his spare cash was being channelled into the building of Timmy and Tricia's new house and so unfortunately he was unable to step in.

Evie told Mr Smith that she hadn't expected that and of course he wasn't to give it another thought.

She felt downhearted, though, and after she had hung up the phone she was honest enough to admit to herself that she had been quietly hoping that Mr Smith would indeed ride to the rescue. She had got used to him sorting things out at her every whim, and so she had secretly rather hoped that this latest request on her part would be another example of this.

Later on at the sewing circle Evie intimated as much to Julia, who told Evie that at least she had tried, and while it was a pity, some things just weren't meant to be.

Evie had another telephone call. It was from Fiona, who spoke with an abrupt efficiency, and the result was that they arranged to go for coffee after the next of the fundraising talks, which was Linda's.

The talk went well. There was something very likeable about Linda, and it helped hugely that she knew her subject inside out. She had made the long-suffering Sam lug a lot of her equipment into the hall so that she could illustrate what she said with a practical demonstration of her various farrier's tools.

What worked particularly well were some large drawings Linda had done of the underside of the hooves of the various animals, that were passed around so that the audience could see the difference between, say, a sheep's foot and a cow's. Linda also brought with her a selection of horseshoes, from the tiniest Shetland pony shoes, up to a hunter's, and then a gasp went up when she revealed the gigantic size of a shoe that she had taken off one of Hector front legs – it was massive, easily as big as a generous-sized dinner plate – and there were several gasps from the audience when Linda described how a glancing blow when dear gentle giant Hector had panicked when the German aeroplane had strafed him and his partner Mabel had resulted in her hospital stay.

Linda proved to be a real natural on the stage, and Evie felt incredibly proud of her friend as this was the very first time that Linda had ever attempted any sort of public speaking. Evie was gratified too to note that this was the best-attended talk so far, and she wondered if it might be because Linda was that rare beast – a woman competing on equal terms in a man's world.

Evie knew that Linda was still suffering from morning sickness, and so on Susan's advice, she had prepared the evening before some ginger biscuits that she had made Linda eat twenty minutes or so before the talk began, as Susan promised that ginger was very good at easing nausea.

Linda started off her talk by saying she was in the family way, with a coy smile and nod in the pink-faced Sam's direction, and so if she had to make a dash for it, that was the reason, and if that happened would everyone please remain seated as she would soon be back, to which everyone in the audience laughed. Her tummy was now quite large, and so Evie thought people would have guessed in any case she was pregnant, but she supposed it wouldn't do any harm just to be clear on the matter. Luckily the biscuits did their stuff and Linda was able to talk for nearly an hour without a single undignified exit.

Tom didn't accompany Evie to the talk this time, as he wanted to catch up on some work, and Evie was quite relieved about this as she was going to see Fiona, who wasn't at the talk either, right afterwards in a café nearby, and this neatly avoided Evie having to tell Tom who Fiona was.

When the two women first sat down together, it was all terribly awkward between them, so much so in fact that Evie really regretted coming up with the idea. The conversation was unbearably stilted, with neither of them able to give answers to any questions the other had asked that were anything much more than monosyllabic.

Fiona lit a cigarette, and offered one to Evie, who was so tense and uncomfortable that she very nearly took it, just so that she would have something to do with her hands, although she wasn't quite tense enough not to wonder if the smoke from Fiona's cigarette would make the expensive kid leather gloves Fiona was still wearing smell unpleasantly like an ashtray.

After about ten minutes of this torture Evie looked across the small round table at Fiona, and said, 'This isn't going very well, is it, Fiona? I do apologise, most sincerely. It seemed a good idea at the time, but now we are both here I really don't know what to say.'

Fiona gave a terse nod of agreement, and Evie felt a little of the tension between them dissipate.

They sat in silence for a short while, each looking at the cup and saucer in front of them. Evie began to swivel her cup slowly around in its saucer, and then she took a sip.

'Fiona, why has somebody like Peter made such fools of each of us?' Evie broke the hush. 'He's not much to look at, and he's pathetic at dealing with either of us at the moment.'

'He's ... he's...' managed Fiona.

Uncertain of whether Fiona had been going to slate or admire Peter, Evie thought she would give credit where credit is due as it felt against her nature not to look for the positive attributes in someone, and so she went on, 'Peter is very clever, I suppose, and reliable too, as long as one doesn't need that reliability in an emotional sense. And he can be fun as well.'

'Evie, I was fourteen when I met him, and I had had a most difficult and unhappy childhood. I had done some things of which I'm heartily ashamed of now – and the fact that Peter seemed to like me anyway, despite his stutter and his bad skin back then, gave me what felt like all those years ago a reason for living,' said Fiona in an oddly confiding tone, although she was speaking very quickly and she wouldn't look in the direction of her companion.

Evie thought Fiona might be alluding in some

way to the silvery slits on her wrists but she felt that she mustn't acknowledge in any way that she had seen these scars.

Fiona went on, 'Peter was the very first person who seemed to appreciate exactly the person I was, and who didn't seem to want to blame me for some bad behaviour or other. I think he made me a better person, or at least until I jilted him. And what a mistake that turned out to be – I realised very quickly that the man who had turned my head so badly had very few of Peter's attributes and that he was only interested in me because my mother is rich. But in the meantime Peter had met you and I think you broke his heart.'

To hear Fiona say this out loud shook Evie badly; it was true, she knew, but it felt nothing short of an unnecessary and brutal assertion, and as if Fiona had plunged a dart right into the centre of Evie's mournful heart.

Fiona went on, 'And when Peter and I ran into each other by accident, coincidentally on the evening he arrived in London in July, it seemed you were to be married to Timmy Bowes and so perhaps it was destined after all that Peter and I should be together.'

Evie couldn't prevent her eyes filling. She looked at Fiona, who appeared sad, but dry-eyed. Evie hadn't expected it'd be herself who would cry.

'Of course,' Fiona continued in a defeated tone that also managed to convey to Evie a searing self-honesty, 'once Peter realised you weren't after all going to marry, it made him feel differently about me. I felt him slipping away, although he never said as much. And so I hated you, Evie, I really hated you, and I blamed you for taking him from me, when really it was this very attitude of mine that was pushing Peter back once again towards you. I see that now.'

Evie expelled air through her nose, and then she told Fiona that she had felt awful about the whole thing, and that she'd come close to disliking Fiona very much too.

'But I don't know,' said Evie as she tried to be as honest as she felt Fiona had just been with her, 'since that evening when you came to see me after school, I feel differently about you. I suppose I think that – to my shame – you, me and Peter are all victims in this, almost wholly because of me failing to make it clear to Peter when I met him that I was engaged but that Timmy had made Tricia pregnant. And I have to live with my error of judgement. I try to tell myself that it was because I was trying to protect Mrs Smith and Timmy and Tricia, and that they all needed to be sorted out first, but really that's an untruth. I didn't mention to Peter I was engaged when I met him because the truth of it was that at first I hardly noticed him and I didn't really talk to him at all. And then when I did, and I realised I had feelings for him, it seemed much too late at that point to tell him about Timmy – I was simply too much of a coward. I feel I behaved very badly, and that I should apologise to Peter. And by association to you.'

There was a silence. Fiona said then, 'My behaviour when I came to see you that evening in the village hall was nothing short of despicable. I don't know what got into me. I had a drink for

279

courage, and then another and ... well, you know the rest. Every night I lie in bed and shame washes over me. I can't remember anything from touching you on your shoulder, until I came to when Peter was driving me home and he had to stop the car so that I could vomit, although I assume that I wasn't very nice when I was with you. If it's any consolation to you, I know now that when anyone says my name to Peter, the memory of me being sick again and again is the one that will be foremost in his mind.'

Evie reached across the table and patted Fiona on the forearm, and said that Fiona should think better of Peter than that – he was the sort of person to make sure he filed that sort of unpleasant memory in the waste paper bin, she was sure.

Fiona clutched Evie's hand back, just for a moment, as they stared at each other.

Evie couldn't say they would ever be friends but as they looked at each other with an understanding that hovered between resignation and a shaky kindness, she thought they were both older and wiser than they had been only a few weeks ago, and that somehow they had dredged out of nowhere a tentative feeling of respect for each other's honesty, as well as a sliver of empathy for each other too.

On the way back to Lymbridge, Evie realised that before the coffee with Fiona she had assumed that the pair of them would put each other in their place as to Peter and his intentions towards either one of them, and that perhaps some angry words would be exchanged between them. Evie's motivation for asking Fiona to meet her had been to reduce the hulkingly large and angry Fiona of Evie's vivid imagination into a smaller and more containable Fiona; in short, to turn the other woman into a sort of satellite person to Evie's life about whom she wouldn't have to spend very much time thinking at all. Fiona had loomed too large and too long over Evie, she had felt for months.

But what had happened had turned out to be much more positive than Evie could possibly have anticipated. Both she and Fiona had each acknowledged their own shoddy past behaviour when it had proved to be sorely wanting. And then they had both done the other the courtesy of not shying away from facing unpleasant truths the other woman was saying, or condemning the other for falling short at certain times of what one would hope for.

It felt like a small victory for common sense and, Evie hoped deeply, it was an indication that both Evie and Fiona were leaving behind their silly and naive views on relationships and love in order to adopt a stance as they headed further into their twenties that felt kinder and less rigid. A stance that would, Evie trusted, allow them each to find a more adult and a more satisfying sense of happiness when either of them dared to think they were in love once more.

How peculiar it was, thought Evie, that the one person in the world she had the courage to strip herself totally bare before, in the emotional sense, was the very person in Evie's whole life who had once wanted to do her the most harm.

And although nothing concrete had really

changed between them – both of them probably wishing they could enjoy a proper relationship with Peter – Evie felt nevertheless comforted and enriched by having shared a cup of coffee with Fiona.

Whatever would Peter say about it all if he knew?

Evie had no idea, and she thought then that she didn't really care what he might think.

It was time she stopped filtering herself and her actions through the opinions of others. That was what young women did as they lived those difficult years that covered the period between being a child and becoming an adult.

Now, Evie felt it was time she embraced being a fully grown woman and stopped hankering back to a time when excuses for poor behaviour might be laid at somebody else's door.

She was Evie, and she was going to get things wrong at times, and she certainly wouldn't please everyone in whatever she did. But as long as she remained true to the ideals of kindness and honesty, and she always tried to treat others as she liked to be treated, then Evie decided that she would just make a pact with herself to always hold her head up high, and to stop worrying so much as to what everybody else was doing or what they might think of her.

It was a lot to mull over, but the fact that later during that afternoon a blizzard came in and marooned Lymbridge meant that Evie had few distractions to prevent her replaying in her mind the talk that she and Fiona had had again and again. It managed to be both a sobering and an enriching memory.

Chapter Fourteen

Little Hettie's christening had had to be post-
poned still further because of the snowy snap as
there were going to be some guests coming from
outside the village, and for a few days Lymbridge
was completely cut off, with all roads to it im-
passable without chains or without the deep tread
of tractor tyres. It also meant Evie had to miss two
of the Saturday Spitfire fundraising talks in Plymouth, which she felt sorry to have to do.

Mr Rogers was stranded down in Plymouth as
he had been there when the snow came down in
earnest. He was put up by the newspaper in the
city during this time in order that he could work,
and he told Evie by telephone that with each talk
for the Spitfire fundraising effort, the audience
swelled, and so there was going to be another
series of guest speakers over the summer, although
for these talks – as long as Evie had no objections,
which naturally she didn't – they would be organised by one of his colleagues working at the
Western Morning News.

Mr Rogers had been in touch with Mr Worth
and with Peter and Mr Smith meanwhile as apparently there were now a host of fundraising events
that were being co-ordinated across the whole of
the West Country, with the result that some people
were even starting to wonder whether by the time
1943 was rung in the whole £6,000 for the Spitfire

could have been raised. Evie was delighted; it might be bitterly cold outside, but she felt warmed through and through by the generosity of others.

Once Hettie's christening had been rearranged for a new date, and Tricia had triple-checked with Evie if it was all right if Peter was going to be there, seeing as how he and Timmy were now increasingly friendly which had (inevitably, Evie groaned quietly to herself) led to Timmy giving Peter an invitation despite the history that Peter and Evie had together, Evie realised that much as she loved Hettie she wasn't looking forward to the celebration very much, as for the first time that she could recall she didn't really want to see Peter.

What made matters worse was that Mrs Smith had asked Tom to come along to the christening too as a guest, and so Evie imagined that Tom would assume she and he were there as a couple. Evie wasn't quite sure what she felt about that scenario either, as for all their friends and acquaintances to see her and Tom together at an occasion that would also feature Timmy did, no matter how one might dress it up otherwise, seem to be pretty much some sort of public declaration, certainly as far as her parents would be concerned, Evie was certain.

Her parents rather liked Tom as far as she could tell, but Susan had tentatively cautioned Evie against rushing into anything, and so for Tom to be by her side during such a public afternoon would fly in the face of that advice. Evie could only give another little inward shrug of disappointment at the thought of this, but she didn't see how she could uninvite Tom or suggest to him that she really would prefer it if he had to be busy elsewhere that day.

And it wasn't as if she could duck out herself and avoid going, as she was going to take pride of place at the ceremony as one of Hettie's godparents. Annoying as it all was, a slightly battle-weary Evie accepted that she would just have to grin and bear whatever might happen.

Earlier in the week Timmy had instructed her (via Tricia) to grasp the nettle, and to have a word with Peter beforehand about Tom being there, as that was the most likely way of preventing any awkwardness, at least as far as the Peter situation was concerned. Timmy had offered to say something to him on Evie's behalf, but Tricia had absolutely forbade him, apparently, saying that with his ability to put his foot in his mouth, he'd only make a sensitive situation worse by saying something inappropriate. Tricia added that Timmy had asked her to say to Evie, 'Pev', and so she was passing the message along to Evie, although the puzzled kink to her full eyebrows revealed she didn't have the slightest idea of what Timmy meant. Evie told her the 'Pev' was just Timmy being silly and Tricia wasn't to pay it any mind.

It was the final Friday of the snowy snap, and as the heating fuel still hadn't been able to get through to the village Mrs Smith had decided that there would be no school that day as everyone had had enough of wearing coats and hats for hours on end in their classrooms. Instead the children were given tasks to do at home in lieu, and this work would be handed in to their teachers on the Monday.

Evie and Leonard Bassett said they rather doubted that would actually happen, but Mrs Smith said it probably didn't matter very much, although they weren't under any circumstances to tell the pupils this. In the tests that all the pupils had taken part in earlier in the week, the marks had been so strong – barring Bobby Ayres spelling of 'cat' as 'Keith', of course, although Evie thought he was merely being playful, rather than it being a genuine mistake – the children across the whole school had excelled themselves to the point where they were now ahead of where Mrs Smith had anticipated. The upshot was that Friday would be in effect a day's holiday and this wouldn't be a bad thing, Mrs Smith felt, as it had been a busy term up until then, and some of the children were looking very tired as they were going to school and leaving for home in the dark, and generally it seemed as if an extra day to run about at home really wouldn't go amiss.

Evie said in a flash that was certainly the case for the teachers, but what about the pupils?

Mrs Smith shot Evie back a beady look even though she suspected she saw the tiniest twinkle to the headmistress's eye.

Leonard Bassett couldn't resist a tiny smirk, and then he mentioned in a casual voice that Evie's resolute maypole dancing instruction was probably to blame for any tiredness the children might have. Evie thought his deadpan and deliberately casual voice meant that Leonard may well have been joking too, but Mrs Smith's hectoring boom of 'Nonsense!' brooked no further discussion in this vein, and so Evie couldn't be sure.

Anyway Evie was glad for the unexpected day off. She had breakfast while still wearing her dressing gown belted over her warmest winceyette nightie, and then after everyone had got off to work or were engaged in their usual morning activities she crept back to bed for a nap. It was noon before she woke, but her batteries felt much better charged.

As the snow had mushed down more to the state approaching lumpy slush than anything else, albeit with a thin ice crust from night-time drops in temperature, Evie put on her galoshes over her boots and tramped off in the direction of The Grange, bearing Timmy a gift of some of her latest batch of biscuits. She was lucky that she hadn't gone too far on her way beyond the village when one of the lorries with chains on its wheels on the way to the site of the new Nissen huts stopped beside her to offer a welcome lift – Evie's thigh and calf muscles were already complaining vigorously at the extra effort needed to wrestle through the slush, and she hadn't even come to the hilly bit yet – and she was dropped off most conveniently right at the bottom of the drive that heralded the final trek up to the recuperation hospital.

When Evie arrived at the now familiar hospital ward it was to see that Timmy had just finished his lunch, and Mrs Smith was sitting with him, regaling him cheerfully with tales of the antics Keith's two black and white kittens were getting up to since their arrival at the Smiths' cottage several days earlier.

The kits had been duly named Mountbatten and Montgomery, which Evie thought quite a mouthful, and not particularly appropriate as they were two little females (although she knew she hadn't much of a leg to stand on in this respect, seeing that Keith was also a female). As it was, Tricia had already joked privately to Evie that they'd soon learn to come to her calls of Batty and Monty, and if she had her way she'd be taking the both of them to her and Timmy's new home.

But to hear Mrs Smith's jolly description to Timmy of Mountbatten and Montgomery stealing one of Hettie's bootees and hiding it behind the coal scuttle, and then going to sleep curled up together in Mr Smith's sock drawer, Evie thought that Tricia might face a bit of a tussle to wrest either of the kittens away from Mrs Smith, which was ironic as Mrs Smith hadn't been that keen on having them at her cottage in the first place.

Keith had spent a day searching for the two missing kittens, and a pitiful hour crying to Evie, with her green eyes firmly closed as if in real anguish, in the evening of the day Mr Worth had driven Evie over to Mrs Smith's with the kittens in her arms as the car slip-slided around on the treacherously icy surface. The sound of Keith's distressed mewling damn near broke Evie's heart, although she knew that cutting the bonds between mother and kittens simply had to be done if the little ones were going to have a good new home.

Happily, after this vocal outburst, Keith seemed to forget about her missing youngsters as she concentrated on giving the remaining tabby and white a top-to-toe wash and brush-up. The sight of this soon made Evie feel a bit better, especially as when she and Mr Worth had been driving

288

home again she'd pounced on the opportunity it afforded to make a good case for the tabby kitten Laszlo remaining at Pemberley, Evie later noticing Mr Worth have a quiet five minutes scratching the kitten under the chin as the pair of them sat together by the kitchen range, while Keith kept a watchful eye on proceedings from the floor beside Mr Worth's feet.

As Mrs Smith bustled away now to find a chair so that Evie could sit at Timmy's bedside alongside herself, Timmy and Evie shared a look that intimated they were thinking the same thing about the kittens that Tricia wanted.

'Two bob on Ma keeping them both,' said Timmy, to which Evie replied 'Done', and they shook on the bet just as Mrs Smith returned with a puffing orderly trailing in her footsteps who was lugging across to Evie a very big and heavy-looking armchair.

Evie thought Timmy wouldn't have seen as much of Tricia in action as she, and so she believed that despite Mrs Smith being used to getting her way and thus a formidable bet, Tricia was even more of a dead cert as far as the future ownership of Batty and Monty was concerned, as there was something opportunistic and nimble-footedly clever about her that would probably ultimately stand Tricia in firmer stead in the contest for ownership of the pusses.

Mrs Smith, Evie and Timmy spent a very companionable hour chatting about this and that, during which Evie asked Timmy what he thought of the plans that Tom had drawn up for the new house. She was pleased that both Timmy and his mother seemed delighted at the design, with Mrs Smith even going as far as to say, 'Honestly, Evie, what that clever young man has come up with is quite remarkable, it really is. He does seem, without doubt, to have thought of everything Timmy could possibly want or need in a home. Timmy had some very excellent ideas too, of course, but it's been your Tom Drake's touch that is bringing them to life for us all.'

Evie was pleased that Tom appeared to have done a good job (and had managed to keep on Mrs Smith's good side, which couldn't always have been easy for him to do), as she felt in some way this reflected on her just a little, and was a small indication of Tom proving to be of suitable potential husband material for her. Still, she told herself not to read too much into Mrs Smith's phrase 'your Tom Drake'.

For in spite of Mrs Smith's endorsement, Evie knew that she still had her niggling doubts about Tom as a life-long partner as her heart never beat faster when she thought of him, although she was trying very hard to follow Sukie's advice and to give him a fair and fighting chance.

When thought of in the round, Evie knew that she found Tom to be handsome, as well as a relaxing and undemanding chap to be around. He was funny and he seemed unfailingly kind, and he was very interested in the world around him which meant that he was a good conversationalist, a trait that Evie was most appreciative of. He seemed to think Evie was intelligent and amusing too, and a nice person to be with, which was a bonus, of course. Evie quite often found herself laughing when she was with him, although not with the sort of bellyache yelp of humour that Timmy could induce in her. And so far they had never quite had the shared moments of intuition that she had so enjoyed with Peter, moments that would have felt as if she and Tom were perfectly attuned to one another, or as if they were jigsaw pieces designed to be slotted together.

Although Evie and Tom were spending a fair amount of time together, for quite a lot of it they tended to meet in a group with other people there too as Tom was a gregarious soul, meaning that he often invited Sam and Linda along, or when Wesley came down for a visit, Wesley and Sukie.

In fact, Tom and Evie hadn't spent much time at all on their own together, and when they had been, their hours beside one another had been chaste in the extreme.

Tom was very reserved when greeting and saying goodbye to Evie. They had stopped shaking hands, which was a relief to Evie, as that had come quickly to seem unnecessarily formal. The situation had progressed between them to occasionally when he dropped her off, Tom would park and then rush around the car to open the door for her, and then he would plant a single, slightly awkward goodnight kiss on her cheek.

Evie wondered when he would graduate to kissing her on the lips. She also wondered whether she would allow him to do so, or not. Finally she asked herself that if he kissed her and she kissed him back, whether she would enjoy it. She couldn't decide.

Tom was most good-looking, certainly – with

movie-star looks that outshone those of Timmy and Peter – but Evie found it rather difficult to think of him in that way, and this puzzled her.

She remembered all too clearly how she had been desperate for Peter to kiss her again, after he had kissed her the first time (in fact, she had felt so swept away by the passion of the moment that although those first kisses had lasted mere seconds, she felt as if her world had from that point on, quite literally, shifted on its axis). And so Evie knew she liked kissing.

And with Timmy she had certainly enjoyed his overtures, although at a more restrained level than with Peter. Indeed, if Evie were honest, she had enjoyed just as much as Timmy's embraces, leading him instead a merry dance by contriving that they never be alone for long, as she felt it dull of her if she had to keep removing his inevitably wandering hands to a safer part of her body – the middle of her back maybe? – as Timmy's fingers would start what felt like a preordained journey towards the buttons on her blouse in a surreptitious attempt to inch his fingers close to her bosom. Occasionally alone at night, when she and Timmy were engaged but before the spectre of a pregnant Tricia had loomed, Evie had thought about what it would feel like if she did allow Timmy's hand to slip inside her blouse. But these were thoughts that would leave her feeling hot and bothered, and with a sense of frustration, although whether this was frustration at her own mealy-mouthed attitude, or Timmy's decidedly lusty one, she could never quite determine.

As Mrs Smith continued to prattle on about

Timmy and Tricia's new home to her audience of two this Friday afternoon, and Evie thought anew of the kisses she had shared with Peter and Timmy, she saw suddenly that she couldn't imagine ever having the same stirring thoughts about kissing Tom. It was strange as he was so easy on the eye, but there it was.

However, these thoughts of kissing reminded Evie of the main reason she was at the recuperation hospital that day, and it wasn't to stay chatting with Timmy and his mother.

She bade a somewhat reluctant goodbye to them, and traipsed off with rather a heavy heart, going outside the grand door at the front of the house and then around the side of the property to the much less grand and virtually hidden entrance to the shabby-looking basement level below the hospital. It was a while since she had walked this way.

Evie rang the doorbell, and after what felt like an inordinately long wait, a young woman with a put-upon attitude came to answer the door. She looked at Evie with a slightly challenging expression, and when Evie asked if she might see Peter, the look changed from challenging to one Evie felt could only be described as pert.

'And who may I say is calling? I don't believe you have an appointment?' said the young woman quite insolently, Evie thought.

'It's okay, Miss Grey,' called Peter's voice from further down the corridor, although Evie couldn't see him yet in the murk of the dimly lit passage. 'I've got this.'

With Miss Grey casting a final look in Evie's

direction that suggested she thought Evie probably as no better than she ought to be, Evie shifted her weight from one foot to another.

Peter came to the door and stood before Evie, and they appraised each other carefully.

'Peter, do you want to get your coat, and then you can walk me down to the bottom of the drive? You needn't be away from your desk long,' said Evie.

Without a word he turned and headed off into the basement, to return a minute later very wrapped up and with his galoshes on.

They walked around the outside of The Grange making some idle chit-chat about how cold it was.

As they turned down the drive Evie took the plunge. 'Two things, Peter. The first is that Fiona and I had a coffee in Plymouth the other Saturday.'

'Why ever in this world would you want to do that? Have you taken leave of your senses?'

'That's not at all gentlemanly of you, Peter! I asked Fiona to meet me because I was thinking too much about her, and I think she was thinking too much about me, as well. It was a coffee that I hoped would clear the air between us. And actually I think it was a ... an interesting experience, for both of us. We didn't argue at all, and we talked about ourselves, rather than you,' said Evie, ignoring the sarky timbre of Peter's comment as she chose her words most carefully.

'And did it clear the air?' Peter's tone was dismissive.

'I think we both found it a rather valuable half an hour. Certainly I don't have the dread of running into her that I once did.'

'Well, I suppose that is a relief. I can't for a second imagine, though, that it was a pleasant conversation for either of you.'

Evie looked at Peter in a way she hoped would indicate that she thought he should take a more open-hearted view. But she didn't say anything further on the matter, and neither did he.

They walked beside each other for a while, with Evie thinking then that her feelings were pretty equally balanced between a part of her that was irked at Peter for his response to her and Fiona meeting, and a harder to fathom part of her that suggested a growing exhilaration at having Peter beside her once again, as a result of which a flush was slowly beginning to seep across Evie's skin. She realised the second feeling was inexorably submerging the first.

'You said there were two things you needed to say, Evie,' Peter prompted her.

Tom!

Evie had forgotten completely that she and Peter were together right at that moment expressly for her to break the news to him that Tom would be at the christening.

She swallowed apprehensively. Evie didn't for a second think that Peter would be devastated that she was going to be somewhere he was, on the arm of another man; but neither was she so careless of his emotions these days that she expected Peter not to experience a pang, even if only a little one.

'Tricia tells me that Timmy has invited you to Hettie's christening, and that you are going to go,' Evie began cautiously.

'I think it's because that baby so very nearly made an appearance while I was driving, as I'm sure you'll remember,' said Peter. 'I know you will feel awkward about me being there, Evie, but I don't really see how I can refuse to go, and especially so when I play chess with Timmy every few days.'

'I know you do, and Timmy loves it; it's very kind of you to spend time with him as he finds boredom the biggest hurdle of him being still at the hospital,' replied Evie even-handedly. 'But the thing is, Peter, Mrs Smith has asked the architect who is drawing up the plans for Timmy and Tricia's new home, Tom Drake, to come to the christening too, and he has also accepted his invitation. You might remember you sat near him at the Spitfire fundraising talk at The Grange that night. I wanted to tell you this because, er ... because Tom and I have been together to the cinema a couple of times, and we've been out in Plymouth to the fundraising talks along with Linda and Sam, and Sukie and Wesley. I've not told Tom about you and me, or Fiona, and I am not sure that me and him can ever become a serious relationship. But I didn't want you to be surprised if you saw us talking together at the church for Hettie's christening or afterwards.'

There was a stagnant-feeling silence, and Evie became transfixed by the sucking and squelching sound her galoshes made with each step as she trudged along through the slush. Her calves and thighs were equally indignant at Evie's treatment of them as they had been earlier.

'Message received and understood,' said Peter eventually. He sounded depressed, and unhappy – Evie discovering there was a difference between those emotions. 'I suppose Tom is the young man who had you with him when he brought Timmy back to the hospital after a trip out the other day.'

They reached the bottom of the drive, and they stood facing each other. Neither of them seemed certain of what to do.

As Evie stared at Peter's once dear face, she felt saddened, and as if she had just crushed the butterfly wings of something very special.

She was surprised, but undeniably thrilled too, when the wind blew some stray tendrils of hair escaping her hat across her face, and the indelible connection between them was winched tight as Peter took a small step closer to her, and after gently brushing her locks aside, cupped her chin softly in a leather-gloved hand and brushed her lips with his.

Evie drew back and looked once more into Peter's eyes, now almost hidden by the long shadows of the dying afternoon, to discover an intensity she hadn't felt a second or two before. Those strange gold flecks on his irises shone out at her, she fancied, pulling her closer.

It was Evie who made the first move this time.

Their kisses turned passionate, and Evie's body felt washed and then cleansed by heat, and she was unable to prevent herself responding with an equal fervour to Peter's obvious excitement as they held each other tightly.

The sound of an ambulance bumping its way down the drive in their direction reluctantly made them move apart.

It only took a second, but the spell was shattered.

'Evie, I'm sorry – do please forgive me. But I couldn't say goodbye to you for ever without that one last kiss,' said Peter. 'I wish I'd fought harder for you, but I think you'll be better without me. Our chance has passed, I fear. Good luck, Evie Yeo, and when you see me at the christening, it will be as if there has never been anything between us, I promise. Thank you for telling me about Tom; it must have been difficult for you, but I wish you both every happiness.'

Despite Peter's unnecessarily melodramatic and tallow words, there was something final in his tone that told Evie she was being dismissed perhaps for the final time from his life.

She understood properly at last that this was how it was to be between them now. She had started the process that afternoon, and Peter had gone on to finish it.

She didn't regret that kiss of seconds earlier, but with a dipping heart, she saw it now for what Peter had intended it to be: a mere kiss – or, more exactly a series of kisses – of farewell. A kiss that was nothing more nor less than a blip along the way of them disassociating themselves from one another.

Evie gave Peter a half-smile in the twilight, and swiftly turned towards Lymbridge so that he wouldn't see her anguish.

If Evie cared to think about it, which she couldn't summon up the energy for anyway, there hadn't been much to do in Lymbridge since the start of the year, other than some meetings of the sewing circle, and of course the usually drudgery of the working week. A moorland village in the short days between New Year and Easter always seemed a dull place to be, at least when compared with other times of the year.

And so it was no surprise that Hettie's christening was very well attended as it gave like-minded Lymbridgers a chance to let their hair down a little, and as Evie entered the church for the ceremony she thought that everybody other than herself looked determined to have a good time at the reception in The Haywain that would follow the church bit.

Evie mustered a smile, and thought she'd just get through the day as best she could.

At least, despite the cold water dribbled onto her head by Rev. Painter, Hettie evidently loved being the centre of attention. She smiled up at Tricia during the ceremony, although there was a dicey moment when Hettie swung her head sharply to peer rather aghast at Dave Symons, who stood beside Evie as they were gathered around the font, as he gruffly said his promises in his broad Devonian accent. Evie and Tricia shared a smile, and then Hettie looked once again across at Evie, giving a massive grin at the funny face Evie pulled at her. So that Timmy didn't look out of place in his wheelchair, Tricia and the godparents were allowed to sit in chairs, although the Rev. Painter asked the godparents to stand when they had to speak.

Hettie looked as sweet as anything, although

rather swamped by the fine lawn long skirt and delicate lace of the traditional Bowes' christening robe that adorned her and that both Timmy and Mrs Smith had worn for their own christenings.

Pattie chaperoned Tom during the church part, while Peter sat with some of the patients from the recuperation hospital who had become friendly with Timmy. Evie made sure not to look in the direction of either Tom or Peter, which was easy to manage during the actual christening although a bit less so later.

'Well, Evie, you did that so well,' said Linda as they stood in the churchyard afterwards, with a glance down at her expanding girth, 'that Sam and I are very much hoping that you'll be wanting to go through it all over again in a couple of months as godmother for our forthcoming event.'

Evie told Linda she'd be very flattered and she'd love to, but then she added that she'd be very miffed, though, if Linda went on to have twins as that would be a lot of Christmas presents and Easter eggs that Evie would have the responsibility of rustling up each year.

Linda didn't respond in quite the light-hearted way that Evie had expected, and in fact her expression was unsmiling and serious, with the result that Evie had a sudden rush of self-doubt as she thought that maybe Linda knew something that Evie didn't, and that maybe she really was expecting twins, meaning that Evie would well and truly have put her foot in it.

At the sight of Evie's momentarily stricken face Linda guffawed and then said, 'I got you going there, Evie, just you admit it!' And Evie had no option but to acknowledge that yes, she had been well and truly wrong-footed by her friend.

Tom escorted Evie across to The Haywain, and as they were about to go in they paused to allow Tricia to pass Hettie down to Timmy, in order that he could wheel his daughter up and over the little ramp that had been constructed especially for the wheelchairs of Timmy and a couple of the patients from the recuperation hospital into the ladies' bar, which had been reserved for the Bowes' party.

As he swivelled his chair to a halt once he was in the bar, Timmy said loudly so that everyone could hear, 'That's my girl, Hettie – this is one of your daddy's favourite places in the world.'

Tricia gave her husband a mock cuff on the ear, while quite a lot of guests smiled at Timmy.

It was a special day for Tricia too, as besides Hettie's christening and after-party, today was the day that Timmy was spending his first night away from The Grange.

In view of Timmy's sterling support over his formative years, Barkeep Josh had given the couple a free night in the inn's best bedroom as a present, with the promise that he personally would make sure that Timmy traversed safely the stairs up and down to the bedroom and that a commode had been installed behind a curtain.

Hettie's crib had already been installed as Tricia was still breastfeeding, and at Hettie's first grizzle, Tricia and Evie took the baby to the room they'd been allocated, where Tricia fed her, and then Evie changed her nappy under Tricia's instruction – Tricia saying she wanted to see that Evie could do this properly, just in case she and

301

Timmy were knocked over at the same time by a bus, as there would be a good chance in that case that Evie would have to double-up as Hettie's parent – after which Evie popped the little girl into her crib for a nap.

Tom and Peter were talking to each other when Evie and Tricia went back to the ladies' bar, having left the door to the room ajar so that if Hettie cried she could be heard. Although Evie's heart gave a lurch, Sukie was keeping an eye out for her and she gave Evie a look that indicated Evie wasn't to worry that the pair of them were talking as Peter had gone up to Tom to introduce himself (although Evie hoped not as somebody who had been kissing her with abandon a mere two days earlier).

Evie took a moment to regulate her breathing once more back down to something approximating normal, and then she bypassed Tom and Peter as she headed for the table where the food was laid out.

She put some fancies on a side plate and went to sit down alongside Julia and Leonard as she was doing her best still to make amends for her and Julia's fight in this very bar. As Evie tried not to notice they were inadvertently sitting on the self-same table on which the Yeo sisters had grappled so unbecomingly with each other, she got the impression that there was something that Julia was itching to tell her, but that Leonard was signalling with firm eyebrows that Julia wasn't to breathe a word. Evie assumed that they had managed to find somewhere to move in together, and so she tried to be happy for them.

Evie looked towards Robert and Susan to see if they had wind of a looming change in Julia's circumstances, but they seemed exactly as normal, and so Evie guessed they didn't know about whatever the development was concerning their middle daughter.

When Susan saw Evie staring in her direction, she tipped a shoulder towards James. Evie followed the line of the tip to see that James and Jane Cornish were sitting together at a table as they shared a plate of sandwiches. James looked like he couldn't believe his luck, while Jane looked slightly surprised by having found herself in this situation. Still, they were managing to have a conversation, and actually Jane looked so young that they didn't seem out of place by sitting with one another, and as a result Evie concluded that Jane was big and sensible enough to let James down gently before too long.

Evie chatted with Julia and Leonard for a few minutes longer, before getting up to make sure that she went and sat with Tricia's parents for a little, as Mr and Mrs Dolby were looking awkward and as if they were feeling a little out of their depth; they were farm labourers and, Evie deduced, probably felt that this was a gathering of people all further up the social scale than they were. In fact, Evie was a little surprised to see them there at all, as she knew they still felt very peculiar about Timmy and Tricia 'having' to get married, but Evie thought it could only be taken as an encouraging sign that they had decided to come.

Susan wanted to say hello to the Dolbys too, and

303

so Evie introduced them. And then Linda and Sam got the hint, as did Sukie and Wesley, and so in turn they all tried to make Tricia's parents feel welcome, Wesley being especially solicitous with offers of fetching them some food and drink, and so Evie supposed that Wesley had previously endured many occasions where he had felt the odd man out with the consequence that he would have a special insight on how to make an uncomfortable situation better. She felt rather endeared by his actions, and so she caught his eye to give a smile of thanks.

It wasn't too long before Timmy made a speech in which he thanked everyone for coming, and gave a special thanks to his mother and Mr Smith, and also to Tricia's parents, who looked rather shocked at his public mention of them, although Evie hoped that a part of them would also feel a little pleased at the acknowledgement that Mr and Mrs Dolby were now 'family' too in Timmy's eyes.

Then Tricia – much to Evie's surprise – stood up to say something. She kept it simple, saying that she wanted to thank people for making her welcome in Lymbridge as the new Mrs Bowes, and then she added that when she fetched Hettie in half an hour or so, she hoped that everyone would join her and Timmy in toasting little Hettie's health.

The only fly in the ointment during the reception was Dave Symons getting rather inebriated. Evie realised things had got a little out of hand when he gave a catcall and then roared what felt like an inappropriately enthusiastic 'Hear, hear' at Tricia's request that later Hettie's health be toasted.

Ten minutes or so later Dave Symons went up to Wesley and stood squarely before him, before raising the forefinger of his pudgy right hand to dig it several times into the soft place just below Wesley's collarbone with a slurred, 'Whaddya think you're doin' with *our* maid Sukie, Mr Big-time Musician, you? There's plenty Lymbridge lads who'd willingly gi' her a trot aroun' the brambles, withou' t' likes of you bein' necessary. Not necessary at all.'

Wesley stood there calmly enough, although Evie could see the muscles tighten in his neck and his lips press together, while Sukie's eyes shot pure daggers in the direction of Dave Symons.

But before either Wesley or Sukie could say anything that would throw fuel on an inflamed situation, Robert nipped over and neatly inserted himself between Wesley and Dave Symons, with a quietly firm, 'Remember you're a godparent and should be setting an example, Dave. What would little Hettie think, let alone Timmy and Tricia on their big day?'

Slowly Dave Symons turned a bleary face to Robert with a grudging, 'S'ppose.'

Robert inclined his head and raised his eyebrows, and Dave Symons understood what Robert was indicating he should do, and he offered a reluctant hand of apology in Wesley's direction.

Wesley looked at it with distaste, but then pumped it once in a perfunctory manner, before turning away abruptly. Robert shimmied into position as a buffer to Dave Symons' view of the swiftly departing Wesley.

Evie went up to Sukie, who looked a bit shaken, and she touched the back of her friend's trembling hand. 'Head up, shoulders back, smile and walk on, Sukes, and don't let that ignorant oaf spoil a thing for you and Wesley. He's only a weak poison and nothing to worry about,' counselled Evie quietly. She knew what she was talking about, as she could, with a wince of revulsion, still remember all too easily the nauseatingly joyful manner in which Dave Symons had broken the news to her of Timmy's infidelity, using it as an opening salvo in then trying to paw Evie himself.

When Evie looked away from Sukie it was to see that Peter had meanwhile made sure that Wesley had somebody with a friendly face to talk to by moving unobtrusively into a position where it was very easy for the two men to have a word or two, after which Peter announced that he had to leave as he was working that afternoon, at which point Tom seamlessly stepped forward to take up Peter's place at Wesley's side.

Evie decided to let them all get on with it, and she busied herself with passing around some sandwiches, and then a plate of rock cakes.

Once Dave Symons had been persuaded to go home and sleep it off, and Peter had made himself scarce, Evie found herself relaxing, and she even went as far as to have a port and lemon, rather than her normal lemonade (or if she were pushing the boat out, a weak shandy).

Evie circulated through the guests, and she introduced Tom to the people he didn't know. She had a second port and lemon, and then a third (at which point Susan flashed her what the

Yeo household would rib their mother was The Look, which Evie knew was Susan, very firmly, wordlessly telling her eldest daughter that she wasn't to have any more alcohol to drink).

Tom went to sit with Timmy, and after that he talked to Sam and then some of the patients at the recuperation hospital before sharing quite a loud laugh and some jokey banter with a couple of the pilots and crew from the airstrip who had finished their shifts and recently arrived at the reception, and then he talked to Wesley again.

As Tom mingled with Timmy's friends, several people came up to Evie to tell her that Tom was an exceptionally pleasant young man and Evie had done very well for herself. Without the slightest effort Evie found herself smiling broadly back.

As Evie confided to Sukie a couple of days later, the more people seemed to take to Tom, the more attractive he then became in Evie's eyes too during the course of the afternoon of the christening, she said, although admitting after a pause that the three port and lemons might also have played their part in this.

Anyway, whatever the catalyst, she and Tom began deliberately to catch each other's eye as they were talking to other people, and then to send each other secret smiles.

After a while Evie realised that for the very first time in her life she was flirting properly, and Tom was responding to her advances.

And what fun it was, she then thought.

Later, Tom walked her back to Pemberley, and at the doorstep Evie told him that he could kiss her.

He leant towards her cheek as usual, but then Evie said in a peculiarly husky voice that was as low as a whisper, 'On my lips, you chump.'

With that they shared at last a proper kiss.

Chapter Fifteen

It was a fortnight before Evie and Tom got around to what Sukie always termed The Talk, although for several days Evie had been sensing it was looming.

Sukie's theory was that as a couple thought about taking occasional nights out up a notch to some sort of understanding where it was tacitly acknowledged that the relationship might have enough in it to make it lasting, there was first The Talk to be overcome, when they would give each other a sanitised version of their romantic history.

Evie was much less experienced than Sukie, but she thought there probably was a lot of truth in her friend's description of what was likely to happen.

The snow had all but melted, leaving only the occasional sloppy-looking patch of watery white in the lee of a wall or a deep cleft of ground, and for the first time there was just the faintest smell of the coming spring in the air that wafted now and again towards them from across the moorland hills. Evie fancied she could also occasionally sniff the tang of salt water in the air, drifting its way from the coast down near Plymouth. And although the wild ponies who had wintered out on the moor were quite thin as they had had to forage hard for their food over the past few months, and the moors themselves still looked dark and unyielding, Evie could detect the subtlest shift in colours around her that she knew meant that it would be very soon now that the new grass would start to sprout, and the various other plants would lose their dejected winter appearance and start to stand tall as if ready to herald the approaching spring weather. The tors themselves looked several hues lighter in the brighter skies, and the birds had started to sing more chirpily while the moorland ponies were definitely neighing to each other more often too, as if to renew old acquaintances and squabbles.

Tom and Evie had decided to walk over to Bramstone one Sunday to have a lunchtime drink in the public house there. Before they set off Evie pussy-footed around whether Tom would find the couple of miles to get to Bramstone to be a bit too far on his prosthetic foot, especially as they would then have to walk all the way back to Pemberley where he had left his motorbike.

Evie gave Tom several opportunities to say he didn't fancy quite such a long trek but (she hoped) these were delivered in a way that meant he wouldn't lose any face. James was very impressed that Tom had both a car and a motorbike, and Evie had told him that Tom liked the motorbike best as long as the weather wasn't too cold, but because of his work with people returning disabled from fighting he had been allocated petrol to run a car, and so that was why he had the use of two vehicles. James dropped clumsy hints about the possibility of Tom teaching him how to ride the motorbike in order that James could deliver it over to the public house so that Tom would only have to walk one way, but in response to Evie's stern expression of disapproval at the very idea these remained hints that Tom took care not really to rise to.

Eventually Tom put a stop to all the skirting around the subject, with, 'Evie, you must relax. I promise you I will tell you if you are suggesting something that is going to be too much for me. But as long as you're not intending to run all the way there, I should be fine. And I'm looking forward to a chance to clear the pipes with a pleasant walk and with the prettiest of the local young women beside me. It's looking set fair, and so I think we should soon be off as I am looking forward most definitely to my pint of scrumpy.'

Evie tried to apologise for being too cautious, but Tom raised his eyebrows and so she decided her best move would be to keep quiet on the subject of what Tom should and shouldn't do, at least for a while.

They put on their coats and scarves, and then had a debate over whether 'to galosh, or not to galosh', deciding eventually to stick to the road to Bramstone rather than heading the slightly shorter way across the moors, and therefore not needing 'to galosh'.

They walked companionably along and then, for the first time, Evie slipped her gloved fingers into the crook of Tom's elbow, and he looked down at her with a smile and then he gave her hand peeping around the nook of his elbow a pat.

The afternoon before they had been over to Oldwell Abbott, where Tom grew up, to take tea with his parents, and his older sister and her two children. The Drake family home was quite close to Tom's digs, which rather surprised Evie, although Tom explained he'd wanted to move out after he lost his foot as he was worried that if he didn't, he'd never be properly independent as his parents would find it very difficult not to help him too much. The house where Tom grew up was large and extremely comfortable, and Evie was made to feel very welcome by his family.

It was no surprise that she definitely detected a hint of being interviewed as possible wife material, and so she tried to acquit herself well and not to think of the tea as a daunting event. Tom kept giving her encouraging smiles, and after a while everyone seemed to unbend a little, and thereafter Evie only had to remind herself very occasionally that it was just a tea on a Saturday afternoon, albeit a tea with her possible parents- and sister-in-law, all of whom she wanted to see her as the sort of person who would very possibly be a suitable prospective wife for their only son and brother.

As they strolled along towards Bramstone the next day it was Tom who decided to take the plunge. 'I suppose that now is the time we should speak of our pasts. Er, I mean, in the romantic way,' he said, 'although actually mine is very simple, as I have never had a sweetheart. I suppose I never met the right girl before.'

He gave her another smile, and Evie supposed

311

that he meant that he thought she was 'the right girl'.

Evie was rather taken aback, though, at his lack of experience, as Tom was twenty-nine and certainly dashing, and so she found it hard to believe that rather a lot of young ladies wouldn't have been chasing relentlessly after him.

He laughed at Evie's look of while not quite disbelief, certainly confusion, and so then he added, 'I don't know why it happened like that, but it did, and time ran away. I suppose I was at school, and I worked hard in a very single-minded way at university thereafter to qualify as an architect, with no time for women, and after *that* I found all my energies diverted to my first job. The war came, and within a couple of months I was in hospital before going to my parents' for a long time to be looked after. I've been in digs and working properly getting on for two years now and trying hard to establish myself as the very best architect specialising in designing properties for the injured returning to civilian life. I suppose that along the way I forgot that at some point it might not be a bad thing to pay attention to finding a wife and to think about having a family. It just seemed easier for me to concentrate on my work, and when I wasn't doing that, to socialise with the friends I already knew. But I've noticed these chaps are virtually all hitched by now, and although I do spend time with a variety of people I've met more recently, it's not felt the same. And my family were just starting to make the odd pointed remarked about my laziness in seeking a lady companion, in part as I suspect they were worried about the Drake family name not getting passed on to the next generation, when I had the great fortune to run across you at Mrs Smith's that January Sunday.'

They smiled at each other once again, and Evie supposed it was her turn to give the lie of the land in the emotional sense, not that she found the thought particularly enticing.

'Has Timmy told you much about me, as I know you've been spending time with him and his new friends at the recuperation hospital, and so I wonder what gossip about me has filtered through?' asked Evie, to which Tom shook his head to indicate, she thought, that Evie was very much a clean book as far as he was concerned.

'Well, it's common knowledge around here that Timmy and I were engaged last year, and it was during this time that Timmy made Tricia pregnant,' explained Evie. 'And this is where it gets a little bit complicated as I found out about Tricia when Timmy had only recently left to fight, and until we had sorted that out between me and him, it meant, I thought back then, that I shouldn't say anything about Timmy and Tricia to Mrs Bowes, as she was then, although now of course you know her as Mrs Smith.

'But this has caused no end of problems, as then Timmy was badly wounded, and although by that point I knew it was over between Timmy and me, and I had rather fallen for Peter Pipe, whom you've met too, the result was that I felt caught, unable to go forwards or backwards. I thought that even though it had been apparent from before he left Lymbridge to go on manoeuvres that Timmy and I were poorly suited to one another, in spite of this local people would expect me to stand by him once he had been hurt. And in any case I had been awful to Peter as I never told him I was engaged or that Timmy had made Tricia pregnant, and I know that I upset him needlessly and hurtfully at the time.

'I went to Stoke Mandeville Hospital to see Timmy – it's hard to think it now, but he was really very poorly back then – and the upshot was that the decision was made that he and Tricia were to marry, and this meant that I was released from our engagement. I dashed straight back to Lymbridge to tell Peter, but he had left to work in London on the secret work he does that I still am not sure quite what it is.'

'Oh, I can tell you about that. He's designed various systems to help pilots with night flying,' chipped in Tom. 'I was talking to a pilot the other day who's been studying with him – apparently they use acetate cylinders that shoot images onto photographic maps to replicate what a pilot might see according to various weather and on various routes to cities or targets in Germany or wherever, to help them learn landmarks. It's easy – well, pretty easy – apparently the other way around: for the Jerrys to follow the River Thames to London, as it's so distinctive even on the blackest moonless night, or to fly along the coast to Devonport or wherever, as the landmarks are obvious. But for our pilots, who might have to fly for many miles across land, it's much more problematic and navigation can only get you so far if you're looking for a specific target, so I hear. Anyway Peter designed the system and worked out how to train the pilots. My pilot chum says Peter's systems are fantastic, and so he's saving a lot of lives as he's taking some of the pot luck out of the sorties. He trained some people in London to then be able themselves to train pilots on the East side of the country. But he's here on Dartmoor working on various developments to the systems, apparently.'

To judge by the sudden guilty and crestfallen look on his face, Tom apparently remembered at that point that he had been given this information in confidence and that he shouldn't have said anything to Evie.

But she laid a gentle hand on his arm and raised the forefinger of her other hand to her lips to indicate she knew this was sensitive information that mustn't be passed on.

The pair shared then a complicit smile, with the result that Evie felt they were well suited to each other after all, as they had just shown they were able to communicate when it mattered without the need for words.

There was a pause as momentarily they each seemed lost in their own thoughts, and then Evie said, 'Ah, that makes sense, as I've glimpsed a couple of the rooms where Peter works below the recuperation hospital and seen some odd contraptions, and so I suppose what you describe is what they are. How simple they look, but I never would have guessed what they were for.'

Evie felt rather in awe of Peter – there was something slightly bumbling and hopeless about him, which she'd always found a bit boffinish and endearing, but actually it seemed to her now as if

Peter's days were spent doing something unsung that was also undeniably heroic, and she'd never guessed quite how clever he was.

'Anyway,' Evie went on, gathering her thoughts back to what she had been saying before Tom had distracted her, 'by the time Peter and I had run into each other again, he and Fiona, his former fiancée, were an item again once more. Peter has ended their association now, but Fiona has been discombobulated, and so he told me at New Year that he doesn't want to have a relationship with anyone else, and that includes me.'

Evie thought this simplified version wasn't too far from the truth, and was about as far as she needed to go. She felt she had summed it all up rather well.

'And how might you feel about that?' said Tom.

'I'm not sure I feel anything to be honest. Or to be more accurate, I don't feel anything that you need to be worried about. It's not the case that if you weren't here, then Peter and I would be involved once again, I do promise you that.'

Evie hoped at this point that she had been honest enough with Tom. She hadn't gone into all the ins and outs of the past year, or the complexity of her finely balanced but always conflicting feelings for Peter.

Still, what was true, as she had claimed, was that if she had never met Tom, she wouldn't be with Peter.

Evie wished it otherwise, but that wasn't enough.

'Evie, do you think there's a chance that you and I might be suited for one another if we were to think decades rather than just until next week?'

asked Tom tentatively.

'What do you think?' Evie didn't want to set her cards out on the table without getting at least a quick glimpse of how Tom might feel as regards their relationship.

Tom chuckled at Evie's refusal to be so easily drawn. 'What I feel, Evie, is you're cautious, and understandably so from what you've just told me, but that you and I could very probably make a good stab at growing old together. And I think too that Evie Drake has rather a nice ring to it, don't you? If it gets that far, I can promise you a lovely and comfortable home, and that if I had you at my side, I would never look at another woman.'

'Be careful, Tom, otherwise I might be thinking you're turning our hypothetical discussion into a firm proposal,' said Evie, trying to keep her voice light and playful. 'To be honest, I still feel a bit bruised emotionally and I'm not keen to rush into anything, however much I might enjoy spending time with you.'

Tom stopped walking, and so Evie stopped too. They looked at each other, and Tom smiled his pleasant, easy-going smile.

'What about,' he said, 'we go along as we are, and then when – and note, please, that I say "when" and not "if", Evie – you feel ready to up the ante a tad, you let me know, and then my proposal can be made formally. Does that sound like a plan that might hold some appeal?'

As Evie looked at Tom's open, manly face, she found herself smiling back.

He was so reasonable and rational after Peter, who was naturally a much more troubled, jumpy sort of person. And Evie could see too that she could have a life with Tom that would provide her with all the creature comforts that she could dream of, while in all likelihood he would be most undemanding and ask very little back from her in return. She wasn't an avaricious person by nature, but she would be silly not to acknowledge that Tom was comfortably off.

She needed to see how things went between them over the next month or two, of course. But in theory Evie was rather inclined to think that she and Tom might make a good team and that she could do a lot worse than marrying him.

She leant towards him for a kiss, and after looking at her for a beat longer Tom moved forward to kiss Evie on the lips.

A chirrup of 'what ho!' made them spring apart, and Evie thought she was probably going to have to desist from kissing men in the outdoors as despite there being few people who lived either in or around Lymbridge, nevertheless she had a real knack of choosing a place to kiss that would immediately become a thoroughfare for those very people who were around.

Sukie was the caller of the 'what ho!', and she stopped beside Evie and Tom atop the horse she had ridden the point-to-point on. Wesley was looking very dubious astride a plod of a breeding mare that Sukie had dredged up from somewhere or other and who stopped because Sukie's horse had halted and not because of anything Wesley had done.

The uncomfortable-looking Wesley clearly didn't have a clue when it came to equine matters, and when Evie spied his worried face, she said to him, 'Poor you, so Sukie's got you out and about, I see. First time is it?'

'She promised I'd love it,' said Wesley, as he wobbled precariously in the saddle as the mare wrenched the reins through his hands to have a sniff at the sod below. 'I'm still waiting to find the love!'

Tom laughed and said he didn't care for horses either. 'I think they smell weakness; at any rate, they always know they're the boss when I'm anywhere near.'

'Tom! You'll put Wesley off,' said Sukie.

Tom turned towards Evie, and as one they stared at Wesley and then looked at each other again.

'Yes, Tom, it would be awful if you put Wesley off, seeing as he's enjoying himself so *very* much,' said Evie in a stage whisper.

Sukie bent down and wrenched the head of Wesley's horse up and told it to walk on, and as she moved past Evie, she found a moment to tap Evie on the behind with her whip. 'See you at the public house in Bramstone in fifteen?' called Sukie as she encouraged both the horses to step out in a walk, with Wesley lurching about in the saddle and then grabbing hold of the pommel of his saddle to give himself some purchase and a better feeling of security.

'Yes, and ours are a pint of scrumpy and a lemonade. As long as Wesley isn't relishing his ride so much that he can't bear to get off, that is,' Evie called to their retreating backs.

James came over to Pemberley one evening after school. As she went to the front door to let him in, Evie could definitely notice the lengthening days now, as it was still quite light when he arrived.

Ostensibly James wanted to tell her about the fleet of Hawker Typhoon fighter-bombers that had just flown to the airstrip. And that Frank and Joseph had been told off by the commander of the airstrip for taking the Yeos' ancient cloth kite on its wooden frame too near to it. It was illegal to fly kites near important bases or near barrage balloons or field balloons for showing the direction of the wind apparently, which Evie and James agreed made sense if one thought about it, although they laughed about the fact that most of the local barrage balloons had been lost in lightning strikes and so the evacuees would be hard pressed to find one to fly the kite near, even though there had been a time when they had been all over Plymouth.

James confided to Evie that he'd bunked off school early so that he could go over to the airfield and take a peek at the new Typhoons; and Evie told him to be careful or else – very possibly quite literally – Susan would have his guts for garters if she caught him skipping lessons.

Uncharacteristically James made some idle chat with Evie that seemed to be about he and Frank and Joseph organising a straw collection as the government were adding straw now to paper mulch in the paper mills. The paper was less good, and Susan had grumbled about this to Evie already as she had noticed the difference with the poorer print quality of the magazines the shop stocked, even though everyone accepted this was apparently a better use of raw materials.

As James talked he kept looking around him, and over Evie's shoulder and eventually she caught on and understood that he was wondering where Jane Cornish was.

'Whatever is Sukie going to think?' Evie kidded. 'She thinks she's your One and Only.'

James looked a bit sheepish, before he blushed an impressive shade of raspberry as Jane put her head around the door to say something about the tabby kitten having caught a mouse that Evie might want to deal with before Mrs Worth saw.

Rather to Evie's surprise, at the sight of her brother Jane gave a little sound, one that Evie could only describe later to Sukie as a simper. Then Jane came into the room properly, and went to sit down as she patted her hair into order. She and James didn't say anything, but they were obviously very aware of each other.

At that point Evie had the feeling she was rather superfluous to requirements and so she toddled off to deal with the Laszlo-and-mouse crisis, while thinking that an eleven-year age difference between her brother and the pretty PG might be insurmountable, or it might not. There was a shortage of men and James was filling out nicely, and naturally he had been trained up hard by the three Yeo sisters in the art of talking pleasantly to a woman, and so perhaps he did have something to offer Jane Cornish that wasn't to be easily dismissed.

All the old rules were being broken, and although Evie didn't think it was yet time to think wedding hats for her little brother and Jane, who could tell how this crush was going to work itself out?

Certainly James was getting to be rather handsome, and actually Evie thought he and Jane seemed rather well suited in terms of their personalities. However, she doubted that if they were to progress to walking out together, that Susan would be quite so supportive of an older woman, presumably with at least some experience of the opposite sex (even if only of the minor variety), swooping down on her baby boy presumably with lascivious thoughts.

The Spitfire talk the following week had to be cancelled the evening before as the speaker was poorly, and so the next day Evie and Tricia decided to take Hettie out in her perambulator as the weather was positively balmy for the time of year.

They walked a long way, almost right over, in fact, to the village with the church with the famously wonky spire.

There was the toot of a car horn and Peter pulled up beside them, and Evie was flabbergasted to see Tom sitting in the passenger seat.

Peter said good morning to Tricia and Evie, and Tom leant across to say that he had had a puncture a way down the road, and when he opened his boot he had made the unwelcome discovery that his spare tyre was also flat.

Peter turned off the car engine and climbed out of the car and peered down to have a look at Hettie in her pram, and so Tom got out of the car as well; he offered Peter a cigarette and the two men lit up.

Tom explained that he'd just been standing beside his motor, wondering what he should do, when Peter had driven along and stopped. The upshot was that Peter was taking him to the airstrip where he should be able to borrow, Peter thought, a manual tyre pump which hopefully would get enough air into the tyre so that Tom could drive the car to the airstrip, where it was likely that one of the mechanics there would be able to sort it all out properly.

Evie thought that that probably was the case, but before she could say anything, there was a hum that suddenly developed to a thrumming in the air above, and all four of them, and little Hettie too, looked towards the direction of the noise. It was to see two Typhoons, which must have taken off at the same time, now cresting the breast of the little hill they were all in the lee of as they stood chatting to one another at a dip in the road at the hill's bottom.

The Typhoons flew on, with Hettie crumpling her face at the loud sound of their engines.

Nobody had ever seen a pair of planes flying so closely together before, and Evie was sorry that James wasn't there to watch it with them as he would have found the beautiful symmetry of the aircraft, with the sunlight making the metalwork softly shine, to be a thrilling sight.

The aeroplanes were juddering overhead very slowly, though, and were flying exceptionally low, as if they had been instructed to remain in formation at a uniform height above the ground, be it up hill or down dale, and so Evie thought they must be doing some practice for a particular sort of flying raid.

The aircraft banked at the same time and changed course slightly so that they were flying together directly towards the village.

Suddenly Evie had a terrible premonition as to what was about to happen.

She looked hurriedly about her, and she saw that, to judge by the dismayed look on his face too, Peter was thinking exactly the same thing as she.

'The church spire!' Evie and Peter cried as one, and they both dashed to get into the car. Tom looked to have no idea what was upsetting them so, but the alacrity with which both Evie and Peter had moved made him throw his cigarette to the ground and leap towards his seat quickly too.

'One of those planes looks as if it is going to hit the spire,' Evie shouted out of the window in panic in Tricia's direction as Peter shoved the car into gear, reversed into a gateway to turn and then drove off in pursuit, leaving Tricia and Hettie standing gawping in the road, with Tricia holding the handle of the perambulator as she watched the car bucket away from her and Hettie.

As Peter and Evie and Tom took the corner half a mile or so down the road, it was to catch the horrible sight of, after looking for an instant as if after all it would miss it by inches, the tip of the wing moving inexorably towards the spire.

From this slightly different angle Evie could see at once that the flight path must have appeared as an optical illusion from the pilot's point of view, because from the position they were in just then the spire looked to be straight. But with the aeroplanes having banked, the angled spire meant that in reality, Evie knew, it was leaning across and into the trajectory of the wingtip of the plane flying on the right.

With a crack and then the sound of breaking tiles on the spire's roof, and then the scream of wood splintering, Evie watched the Typhoon nudge against the spire, and then the spire and the Typhoon spiralled in a tumble together towards earth in what looked like a jagged yet almost beautiful plummeting dance in slow motion.

There was a dull thud, and then a crescendo of smaller crashes. Evie knew she'd never forget the precise intonation or order of the sounds. As Evie thought the final crash had come, after a beat there was the sound of clutches of tiles still falling from the church.

While the dust rose from the accident Peter had slewed the car to a halt, and he and Evie were running towards the scene with Tom hobbling as fast as he could in their wake.

The aircraft didn't look completely destroyed. Certainly its body seemed more or less intact, although it was on top of debris from the spire and at least one of its crumpled wings.

Evie could clearly see the face of the pilot propped still and bleeding against the clear dome of the windscreen, as he held an arm across his chest. There was a splatter of blood across where the pilot should look out from the cockpit.

She stood transfixed as she stared at the young man's face. He looked in agony but very still.

Peter and Tom knew exactly what to do. Tom put his hands together to give Peter a bunk-up, and Evie saw Peter wrench apart the opening to the cockpit and fiddle with the knobs presumably to make sure the engine was turned off. Evie could smell the fuel leaching from what would have been a full fuel tank to the ground.

Peter looked at the pilot and touched him, and his hand came away bloody.

'He's breathing, but I daren't move him while he is unconscious in case he has broken his back,' yelled Peter. 'Evie, you must drive my car to the hospital to get a doctor. The other plane should have radioed through, but the granite in the tors between us and the control tower might mean that from here there's no communication.'

Evie was already racing to Peter's car, trying to remember Jane Cornish's instructions as to how to start a parked car.

Peter's car was huge by comparison to Jane's, and it was powerful, and Evie lurched terrifyingly along, her heart pumping nineteen to the dozen.

There was an awful moment when Evie nearly ran Tricia and Hettie over when she took the first corner far too fast, missing them and the oncoming hedge by no more than a whisker, and she nearly lost control of the veering vehicle.

As fast as she could go, Tricia was pushing the pram to the scene of the accident to see if there was anything she could do.

Somehow Evie swung the behemoth of a car around the mother and child.

Tears were coursing down her cheeks when eventually she got the car to the hospital and stopped it with a crunch of gears, stalling the engine, and leaving it half on and half off the decorative flower bed at the centre of the gravel circle at the top of the drive.

Timmy was in his wheelchair on the front door-step to The Grange. As Evie staggered in his direction, he looked to her as if he had been just about to wheel himself down the wooden ramp on the side of the steps up to the main door.

The moment he realised it was Evie who had arrived so dramatically and in such a panic, Timmy immediately turn the chair in a small semicircle so that he could furiously ring one of the bells that had been placed on posts at the top and the bottom of the ramp, Evie presumed so that if somebody in a wheelchair was on their own and couldn't traverse the ramp, they could summon help.

When an orderly arrived Evie explained about the crash, her voice getting swallowed by gulps, and very soon afterwards a doctor and driver jumped into the ambulance parked in the drive and hurried off.

Sure enough, nobody at The Grange had been aware of the Typhoon crashing, although the church could clearly be seen without its spire from outside the recuperation hospital and Evie fancied she could see a cloud of dust in the distance still rising from the crash site, or would that be a wisp of smoke?

Timmy wheeled himself inside in order to phone the airstrip.

Evie found her teeth chattering and her hands trembling, but she was too dazed to think much.

It seemed an age before Timmy returned, after which he and Evie sat together for a while in a patch of sunlight, Evie shocked and shaking, but no longer able to cry, and with Timmy doing his best to reassure her.

He told her that Peter had been right, as the control tower at the airstrip were only just realising something was wrong when Timmy phoned, mainly because they were able to pick up only the one dot on their radar, when of course there should have been two. Evie had been very brave to alert the authorities, and to send help, Timmy added, to which Evie shook her head vehemently in disagreement.

After a while Evie realised that Peter would need the car to ferry Tom and Tricia and Hettie to where they needed to be.

But one look at her scarily pale face made Timmy say, 'I think you've done enough driving for today, Evie,' and he wheeled himself back inside the hospital again to see if there was someone available who could drive down to the accident with Peter's car.

Evie refused to move from where she was sitting, and so Timmy came back to her with a blanket he made her wrap herself in as he parked up his wheelchair to keep vigil alongside Evie. Later Sukie came out with a glass of water for her friend, but Evie was staring unseeing into the distance across the moors and didn't notice the anxious looks exchanged between Sukie and Timmy.

It was well over an hour until Peter drove back to the hospital. He was on his own, and his coat was smeared with blood. As he walked gingerly in a none-too-straight line towards Evie and Timmy, Peter called that Tom had managed to get himself a lift back to Oldwell Abbott and he'd be in touch with Evie tomorrow, while Tricia had been offered a lift too by one of Mrs Smith's friends who lived in the village; Hettie had been crying and was obviously desperate for a feed, and so Tricia had been grateful for the offer of a ride.

When he was close enough that she could see his expression, Evie looked at Peter's face, and instantly she could tell that the poor pilot hadn't made it.

'He was only nineteen, Evie, only nineteen,' said Peter then as he stood before her, one of his legs quite obviously quivering so violently that the material of his trousers was fluttering on that leg. Peter's voice cracked as he added, 'I held him as he died.'

Timmy looked up at Peter, and touched his coat, but he didn't say anything.

'Come with me, Peter,' said Evie quietly. 'I think you need a tot of your whisky.'

As she took Peter's arm and gently guided him unprotestingly towards the entrance to his workplace, Evie felt tears trail down her cheeks once more, and a physical ache deep within her heart.

What an awful day.

That poor, poor brave pilot.

Evie's spirit felt crushed.

And to look at Peter's traumatised expression, he seemed as if he would never recover from having felt the young man's life ebb and then slip softly away as he held him tight in his arms.

Chapter Sixteen

The ramifications of the dreadful day of the Typhoon crash seemed to go on for some time.

Evie suffered nightmares, and Tom told her he had had them too.

He and Evie seemed not as patient with each other somehow, and a bit less happy with one another when they were alone together than they had been previously.

Evie could understand why this might be, but she hankered after her and Tom's former easy conversations and the agreeable hours they had spent together.

It wasn't long before Evie was short-tempered with Timmy when he tried to make a Pev joke, responding with a sharp, 'Be quiet, Timmy. Pev is long laid to rest for me, as is Chad too. The Evie who laughed at that feels now to me like nothing more than a child, and the Evie I feel I am today hardly recognises that old Evie.'

Evie went to give Timmy a stern look, but then she saw how lined *his* brow was getting, and immediately she felt guilty as Tricia had told her that Timmy had started to suffer bouts of pain in his legs, but that he hadn't wanted to make a fuss when everyone was still so upset over the loss of the young pilot.

And when Evie cared to look anew at Tom, she noticed purplish shadows under his eyes, and a papery cast to his skin, and at one point he confessed that he was now getting unexpected but terribly vivid flashbacks to the incident when he had sustained the injury on the foot he had lost – apparently that had also been in a small-aeroplane accident with a church nearby.

One evening Evie gazed at her own reflection in the mirror and decided that she was also looking much less fresh-faced than she had a year earlier.

She appeared now to have come of age, and to be very much a young woman, rather than somebody only just leaving her teenage years.

She felt different inside as well: less excitable and more resigned to the complexities of the adult world, and certainly much less optimistic than she had once been of a happy outcome for any of them.

It was a menacing thought.

Meanwhile Timmy told Evie that Peter had been recommended for a commendation for bravery because although he had tried to turn the engine of the aeroplane off, the crash had made this impossible to do, and yet Peter had refused to leave the dying pilot even though the danger of the leaking fuel exploding and making the Typhoon ignite in a ball of flame was very real.

Timmy added that Peter was refusing the commendation.

Peter wouldn't see Evie, or anyone else, and even Timmy admitted to being concerned about Peter as he was so out of sorts.

The *Western Morning News* wanted to do an interview with Peter, but Mr Rogers told Evie that Peter had been very curt when he had declined the offer, telling the reporter to get lost or suffer the consequences.

Evie mentioned Peter's uncharacteristic withdrawing from everyone to Susan, and her mother counselled that perhaps he needed some time alone to think about, and to come to terms with, the tragedy.

Evie told Susan that Peter was helping teach pilots about night flying, and mother and daughter discussed how this accident would have been a shocking example to Peter as to how dangerous it was when an aircraft crashed and how narrow the difference between life and death could be. And Susan pointed out, not that Evie needed telling, how anybody with any sort of conscience would find it hard to recover from watching at such close quarters a courageous young man die so needlessly.

A host of letters were written to the *Western Morning News* about the spire. The church had been asked to take it down over a year earlier when the construction of the airstrip was announced, as some doom-mongers thought it very possibly posed a problem to the aeroplanes. But because the spire was so characterful and historically interesting, and the risk was deemed small, the church had refused to do so; and there were letters both condemning this but also some in support of the church's decision.

Tricia told Evie that she had seen that both Peter and Tom had done everything they could to save the pilot, but she could see too that well before they stopped trying it was a hopeless cause. And after it was clear the pilot had died, it had been very difficult.

Tom had punched the aeroplane, gashing hand badly, and Peter had vomited. Tricia added she hadn't known what to do for the best, so she had lifted Hettie out of the perambulator and thrust her into Peter's arms, and he had seemed to find it soothing to have something to hold until help arrived, and this had given her time to bind Tom's hand with a portion of her skirt that she had ripped into a makeshift bandage.

The accident had even affected Sukie. She had been unaware of what had happened, and so had gone for a solo horse ride on the hunter she liked so much. Late that afternoon she had been on a narrow piece of road with coppiced barriers on either side and she was heading downhill when a gigantic lorry had chugged up the hill towards her with the fuselage and tail and wings of the Typhoon, now in bits, roped in sections on the flat bed of the rear portion of the huge vehicle. The incline was steep and the lorry unable to stop, and with its engine revving and the driver crashing the gears as he changed down to the lowest, even Sukie's experience couldn't prevent her horse panicking and he shot off back up the road, his metal shoes not giving him enough purchase on the tarmacked corner, with the result that he and Sukie crashed to the ground before skidding on their sides across to the verge. Luckily there was a gate and although Sukie was in agony as her hip had landed on one of the metal stirrup irons, she was able to get the gate open just in time so she and the horse could be on the other side of it when the lorry inched itself past with the driver

sorry but the incline was so
n't dare stop. Horse and rider
npleasant friction injuries on the
kie had to wear a sling for a fort-
ant she couldn't work as one of her
as very cricked.

She . Evie that she thought it had been such
a fright for the horse that she doubted he'd ever
be trustworthy in traffic again.

There was a funeral for the pilot, and Rev.
Painter excelled himself by pitching his eulogy to
the sombre mood of the packed church.

Evie had never been to a funeral before, and
throughout it, all she could see was the young
man's face leaning against the windscreen, and
Peter's hand dripping dark with blood as he lifted
it away from the poor man's chest.

In the weeks afterwards Evie felt as if she was in
a dream. The end of the spring term, and then
Easter and the Easter holidays, and James's, and
Frank and Joseph's birthdays – which were all
within four days of one another's – passed in
something of a blur.

One evening Tom came over to see her at
Pemberley.

Evie hadn't been expecting him but she rather
guessed what he had sought her out to say.

'Tom, you don't need to go through with what
it is you want to tell me,' Evie said. Her voice was
flat and quiet. 'I'm guessing that what you mean
to say is that the death of that pilot has stirred up
a mass of feelings in you that you didn't know
you had, but they are very powerful emotions;

334

and the long and short of it is that you don't want to go on walking out with me. I don't think I am wrong, am I?'

To Evie's dismay Tom's face furrowed and he began to sob, his shoulders heaving.

Evie felt very rattled at the sight, but his obvious distress touched her deeply, and so she stepped forward to hold him close as he wept as she stared out of the window at the trees coming into bud in Pemberley's garden.

Afterwards, she didn't feel particularly regretful at the demise of their relationship, but she put this down to the fact that both she and Tom were still coming to terms with what they had seen when the plane crashed.

But what was more challenging was that over the next week or two Evie had to keep reiterating that she wasn't too cut up to be single again to her friends and family, who all seemed to assume that she was much more upset about it than she actually found herself. It was all immensely tiring. In fact, Evie couldn't believe the difficult time she had in getting people to believe her, as whoever she was speaking to's next response was invariably to assume erroneously that Evie was merely putting a brave face on things and that really she was still hurting deeply inside.

All except Timmy, that is.

'Evie, since the accident, I've discovered that Tom isn't quite the man we all thought he was, and I've worried myself sick on how to broach this with you,' Timmy confided after Evie explained the situation.

Evie frowned at his serious face and tone, as

she couldn't remember Timmy ever talking with such solemnity. She didn't feel particularly in the mood to hear more bad news.

Timmy was sitting up in his hospital bed as they spoke, and he reached across to clutch Evie's hand, holding it gently as he said that Tom had told him a week or so after the accident that he had been contemplating living a lie. The pilot's death had, however, loosened something in Tom, and had made such a course impossible for him to consider.

Timmy told Evie he had then been let in to the confidence that it was men Tom was really interested in, and not women. And aside from the fact of witnessing the aeroplane so soon after its tragic descent as the fuselage lay on the ground along with the remnants from the broken spire, which would have been traumatic in any case, Tom had been thoroughly devastated by the death of this particular young pilot.

For they had been an item – an item shrouded in the utmost secrecy, but an item nonetheless. In fact, Tom had dared to use the word 'love' to describe to Timmy how he had felt about the young man, Timmy explained now to Evie gently but clearly.

Timmy didn't seem especially shocked by Tom's revelation, and so Evie supposed that Timmy had come across other young men of this persuasion, even though the general assumption was that such people would go to any lengths to conceal such inclinations.

Evie's mouth was dry and even though she heard Timmy's words, she couldn't quite comprehend for some time exactly what it was that he was telling her.

Timmy explained everything to her again, as Evie looked at him with her brow clenched into a frown.

So Tom had cared for the *pilot*, the dead pilot, and not her? In fact he had *loved* the pilot...

But of course!

And suddenly everything fell into place, and made complete sense to Evie.

She saw in a flash that she had been the respectable cover that Tom required, the prospective wife he needed in order that his real affiliations wouldn't be blown. Evie guessed that Tom's family had become suspicious about him, and were presumably terrified he would get arrested for lewd behaviour.

Evie had never knowingly met a homosexual before, and she wasn't at all sure as to what it might be they did with one another. But she knew that sexual activity between two consenting men was illegal, and when she thought of how nice and kindly Tom had always shown himself to be, Evie decided not to think too deeply about what he would have got up to with the young pilot.

For if Tom had loved him truly and honestly, and according to Timmy this seemed to be very much how it was, how on earth could that be wrong?

Tom was a decent man, Evie knew, and so how incredibly tragic for him to have to consider a marriage, and presumably the distasteful act of love with a woman, purely to keep society, and his family, happy.

Tom had promised to Evie that he would give

her a comfortable life, and she didn't doubt for a moment that he would have worked hard to make sure this happened, although it would have been a life without passion or true love for either of them. A deep fondness for each other would have been the best either of them could have hoped for, and that wasn't really enough, was it?

Maybe the young dead pilot had loved poor Tom back.

Evie very much hoped so – Tom was a decent man and deserved to have somebody care for him exactly as the man he was.

And as Evie sat beside Timmy and thought about it further, once more she gave into a barrage of tears.

She just felt so damn sorry for Tom, for wheel-chair-bound Timmy, for vulnerable, damaged Fiona with her ladder of scars on her wrist, and – at the end of the queue of sorry – for herself, as she seemed to get it wrong so much of the time.

For the first time that Evie could remember, Timmy chose to remain silent, and as the nurses surreptitiously put up screens around his bed as they could see the pair needed to be in private, Timmy passed a hankie to Evie and then let her silently sob herself to exhaustion.

'Well, I know now why the kisses that Tom and I had never felt like real kisses,' said Evie at last, as she lifted her head to give Timmy a very damp and exceptionally tiny smile. 'They always felt to me like they were kisses that were merely going through the motions, kisses that were without any sense of depth or passion about them. And that's because that is precisely what they were.

Tom was handsome and debonair, and yet although I liked him very much, I didn't thrill to his touch. I knew there was something amiss all along; I just didn't know what it was.'

Chapter Seventeen

Bad times can't go on for ever, though, and with the days in double summer time, the lengthening, light evenings definitely heralded a shift in the pervasive gloomy atmosphere Lymbridge seemed mired in.

But oddly it was the day of the dress rehearsal for the maypole dancing competition when Evie felt the clouds break above her, and a burst of sunlight first warm and then ease her fractured spirits a little.

It was only two days to go until the maypole competition, and both the simple dance for the infants, and the more complicated 'The Gypsies' Tent' for the juniors middle and top were riddled with so many mistakes that they were a complete disaster.

In fact, so much so that Mrs Smith had to say cheery words to buck Evie up along the lines of, 'It's not the winning that counts', 'Chin up, Evie, worse things happen at sea', and 'Maybe you should rename our version as "The Gypsies' Catastrophe",' and so on.

Evie sighed – it *was* the winning that counted! – and then she thought the children would have a good time regardless, even though they were almost certain to come last in the competition, and if they didn't, then pity the poor judges who would have to watch a whole competition of such hideousness.

Really there were different types of winning, she reminded herself.

Winning didn't always come with a rosette, or a medal. Look at Peter, for instance, and his refusal of the bravery commendation. He was a winner, in Evie's opinion, even though he didn't have a piece of paper to prove it.

Tom too was a winner, in that he had found the courage to open up to Timmy about difficult personal feelings.

And Timmy was a winner, for being, well, for just being the irrepressible Timmy, but also for facing up to a devastating setback to his hopes and dreams with equanimity and good humour, at least most of the time.

As she walked over to Mrs Smith's cottage after school had finished that evening to collect Tricia, as they were going for a drink at The Haywain, already Evie was thinking about her next term at the school (still as a temporary infant teacher, of course, mind, Mrs Smith had told her, but at least she was still just about hanging on to her post with her knees wedged as firmly as she could get them under her teacher's desk), and Evie realised that for the first time she felt well on the way to becoming a fully fledged infant teacher.

No longer did she doubt her ability. Instead she revelled in the challenge of taking small children unused to being separated from their mummies, and helping them settle in to a new routine and learn their letters and sums so that when they moved up to the juniors middle they would be ready to pick up the pace of their learning. The pupils seemed to have enjoyed her teaching over the whole of the school year, and she felt privileged to watch them growing in confidence and knowhow, and to understand that she had played a large part in this process.

What a difference a year makes, Evie thought. This time last year I felt I got everything in the classroom wrong more often than not, while now I feel much more able to cope with anything those dear little tots throw at me.

An instant later Evie's thoughts turned to how she felt about her own behaviour in the romantic sense over the past twelve months. She laughed at how naive she had been, and how judgemental.

Goodness knows what the future holds, she smiled, but I will face it with an open heart and a determination to think well of everyone and to behave as decently as I can.

As she walked along suddenly she thought of her next project for the village.

It was to be a panto!

She would start work writing the script the very next evening, so that rehearsals could start mid-summer for the panto, and it would be staged between Christmas and the New Year.

It was going to be the best, the biggest fundraising panto ever... At least, that would be the plan.

Evie paused for a moment to stare around her at the beautiful moors in the hazy evening sunlight, and at a herd of ponies all with their heads up and looking back at her. The little stallion who had so enjoyed the reconstituted eggy mixture on the day of the tea for the military recruits looked for all the world as if he recognised her, as he lifted his nose and let out such a deep reverberating neigh in her direction that it was hard for Evie to believe his small frame could bellow so loudly.

She smiled to herself. Perhaps she'd never been the hopeless failure she'd so often felt herself to be. At least not if the look in the stallion's luminous eyes was anything to go by.

An answering strangulated goaty scream to the stallion's call came from the direction of Elizabeth and Margaret, and the beauty of the moment was broken.

Then Evie thought back with a smile to the previous evening.

After laughing at Lymbridge Primary School's poor showing at the maypole dancing competition, which had gone as badly as Evie had feared, Robert had told her that unless something disastrous happened, which didn't look at all likely, they would definitely have the whole £6,000 for the Spitfire fund by Christmas.

He added that Evie should feel very proud of herself, as without her none of this would have happened. She had had the idea, he pointed out, and her idea had inflamed the imagination of a whole host of small committees and teams, with the result that groups as far away as Bristol – helped along there by the support of Wesley, who lived in the city – and way over to Bath, and right down to the tip of Cornwall had all joined the campaign, each determined to make a difference as they united in a common cause for the war effort.

'You make me proud, Evie, you really do,' said her father, with just the tiniest crack in his voice.

There was only Evie and Robert sitting at the kitchen table at Bluebells, and unfortunately Shady had broken wind so there was a rather noxious taint swirling in the air around them, but Evie felt as proud as a queen.

She knew Robert would never say anything he didn't mean, and so she smiled warmly at her father in thanks.

Tricia was looking rather pleased with herself once she and Evie were meandering towards The Haywain, and with a jovial look on her face she looped her arm through Evie's.

'Evie, I wanted you to be first t' know, after Timmy that is; an' I tol' 'im this mornin'. It's early t' know for sure, but I's in the family way again! I know I am as all's I wants t' scoff is eggs, an' I were jus' like that wi' our 'Ettie. An' my wee smelt like sugar, so it's fer certain.'

Evie looked at Tricia, and now Tricia had said it, she could see it was obvious. Tricia's hips had spread, although her belly was still smooth, while her chest was insistently bigger. How on earth had Evie not noticed?

She hugged Tricia, and then said in her ear, 'So the doctors got it wrong then, did they, about what Timmy might be able to manage as a husband? You'd better be asking Tom to make sure to add another three or four bedrooms to the design of the house as I think you're going to need them.'

343

'Too bloomin' right those doctors did. It took a bi' o' workin' out, and I were tired after the christenin' – but once we got it sorted, there were no holdin' us back an' I don't think I got a moment's sleep, and nor did Timmy either,' said Tricia happily.

Evie thought she hadn't needed quite so much detail on the conception of the latest Bowes, but there it was. She was sincerely delighted that Hettie would be having a sister or brother before too long.

'Tom had better pull his finger out then to make sure you and Timmy and Hettie are as snug as bugs in your new house before the autumn, and that you've had time to unpack all your clothes and whatnot from when Hettie was a newborn,' said Evie as she threw her arm over Tricia's shoulders.

'If it's a girl, I like 'Ortense,' said Tricia. 'An' for a boy, 'Arry or 'Orace.'

'Of course, you do – they're perfect names,' laughed Evie.

The Haywain was busy, but then it always was these days, with the recruits swelling Barkeep Joss's clientele.

Julia and Pattie were there already, and they had bagged a table (and yes, it was the one that Julia and Evie had fought at), and it wasn't long before Sukie and Linda arrived too.

Sukie and Wesley had got engaged over Easter, and since then Evie found herself several times staring enviously at the sparkle of the single diamond in Sukie's ring in the dimmish light of the former ladies' bar.

Sukie looked at Evie, and gave the look that told Evie not to be downhearted. Sukie hadn't expected to fall for someone like Wesley, and yet he – and love – had come along when she least expected it, was what Evie read into the expression that Sukie was telegraphing her.

Evie decided that she and Sukie's friends hadn't made enough of a fuss about the engagement. Sukie and Wesley's commitment to one another was to be celebrated, and so Evie promised herself that now the maypole competition was done and dusted she would go all out to throw Sukie a wonderful surprise party. Maybe it could be done at The Grange with The Swingtimes performing – Timmy and his pals would love that, and it would be a fitting tribute to dear Sukie as all her work colleagues would be invited too.

With that Evie grabbed Sukie's left hand, holding it up to the light and angling it this way and that so that the brilliance glinted off the diamond and shone deep into Evie's heart.

'Very, very nice,' declared Evie, and then she embraced her friend in a warm hug. When they released one another they laughed when they saw that they had each teared up.

To avoid any awkwardness, a grinning and rounded-tummied Linda joked that when Sukie and Wesley were to be wed, she was sure that Wesley would be able to borrow Hector for the ceremony, as the massive great workhorse had had pride of place at Linda's own wedding and been impeccably behaved for the whole day.

Sukie laughed and said that she had had to promise Wesley that she would never make him go near another horse again, but she added that they were trying to fix a date for the wedding that would be well before Linda and Sam would be due to have their baby as she couldn't bear the thought of Linda possibly not being able to come.

Evie was already hard at work on Sukie's wedding outfit, and also on something for Linda to wear, as Linda only had the one dress and a pair of Sam's trousers that she could squeeze herself into at the moment.

Just as Tricia looked as if she were about to say that she too was expecting a baby, Julia interrupted with a squeal to say that she had news and try as she might, she simply couldn't hold it in any longer, but none of them were to breathe a word...

Tricia sat back in her chair, and Evie thought she looked as if she'd decided to keep the news back of her and Timmy's forthcoming addition to their family for just a little while longer and that she would to tell them all about it another day.

Leonard came from quite a privileged background, they all knew; and breathily Julia described how he and Robert had hatched a plan whereby Leonard would provide Robert and Susan with the injection of cash that they needed, but he would be a sleeping partner in the shop/petrol/garage business, and in return he would get paid a dividend when the business was turning a profit.

The paperwork had been done and almost finalised, with Susan deliberately kept none the wiser as Robert hadn't wanted to get her hopes up in case something went awry with the arrangements.

Instead the plan was that once the contract was ready for signature, Robert was going to get up a little earlier than usual one morning in order to creep down to the kitchen; he wanted to surprise Susan by placing the key to the shop and the contract awaiting signature in a box he would tie up with ribbon and leave it on her breakfast plate ready for her to find when she came in to prepare everyone's breakfasts – sworn to secrecy, Pattie had quipped apparently to her father that she'd better do the tying of the ribbon's bow, as her father's fingers were hardly nimble – and thus a symbolic present of the shop would be made to Susan.

Julia planned on leaving her work at the Post Office to join Susan working at the shop, and Pattie had confirmed that once the garage workshop was up and running, and the war was over, she would be keen to join the family business too.

Evie congratulated Julia for Leonard's altruism, saying it was going to make a resounding difference to the Yeos' way of life, before adding, 'I know a place where following the May Day maypole competition there's been left a rather large surfeit of khaki-coloured ribbon, if that's any help to the wrapping of the present box the key and contract will be in.'

A new round of lemonades were bought to celebrate, and as Evie returned to the table lost in the thought that maybe Leonard had redeemed himself in her eyes to the point where she could start to be genuinely friendly to him, she noticed

347

a telegram delivery man standing next to her empty seat holding an envelope in his hand. Presumably somebody at Pemberley had sent him over to The Haywain to find her.

Everyone was looking concerned, and Evie felt a corresponding slithery downward sensation in her belly as telegrams nearly always heralded bad news these days.

But when Evie ripped the telegram's envelope open after she had remembered to tip the delivery man, she was dumbstruck.

The telegram said simply but clearly: 'IT IS TIME FOR ME TO GO BACK TO HERTFORDSHIRE WHERE I BELONG AND I WILL NOT BE IN DEVON AGAIN STOP PETER AND YOU SHOULD GET MARRIED STOP BEST WISHES TO YOU BOTH STOP AND I MEAN THAT STOP FIONA STOP'

Evie sat open-mouthed as her friends passed the telegram from one to another. At last she said to the delivery man that there would be no reply, and then after a second read-through, just to make certain she hadn't got the wrong end of the stick, she passed the telegram around the table once again so that everyone could read it in case they had missed anything the first time.

Well, there would be a reply, Evie knew, but she couldn't think of precisely what it should be for now. Actually then Evie realised that neither could she think of anything at all just at the moment, or of anything to say. It was as if she had taken a very bad bump to the head and was suffering concussion.

From what sounded like a long way away Tricia

pointed out that the long length of the telegram would have been very expensive for Fiona to send, to which Sukie replied, 'Hopefully so.'

Evie stared down at the flagstones on the floor and wondered what she should do.

But when she looked up again it was to see that Peter had taken the place of the telegram delivery man – he was clutching a telegram from Fiona too, and was staring intently in Evie's direction.

This was absolutely the last thing she had expected.

Peter and Evie didn't say a word – in fact, they'd not been in touch for weeks as in the aftermath of the aeroplane crash Peter had continued to rebuff all approaches from Evie or everybody else – but Evie stood up, and they continued to hold each other's gaze for quite some time as they stood before each other, as Evie's friends watched what would happen in excited silence.

Without once taking their eyes away from one another, Evie and Peter moved towards each other and left The Haywain to have a private talk outside.

As if they were the only people in the world, they walked so closely side by side that their shoulders kept nudging one another's as they headed to the patch of rough ground beside the public house, where the foundations for Timmy and Tricia's house were being laid.

There they stood, united as one, still and silent, as they contemplated with serious expressions the trenches the builders had dug for the foundations to the house, and the mundanity of the

349

piles of wood and fixings waiting to be used.

It might have been a few minutes or it might have been an hour that they wallowed in the mere fact of being near to one another with nothing at all in the world to hold them back.

And so it was only as the first stars started to twinkle high above while from far away across the cosmos an ecstasy of atoms began to dance once more between them, bouncing across from one to the other and back again, that Evie and Peter turned towards one another.

Evie felt full to bursting, and as her heart fluttered and bumped uncomfortably beneath her ribcage she fancied she could see the hazel flecks in Peter's eyes turn golden, and fizz and sparkle in the gathering twilight just for her.

'Evie, my Evie...' Peter began with none of the familiar hesitation in his voice.

It was quite some time before they headed back inside The Haywain again, and Evie's lips were redder than when she had left and her cheeks were flushed. It was as if her lips and her cheeks had been put through a punishing half hour or so, and her giddy expression and mussed hair did nothing to dispel that impression.

Peter looked pretty dazed too, although also quite smiley, and all of Evie's dear friends noted that somehow he stood taller and with his shoulders broader.

Such was Evie's euphoria that she didn't mind in the slightest that her friends looked ready to chaff her, or that in her absence one of them had drunk the lemonade that she had bought but not had time to sip.

Evie had now far too much else to think about, and it was all to do with Peter and how suddenly their stars had aligned and fallen perfectly into place.

If her lips weren't tingling and her blood racing so pleasurably, she would have thought she were dreaming.

She went to say something to her friends, but couldn't find the words. Instead she smiled happily at them and they smiled back at her. Nothing, for the moment, needed to be said.

Evie turned to Peter.

'My Peter,' she whispered in his ear, and as they sat down she saw that the hairs at the back of his neck had lifted at the sound of her voice.

The publishers hope that this book has given you enjoyable reading. Large Print Books are especially designed to be as easy to see and hold as possible. If you wish a complete list of our books please ask at your local library or write directly to:

Magna Large Print Books
Magna House, Long Preston,
Skipton, North Yorkshire.
BD23 4ND